Hope Even After

Heather Greer

Scrivenings
PRESS LLC

©2026 Heather Greer

Published by Scrivenings Press LLC
15 Lucky Lane
Morrilton, Arkansas 72110
https://ScriveningsPress.com

Printed in the United States of America

All rights reserved. No part of this publication may be reproduced, stored in a retrieval system, or transmitted in any form or by any means—for example, electronic, photocopy, and recording— without the prior written permission of the publisher. The only exception is brief quotations in printed reviews.

Paperback ISBN: 978-1-64917-575-5

eBook ISBN: 978-1-64917-576-2

Editor: Elena Hill and K. Banks

Cover design by Heather Greer.

Scripture quotations are taken from the New American Standard Bible® (NASB), Copyright © 1960, 1962, 1963, 1968, 1971, 1972, 1973, 1975, 1977, 1995 by The Lockman Foundation. Used by permission.

NO AI TRAINING: Without in any way limiting the author's [and publisher's] exclusive rights under copyright, any use of this publication to "train" generative artificial intelligence (AI) technologies to generate text is expressly prohibited. The author reserves all rights to license uses of this work for generative AI training and development of machine learning language models.

"He heals the brokenhearted and binds up their wounds."
Psalm 147:3

To those struggling with addiction, there is help and hope. You are created in God's image and are worth the battle for sobriety.

To those with loved ones mired in addiction or on the recovery journey, you are not alone. Find others to support you as you help your loved one through the dark valley.

Chapter One

With a deep inhale to fortify her patience, Daisy Taylor slammed the door of her Ford F-150. This was not the way she planned to spend her Sunday night. She wrapped the loose end of her scarf around her neck as she stalked across the grass. Frosted blades crunched under the hard soles of her cowboy boots as she moved toward the mass of rumpled flesh and cloth in the middle of the otherwise tidy lawn.

"Lord, please." Daisy blew out the prayer on a frustrated breath. "Help me."

The acrid stench of alcohol and bile burned. Daisy swallowed hard against the assault on her own stomach. The last thing she needed was to add to the putrid mix. Breathing as shallowly as possible, she grasped what she thought was an arm and tugged until the figure sat somewhat upright.

"Luke Masters, what have you gone and done now?" She threw his muscled arm over her shoulder, put her own around his trim middle. She was a fit and active twenty-seven-year-old, but Luke had the extra bulk of a man who spent time at the gym. Bracing herself, Daisy lifted with her legs. Though his movements lacked control, Luke wasn't completely dead weight. Good thing. He might have had to lie there in the cold.

Once he was standing, or rather leaning against her, she took a deep breath, instantly regretting it. How was it possible to taste a smell? When, in all of human history, would such a feat have been practical?

Never mind. There were more pressing matters. "What does 'last time' mean to you?"

"Daisy?" Luke squinted at her as his head swayed back unnaturally. "When did you get here?"

Those answers didn't matter either. He wouldn't pay attention in his current state, and he wouldn't remember later. He lifted fingers to her cheek in an awkward pat. She jerked away from his touch.

"What is the matter with you?" She struggled to direct their cumbersome steps toward the plain, little ranch-style house. "You could have frozen to death."

Alcohol and extreme cold did not play well with each other. And though spring was around the corner, early February in southern Illinois was temperamental enough to drop from sixty degrees to thirty in the time it took to take a breath. Luke wasn't even wearing a decent coat, just his stupid plaid jacket, which fit more like a heavy shirt.

What if he hadn't called?

His grin was mischievous. "You could always warm me up, darlin'."

Daisy fought the urge to drop him right there on the steps and march back to her truck even as her eyes burned with a sudden urge to cry. Thinking about all the drunken words he had spewed when he called brought heat to her cheeks despite the cold. These new ones added to the insult.

He didn't understand. Not even in his inebriated state would Luke have been so careless if he knew the truth.

"That's enough of that, fool boy."

"Not boy." His jaw tightened as she opened the door and pulled him through. "Man. How long's it been if you can't tell the difference?"

She sucked in a deep breath and swallowed hard. The need to escape pressed in on her, and she nearly dragged him through the living room and down the hall to his bedroom. It was just the alcohol talking, but it still sliced deep. She'd have to bluff her way through this if she wanted to keep her emotions intact.

"You might look like a man, but you've got all the common sense of a toddler." She plopped him unceremoniously onto the bed. "Pardon me for being confused."

His hand tangled in her scarf, pulling it from her neck before he patted the mattress. "Join me? We can clear up your confusion."

She leveled him with a glare before dropping to the carpet in front of him. *Get his shoes off and get him in bed.* She could accomplish the simple task. But a string of inappropriate comments about her proximity and what they might do brought her to her feet and sent her flying out of the room, his calls trailing her like the tail of a kite.

As the front door slammed behind her, Daisy sucked in a ragged breath and gave in to the sob she'd fought since she arrived. As if her emotional pain weren't enough, the cold sent shards of ice into her lungs, releasing a cough that shook her to her core. Each cough allowed another gulp of freezing air to pierce her lungs. Crying and coughing her way to her truck, Daisy climbed in and turned the key. Warmth flooded the cab. Her head dropped to the steering wheel. The coughing eased. The sobbing continued.

"God, why?" She whispered. She refused to breathe the full question into existence as if it would change the truth. It didn't matter. Spoken or not, it screamed in the silence. Why did she have to love someone she could never have a future with? And why couldn't she extricate him from her life once and for all?

Luke tightened his eyes against the onslaught of light streaming through his bedroom window. At least, he thought it was his bedroom. He cracked one eye open, just enough to see his dresser on the wall across from his bed. Mistake.

The slight movement added an extra row of percussionists to the band rocking out in his head. He shifted his gaze from the window bathed in daylight. Mistake number two.

He wasn't sure what he'd eaten the evening before, but any more movement and he'd get a clearer picture than he wanted.

A groan escaped. Thoughts whirled, but none long enough to grab hold of, and each one added to the nausea. The shrill ring of his cell phone made him forget the drummers in his head. Of course, they were replaced with a searing knife slicing through his gray matter. If any brain cells remained after the previous night.

He dug the phone from his pocket with as little jostling as possible. The small movement made his body hurt worse than an arthritic octogenarian on a rainy day. Squinting, he concentrated on the lit-up numbers and letters on the screen until they formed an all too familiar number. Dread joined the sea already churning in his gut.

Focusing on the time in the corner of the screen, Luke groaned. He should answer. But the Sahara had taken up residence in his mouth and throat. His boss could wait—or not. At the moment, he didn't care. Death was the only visitor he'd currently welcome. Considering how his body ached and the room tilted at the slightest provocation, death might have already come for him. He couldn't be sure.

With slow, deep breaths, Luke forced himself up to sitting on the mattress edge. A few more long inhales, and he was steady enough, he hoped, to open his eyes. Pain begged him to reconsider, but the sooner he made himself move, the sooner he would reach the end of this misery. He needed a glass of water and a few ibuprofen, a shower, and a trip to the local drive-thru for a burger and fries or whatever greasy offerings filled the menu.

What was sticking out from under his bed? He reached down, fighting the room's sudden sway, and pulled Daisy's favorite scarf from its hiding place. Daisy. Now he understood how he got to his room. But why would she leave her scarf behind? He was the incapacitated one last night. Why didn't she look for it when it fell?

Unless ...

Another groan, this one brimming with frustration. What could he have said to run her off? Daisy had seemingly infinite patience, but he knew the truth. There were ways to push her to the breaking point. He could be ugly when he'd been drinking. Most people around him at those times didn't care and were just as mouthy. But considering the discarded scarf and the fact that he was fully dressed on top of the covers, including his shoes, whatever had taken place was far from good.

He'd need to deal with the fallout. But first, his anti-hangover regimen. He needed clarity to figure out what he'd done and how to apologize this time. With answers and a ready defense, he'd call Daisy. No. Wait. He'd return his boss's call first. Beg forgiveness for his unexplained absence this morning. After smoothing things over at work, he'd deal with Daisy.

Chapter Two

"It's one day, Mike. And everything worked out." Luke ran a hand over his stubble-covered chin. "Tim was looking for some extra hours anyway. No harm done."

"No harm?" Mike's laugh barked through the phone speaker. "Funny. Almost as hilarious as thinking it's only one day. It's one day this week, one day last week, and countless more the entire time you've worked here. I can't depend on you."

Desperation snaked through Luke, leaving his muscles jittery. He bounced his heel against his hard bedroom floor. The urge to fight back welled up, but that wouldn't work with Mike. He paused to breathe. "You can. It won't happen again."

"You're right. It won't, because you won't be working here." His boss's sigh sat heavy between them. "Listen, Luke. I like you. I really do. And I consider us friends."

"A friend wouldn't hang me out to dry like this."

"I've got no choice. You're unreliable. As your friend, I worry about you. You've got a problem, and you need to get it under control. Because right now, it's controlling you."

"Whatever, man. Keep your job and your so-called friendship. I don't need them." Luke hit end. No job. And with the way things ended, no decent reference to get a new one. Mike was wrong. The previous night had been a mistake, but he had it under control.

Luke's breaths came quick and shallow. Heat filled the blood pumping through his veins. He worked hard and always accomplished more than was asked of him. So, he missed a day or two every now and then. How dare Mike insinuate he had a problem. And now, thanks to that bleeding heart sticking his nose where it didn't belong, Luke was without money coming in.

An angry growl erupted from his chest. Luke hurled his phone across the room. As soon as it left his hand, he realized his mistake. He crossed the room. Even before picking it up, he could tell the screen was shattered. Not the end of the world, as long as the electronics still worked. He lifted it. The black screen didn't fade to the picture of him and Daisy from their high school prom. He'd have to make do without a phone for the foreseeable future.

No phone meant no call to smooth things over with Daisy. His apology tour would have to be in person. Nothing like adding the complication of face-to-face to what should've been an easy fix.

He considered throwing the broken phone again. Instead, he dropped it in the trash and scrounged through his dirty clothes from the night before to find his keys. See. He had everything under control, no matter what Mike or anyone else thought.

DAISY STARED at her kitchen counter as her best friend poured smoothies from the blender into waiting cups. "What's this one, Bek?"

"Citrus mint." Bekah placed a cup in front of Daisy. "It'll be a hit this summer at the communi-TEA Barn's tea bar."

Daisy moaned as the bright flavor of citrus melded with the

smooth mint. Refreshing. "I chose the right person to collaborate with on new drink flavors, but I have one question. Are you trying to usurp the throne?"

"Definitely not." Bekah's laugh rang through the kitchen. "Communi-TEA is your baby. I'd never have thought to start an herbal tea business, especially one where you're responsible for growing and blending the product."

"You're taking to it, though. Without a doubt. I'd better watch my step or the other artisans will help you oust me."

Bekah playfully shoved Daisy's shoulder. "Don't even start. The crafters renting booth space love the place, because of you." She leaned against the counter and crossed her arms. "Now, enough stroking your ego. You're avoiding, but we've got to get back to the real issue of the morning. It's time to cut him loose. Once and for all. No going back."

"I'm not sure, Bek." She pushed the straw around and around through her smoothie. "This isn't Luke. Not the real Luke."

"I love you, hon, but you're wrong." Bekah took a drink before continuing. "He isn't the boy you grew up with, and he's not the man you fell in love with anymore. He's changed. What you see is who Luke is now."

"Even if you're right, it's not like he's a monster. He's got a problem."

Bekah scooted their cups to the side and grasped Daisy's hands in her own, forcing Daisy to meet her eyes. "Yes. He's got a problem, and it's spiraling out of control. Luke's going to crash and burn, and I hope it isn't literal when he does. But even more, I hope he doesn't take you with him when it happens."

Daisy shrugged. "I'm being careful. I won't let it go too far."

Bekah's raised eyebrow spoke for her.

"I'm serious. I won't. But he needs someone in his corner if he's ever going to beat this thing."

"He doesn't even admit there's a thing to beat." Bekah's

voice climbed higher as she spoke. "You can't help where it isn't wanted."

"I can't write him off like all our years of friendship, everything we've been through together, doesn't mean anything. He's hurting. You know as well as I do, his drinking didn't become an issue until after Pops died."

Bekah moved across the kitchen and leaned against the far counter with a huff. "And Pops wouldn't have put up with his drinking in the first place. He'd have boxed Luke's ears."

Despite the seriousness of the situation, memories of Pops brought the hint of a smile. "You're right. But Pops wasn't aware. And if he were here now, he'd be fighting for Luke. Can I do any less?"

The doorbell prevented Bekah's response. Daisy pushed away from the counter and made her way to the door. Opening it, her stomach dropped faster than it did on the coasters at Six Flags.

"What are you doing here?"

Luke never conducted his after-a-bender apologies in person. She suspected he didn't want her seeing his day after, woke-with-a-hangover look. Too bad that even in his disheveled state, Luke could still catch the eye of any woman he wanted, including her.

"Mornin', Daisy." Luke nodded as he tugged the brim of his raggedy baseball cap. "Can I come in? Or could we go for a walk?"

"No," Bekah spoke from behind Daisy. "She's got nothing to say to you."

"Bekah." Daisy turned to find Bekah glaring at Luke. "It's okay."

Disappointment filled her gaze. "No, Daisy. It isn't. And don't let him convince you otherwise."

"Please." Daisy willed Bekah to see what she saw. "Try to understand."

Bekah rubbed her lips together and shook her head. "I can't. But whatever. I've got to get to *your* store." She swiped her purse from the kitchen table. "Closed on Mondays or not, a manager's work is never done. I'll talk to you later."

A weight settled in Daisy's chest as she moved to allow Bekah's exit. They'd patch things up later. Luke stepped out of the doorway.

"Always a pleasure to see you, Bek." His smug smirk discounted a polite nod in her direction.

She huffed. "I wish I could say the same."

Daisy waited only until Bekah moved out of earshot. "Did you have to provoke her like that?"

"All I said was …"

Daisy held up her hand. "I know what you said." She snatched her coat from one of the pegs by the door. "And in case spending time with Jose or Jack or even the good Captain made you forget, we've been friends all our lives. Your tone was clear, and the spark in your eyes means you were absolutely trying to provoke Bekah. She doesn't deserve it, and I want you to leave her alone. She's trying to protect me."

"Protect you? From me?" Luke ran a hand through his brown hair. "Daisy, I'd never hurt you."

She bit her lip to trap her words inside.

"Daisy?" A crease formed between Luke's brows. "You know that. Don't you?"

Her eyes stung. She blinked the discomfort away, praying as she did for the simple favor of dispelling the tears without letting them fall.

"Daisy?"

She raised her gaze to his. Concern radiated off him like waves crashing onto a sandy shore. It was too much. A tear escaped, trailing down her cheek. She shut her eyes against the onslaught. Warmth chased the coolness from her cheek as Luke's thumb grazed over it, brushing away the moisture.

"Oh, Daisy." His voice was a whisper.

When his arms pulled her against his chest, she knew she should resist. He'd held her a million times. She'd done the same for him. In celebration and in devastation, they'd always been there for each other. She'd found camaraderie and comfort in the arms now holding her, in the hand softly stroking her hair.

Finding herself embraced once more, the issues dividing them almost faded away. Her shoulders sagged as tears continued their silent descent. Nestled against his strong chest, even his coat couldn't keep her from hearing the steady rhythm of his heart. She sighed. It would be easy to believe the Luke she'd fallen in love with stood next to her. What-might-have-been flooded her soul with hopes of happily ever after.

But.

But this was not a fairy tale. A happily ever after wasn't looming. And though she believed with everything inside her that the Luke she loved still existed. He lived hidden away under the man who ran from life by drinking too much. Bekah was right. Who he was now wasn't the man she knew Luke should be.

As if in answer to her silent conflict, Luke's arms stiffened. Cold rushed in where her cheek had been warm against him. Why did he pull away?

His hand gently cupped her chin, raising her face until she looked him in the eyes. His square jaw tensed. His green eyes deepened until they appeared almost emerald.

Daisy tensed, chewed the inside of her lip. In her experience, that look meant anger bubbled under the façade of a calm demeanor.

"Tell me the truth." Before she could do more than open her mouth in answer, Luke continued. "I mean it. No lies or sugar-coating things. Do not protect me. Agreed?"

She nodded as much as his hand under her chin would allow. "Always."

His eyes darted away from her and back again. "Did ..." He sucked in a breath and swallowed hard. He refused to look at her, his focus drifting to something beyond her shoulder. "Did I hurt you last night?"

"Yes."

He swore. His hand dropped from her chin as if he'd touched a flame. He stepped backward, away from her. "No. I couldn't. I didn't."

He spun away and retreated from the porch to stalk over the lawn in front of it. Rubbing his hands over his face and hair, Luke glanced back at Daisy and completed his show with another word that would have brought Pops with a switch in hand. "Tell me. Please. You don't owe me, but please. I need to know."

A sudden realization made the smoothie churn in her stomach. Luke believed he'd taken advantage of her, and anger tempted her to let him think so. After all the crude offerings he'd voiced through the years, he deserved to experience some of the hurt. Besides, if he were convinced of the worst, he might understand the need to address his issues.

No. Daisy couldn't do it. Lying to Luke, even refusing to correct his misconception, was wrong. Pain and disgust mingled in his eyes, and Daisy's hesitation to clear up his misconception was responsible for their appearance.

As much as he'd hurt her, Daisy wouldn't allow him more pain than he brought on himself. The truth would bring him comfort. She took a step toward him, but he shook his head.

"Oh, Luke." She reached out to him, only to drop her hand as he retreated once again. "No. It wasn't like that. I promise, you've got it wrong."

Breath rushed from him as his eyes slid shut. "You're telling me the truth?"

"I wouldn't lie to you. And never about this." She waited

until he looked at her to offer a reassuring smile, weak as it was. "You hurt me, but not physically."

"Will you tell me?"

Daisy climbed the steps and sat on the porch swing. She patted the seat beside her. Luke hesitated before joining her, leaving as much space between them as possible. It was just as well. Sharing last night's phrases and invitations would be embarrassing enough without him right next to her. With only occasional glances in his direction, she filled him in on all the crude details.

Luke hissed at multiple points in the telling but didn't try to minimize his behavior. "I'm so sorry, Daisy. You don't go for those sorts of things. You're too good for that, and I'm embarrassed I said them to you."

She drummed her fingers on the arm of the swing. He didn't understand, not fully. Of course, he wouldn't if she didn't tell him. How far should her assurance of honesty take her?

"What hurt most—" Now it was her turn to look anywhere but at him. "What hurt most was that there was a time I would've married you and given you every part of me."

His jaw tightened again. "You broke up with me."

"You know why. And if you doubt, you can look at last night for a clearer understanding." Whether he wanted to hear it or not, he needed the truth. "But you're right. I broke up with you, and it broke my heart. I've never stopped loving you. That hurt hasn't ever healed. Your crude propositions, the idea you'd take from me what I always wanted you to have, but without thought or reason beyond physical gratification, were salt in the wound."

His dark expression hinted at a storm raging inside. His jaw worked. "You never stopped loving me, huh?"

"Not even one day."

"What about the others?" His lifted brow challenged her to prove her honesty.

She flinched. "Not that it's your business, but I've not dated in the last four years. Early on, I tried. I thought it would help me heal if I moved on. It didn't."

"Jason Price? Zachary Allen? Didn't I hear about you going out with both?"

Her shoulders straightened as she raised her chin. How could Luke think this line of questioning was appropriate? *Father God, give me patience to answer without losing it on him and making matters worse.*

"I went out with them, but only as friends. Once I knew, for whatever reason, you'd taken up permanent residence in my heart, I knew it would be wrong to continue dating. No one who went out with me had any misconceptions about our dates turning into anything more than friends hanging out."

LUKE STOOD and strode to the porch railing. Going on the offensive to ease his guilt over his boorish behavior was a poor choice. But jealousy had left him countering her claims of loving him with the men she'd dated, and the truth was worse than he imagined. Not that her dating would be wrong. He'd dated since they broke up, and not in the chaste way Daisy would have. But she'd not. Because of him. Because she still loved him.

His stomach twisted in knots. Daisy, who'd stood by him despite the choices driving everyone else away. The one person in his life he could always count on. When they were together, she'd accepted every physical display of affection as a gift, even though they were as simple as a kiss, holding hands, or brushing stray curls from her pale green eyes. Daisy was selfless. Good. Better than anyone he knew. Her heart craved giving love and receiving it from another.

But she couldn't have it because of him. Luke struggled to breathe past the squeezing of his chest. The one person most deserving of a Hollywood love story, and she was missing it because she fell for the wrong guy.

Luke hated the title. Wrong guy. He wanted Daisy as much as she wanted him. None of the other women came close to filling the emptiness left by her loss. Daisy was the one for him, but he'd long since made peace with settling for less. It was all he could hope for after she'd ended things between them.

"I'm sorry." One tiny apology when Daisy deserved much more.

"Luke?"

Her soft voice washed over him with what might be called hope. It'd been so long since he'd felt it, he was hesitant to name it.

"I'm sorry, Daise. I didn't know." He joined her. Her hands were small and tense inside his own as he reached out. Emotion highlighted the darker green flecks in her eyes as wariness filled them. "I should never have said those things to you. Forgive me?"

He loosened his hold when her hands twitched to pull away. The choice belonged to Daisy, and he resolved to respect it. Her hands stilled inside his, though her indecision was obvious in the twist of her lips. When her silence continued, Luke nodded. He asked too much. He always did, and he gave little in return.

"I forgive you."

He tightened his hold on her hands and raised them to his lips. Her skin was soft against his kiss. She sucked in a startled breath.

"Then let's make this work." He gave her his most persuasive smile. The roguish one that still drew her like a moth to flame. "We're miserable apart. I love you, and you still love me. Now that we've both admitted the truth, there's nothing stopping us from being together."

Chapter Three

Nothing stopping them? Daisy could list a million reasons a relationship with Luke was out of the question. Well, that might be an exaggeration, but still. The faith he once claimed was non-existent. He declared his love, but if rumors were to be believed, he'd hooked up with half their graduating class since their breakup. Her heart couldn't survive the devastation he left in his wake when things went sideways. And they would go awry. As long as he was drinking, it was a guarantee.

"I can't."

He dropped her hands. "But …"

She shook her head. "No."

Raw need filled his eyes. He viewed her as his salvation. She refused to accept the role. It would only lead to disappointment for them both. Still, the temptation to ignore the truth tugged at her heart.

It wooed her with the lie that Luke wasn't going to fill his emptiness with God, but he could fill it with her. It would be better than nothing. They could both have what they wanted. The love she'd pushed to the background through the last few years screamed at her to listen, to accept what she wanted.

Daisy turned her head and broke the spell his eyes attempted to cast over her. *Father God, I don't have the strength to refuse or to walk away. What do I do?*

You will know the truth, and the truth will make you free.

But God, I know the truth of Your word. Your Son has made me free.

You do.

Luke. He needed the truth. Pain led him to drink, and his drinking blinded him to the Son who could give him the freedom he craved.

"I'm not what you need." She faced him. "I can't be. You've got a problem, and I can't let it into my life no matter what I feel for you."

Light fled his eyes, leaving them dark and cool. "Because I like a drink every now and then?"

"Yes. No. I mean, it's not like that." She sighed. "It's not occasional. You drink yourself stupid more often than not. It's not healthy or safe. And it keeps you from dealing with life."

He swore. His fist connected with the swing arm. "Just like Mike. Both of you act like this is some big issue. It's not."

"Mike?" Daisy frowned. "Your boss talked with you about this?"

He glared at her. "Yeah. This morning. Right after he canned me."

"I'm so sorry." Daisy hurt for him. It couldn't be easy. But surely, he had to see there was a real issue.

He scoffed. "Doesn't matter. I'm done with him and his run-down nursery. Never could figure out how he kept all of us anyway. He couldn't be making any money. Probably needed to let someone go, and I was an easy target."

"You know that's not true. Mike is your friend." His forearm was tight under her own as she rested it there. "But he sees what I see."

Luke flew off the swing and spun to face her, defensiveness

starching his spine. "And just what do you see? Some lousy, no-account drunk?"

Even in the ugliness, Daisy had never regarded him in that way. But apparently, somewhere inside, Luke believed exactly that, though he didn't admit it. A vise squeezed her chest. "No." She kept her tone quiet and steady. "I see a caring, wonderful man who's been hiding behind addiction."

"Addiction?" He raised his hands in frustrated disbelief. "You think I'm an addict? I'm the next junkie they'll find in an alley somewhere?"

Lord, give me the words. "There are lots of addictions. Junkies aren't the only ones letting substances direct their lives. Alcohol, gambling, sex, porn. Anything sinking its talons into a person's brain chemistry can create an addiction."

Luke's eyes narrowed. "I can say no any time I want."

"Do it, then." Daisy sucked in courage. "Because when you're drunk, you turn into a man I don't recognize and, frankly, don't have any desire to."

"I already said I'm sorry for last night. It was a bad night is all. Drinking didn't cause it."

"Then, we have a real problem." Daisy raised her chin. Luke mirrored the action. She'd reached the point of no return, but she couldn't veer from the truth. "Because if your behavior last night was just Luke Masters having a hard day, whether we could get back together again should be the least of your concerns. That's a man I don't even want as a friend."

Daisy refused her building tears and the quaking every muscle in her body cried out for. Luke would see it as weakness. He could not be allowed to see the cracks in her armor. One glance and the battle would be lost.

Luke's jaw worked as he glared, but was that shock and hurt underneath? Daisy felt it as clearly as radiating sun on a summer day. *Please, God. Don't let it harden him.*

"So, that's the way you feel?" He raked a hand through his

hair. When she didn't answer, he shook his head. "Fine. You're the last person I expected this from. But I guess it was just a matter of time before you deserted me too."

Luke strode from the porch, not sparing her even a glance until he opened his Mustang's door and turned to get in. Their eyes met over the distance. His gave her one last chance to take back her words. A slight shake of her head was all she could manage. Anything else would release the torrents. Luke slid low into the driver's seat. A trail of dust followed his exit from her driveway. Was it the dress rehearsal for his leaving her life as well?

Stiff from the encounter as much as the chill in the air, Daisy trudged from the porch back inside. She should call Bekah. Then again, Daisy was in no mood to deal with her friend's good-riddance attitude.

Her coat missed its peg and slid to the floor. Daisy stepped over it on her way to her overstuffed recliner. She sank into it and cupped her hands over her face as the first sob escaped.

What had she done? Luke and her, together. For as long as she could remember, he'd been in her life. Even after dating through her senior year of high school and well into her sophomore year in college, they'd never compromised their friendship. In those early post-dating years, their continued relationship had proved difficult to navigate, especially when new guys entered her life. But none were ever worth losing Luke. They moved on. Luke remained.

Until now. She stuttered a breath between her tears. Was it worth him knowing the truth?

If she went to Luke, he'd take her back like nothing stood between them. Back to the status quo. On good days, they'd enjoy the same easy camaraderie they'd always shared. On the bad ones, Luke would have a few too many, and Daisy would be there to carry him in from the lawn.

At one time, the good days outweighed the bad. Now, they

attacked with greater frequency. Even when he didn't drunk dial her, Daisy knew Luke was still drinking. On nights her phone was silent, ugliness haunted her dreams. Whatever woman he hooked up with was there to help him inside. It didn't take the town busybodies reporting his every move to figure it out.

Cold seeped in with a memory she'd rather forget.

Daisy had arrived at his house with two fresh cups of coffee, oblivious to his activities the previous night. Luke's discomfort as he let her into his kitchen confused her. They'd always seen each other's houses as second homes. The door was always open.

Before she could work out the puzzle, a woman traipsed out of his room in nothing but her bra and panties and wound herself around him with a cat-that-ate-the-canary grin.

"You ordered us coffee." She'd kissed his cheek. "How sweet."

Daisy swallowed and looked everywhere but at the two of them. Dutifully, she held out the second cup. "Um. Yeah. Here you go. Two coffees."

He'd taken them from her before she stumbled back out the door in her hasty escape. He didn't owe her fidelity. They weren't together. But his failure to be even half the man she'd fallen in love with stung.

It was the last time she'd darkened his door without invitation, revoking their open-door policy until further notice.

"God, I can't do this." Not even she was sure what her prayer meant. Her need to cling to the truth butted up against her desire to fix her friendship with Luke. "Help me. Please."

Chapter Four

Luke slammed the cabinet shut, rattling the glasses inside. He filled the one in his hand from the faucet. Eyeing it with disgust, he dumped the water down the drain and left the glass in the drying rack.

In light of his blow-up with Daisy, the fridge offered better options. He took a beer from the top shelf, popped the top, and let the crisp bitterness trail down his throat, bringing him its own unique comfort. He drained the can and tossed it in the trash on his way to the living room.

"She doesn't know what she's talking about." He flopped into his recliner and picked up the remote. Turned it over in his hand. Pointed it at the TV. Sighed. Flung it back onto the side table. Dropped his head back. Swore. "Daisy, how can you mess with my head when we're not even together?"

Attempting to rein in his thoughts was futile. Snapshots of Daisy and him had long since been boxed and shelved in the closets. It was easier than explaining to the women he brought back to his place why pictures of another filled his walls. So, he'd put them away. Too bad purging the images from his mind wasn't as easy.

"Empty." Luke stared at the blank walls. Their starkness taunted him now with every word she'd spoken. With her decree that even their friendship was done, packed away just like the photo evidence, leaving him as bare as his walls.

"Enough." No more pity party. He needed people. Luke grabbed the keys to his old pickup truck before dropping them back on the counter in favor of the Mustang's. It was a muscle car kind of night.

He headed out the door and toward the one place even the Daisy in his head wouldn't dare darken the door. A few games of pool would shake her loose. And just to prove her wrong, he wouldn't even drink.

LUKE LINED UP THE SHOT. Peripherally, he spotted hips swaying in all the right ways as they sashayed his direction. The cue cracked against the ball, drawing his attention back to the felt. His distraction had cost him.

Tim laughed and moved to take his own shot. Not only did the final striped ball find its way to the pocket, but he was also set up to sink the eight ball. He did without breaking a sweat. He clapped Luke on the shoulder. "I think your luck may have run out."

"I wouldn't be so sure." A saucy grin stretched Jessica's glossy red lips. "I think there's plenty of night left for Luke to get lucky." Mascaraed eyelashes dropped in a wink before she moved toward the bar.

Already a few drinks past his resolve to abstain, Luke smirked as he watched her retreating backside. Every swing of her hips emphasized her innuendo. Before the balls on the table were reset, she returned with three beers. Tim took his with a loud kiss to Jessica's cheek.

"Ugh." She nudged him away with her shoulder, sloshing

some of the contents of the mugs in her hand. "Keep your lips to yourself. It's a beer, not a request."

He sneered. "Honey, everything you do asks for that and then some."

Jessica feigned an insulted huff. "You're disgusting." She slinked her way past him to Luke and handed him a mug. "You could sit the next one out. I think Tyler said something about wanting next game."

"Tyler. You're up. I've reached my limit." His words were spoken to the room, but his eyes never strayed from Jessica. Luke followed her to a high top in the corner. Though she took the chair opposite him, it made its way around the table before their drinks were finished.

The hard edge of her manicure traced a path up the back of his neck and into his hair, sparking a familiar pull toward her. Her fingers found their way back to the base of his neck and gently kneaded the muscles.

"What's wrong?" Jessica leaned closer. Her arm rested against his back while her fingers traced lazy circles on the muscles she'd just massaged. "You aren't upset I made you miss your shot, are you?"

Luke let her nuzzle his neck. "Nope."

"Good." She whispered into his ear. "You may have lost the game, but I have a feeling you'll not miss your next shot."

Her hand on his leg stoked the spark into a flame. He turned. Her lips were inches away, waiting for his kiss. Before Luke realized it, Jessica'd slithered around him like the serpent on the tree in the garden of Eden. Her offering was familiar. He'd eaten this tree's fruit and others like it without pause more times than he could count. This night would be no different.

So what if the aftertaste was as bitter as bile in his throat? It was still sweet on the lips, like every innocent kiss he'd shared with Daisy. He edged away from her embrace, but Jessica didn't seem to notice. Rather, she took it as an invitation to trail kisses along his neck.

No. Daisy couldn't invade this place. She was too good for this mess. Yet here she was in his mind, hounding him like she had in the early days after their breakup. He leaned away from Jessica, prompting her to sit up with a pout designed to draw his attention back to her willing lips.

He watched her. She transformed in an instant. The down-turned lips formed a seductive smile. Familiar enticement and an open offer. Not a hint of sincerity. He dropped his eyes to their hands when hers covered his.

"Oh, baby." She purred while batting her eyes. "I knew there was something wrong."

He glanced at her. The back of her fingers traced down his stubble-covered cheek. The fire didn't return. Not even a spark.

"Don't you worry," she cooed. "We'll make everything right again." She leaned close and whispered once more in his ear, detailing all they'd do when they left the bar. He swallowed hard as he realized some of her suggestions were the same ones he'd propositioned Daisy with just the night before. Each suggestion was more vulgar than the last.

Luke removed her hands from his body and set them in her lap. "No. Not tonight. Not any night."

Surprise widened her eyes before they narrowed to slits. "What? You're done with me. Just like that." She snapped. "No explanation?"

"I'm sorry. I can't."

"You have before."

"Well, I can't now." He jammed his fingers through his hair. "It's not right."

Jessica snatched her purse from off the back of the chair and stood glaring at him. "What's turned you into a choir boy? Nevermind. Doesn't matter. You're gonna miss me. When you come crawling back, guess what? The only thing I'll give you is two words. Not tonight."

She turned and stomped toward the restroom with a tirade of hateful words keeping step. Heads swiveled in his direction. Luke schooled his features, hoping for bland and uninterested. He shrugged as he stood and lifted his mug to drain the last dregs. He paused and set it back on the table.

Not tonight. Seeing Jessica clearly, for the first time in years, held up a mirror to the man he'd become. His stomach roiled. It was time for a change. And Luke knew exactly where to start.

Chapter Five

Daisy jerked awake, bolting upright. The pitch-black room offered no clues as to what yanked her from her restless dreams. She inclined her head, shut her eyes, and concentrated on the sounds. Was her alarm nothing more than angst fed by her dreams?

Pounding from another room. Who would be at her front door in the middle of the night?

"Daisy, open the door. Please."

Luke.

She groaned and glanced at her bedside clock. Two in the morning. He'd never shown up at her place after over-indulging. The hammering continued. He was yelling loud enough to wake the dead. Waking her neighbors on the other side of the small field separating their homes would be easy. Explaining to them —or worse, the cops—how Luke was only a nuisance and not a danger was the last thing she needed.

She shoved the covers aside. The cool wood floor chilled her bare feet with each hurried step. Luke's knocking and calling out diminished as she approached the door. He must have heard her approach. She unlocked and opened the door.

"What do you want?" She crossed her arms over her chest. "It's two in the morning."

"Can I come in?"

Daisy's eyelids felt weighted and puffy from crying herself to sleep. She didn't need a mirror to confirm she looked a mess, but with his hair tousled, shirt half untucked, and shoulders sagging, Luke looked worse. Not as bad as when he'd drunk himself stupid, but still not himself. His green eyes, so given to laughter, were lightly bloodshot and filled with something suspiciously resembling defeat. If she had to put his expression into one word, lost would define it perfectly.

God? I need Your help here. Do I let him in or not? Daisy studied him as if the answers she sought would be found in the man before her. He didn't so much as fidget as he waited.

"Please, Daisy." The words were laced with pain.

Doubt fled, and resignation took its place. Stepping aside, she waved him in. She plopped onto the sofa and folded her legs under her on the cushion. Luke stalked back and forth across the carpet. Silence stretched between them. She watched. He paced. The kitchen clock ticked off the minutes in the background.

This was ridiculous. There were far better things to do this early in the morning than sit on her couch watching him stalk back and forth across her small living room. Returning to her bed topped the list.

Her sigh broke the silence. "Listen, Luke. I'm tired, and I've got work in a few hours. If all we're going to do is sit here, or pace here, or"—she waved her hand in the air—"whatever this is, I'm going back to bed. See yourself out."

Luke raked his hands through his short hair and down his neck as he dropped onto the other end of the sofa. His throat moved as he swallowed. "I almost went home with her. Any other night, we'd have hooked up without me giving it another thought."

Seriously? He'd come to tell her about some chick at the

bar he'd nearly slept with? Daisy rubbed her face with her hands. She'd not had enough sleep to deal with this. "Luke …" What could she say? Nothing. That's what. "I'm going back to bed."

His hand over hers stopped her before she stood. "No." He shook his head. "That's not. I mean, I started badly. Please."

Saying no to Luke Masters was never easy. This time, it bordered on impossible. His need was palpable. His eyes begged for a chance to explain. He was lost, but she wasn't his North. Understanding the truth is what convinced her to break up with him in the first place. She could never be his guide, but he refused to acknowledge the only One who could. And while praying, he'd see his True North through her had kept their friendship going, it still inflicted pain on her heart every single time he failed.

"Then start again."

His shoulders relaxed. "I didn't intend to drink. I went to play pool to take my mind off it, off what happened earlier. But I wasn't going to drink. I swear, I wasn't."

How many times had she schooled him on making promises he couldn't keep, much less swearing to something? But given the circumstances, she guessed his broken promise was the least of her concerns. He'd obviously tried and failed. The red in his eyes confirmed it.

"But you did."

His gaze dropped to the floor. His shoulders rose and fell. "Yes." He looked back to her. "I wanted to prove you wrong. I didn't drink as much as I usually do. I guess that's something."

She stared, refusing to acknowledge what he considered a win.

"Right." He cleared his throat. "You're right. But it did mean I wasn't wasted when Jessica joined me."

Great. Now they were back to the woman Luke didn't sleep with. This conversation was progressing perfectly.

"She was willing, Daisy. She doesn't play games and doesn't want a relationship. Jessica puts it all out there loud and clear."

Daisy was going to be sick if he continued. Knowing he hooked up with the women at the bars and hearing about them were two different things. A small but vital distinction.

"I couldn't."

He paused, watching her. What did he want from her? A prize for once-in-a-lifetime celibacy? People made the same choice every day. Not Luke, obviously, but it wasn't an unusual occurrence. Not for her. Still, Luke waited for some reaction. What could she honestly give?

"Seems smart."

A sad smile curved his lips. "I couldn't leave with her, Daisy. Every time she pursed her over-colored lips and batted her over-done eyes, all I noticed was how fake it all was. Her clothes, her looks, her laugh, everything. It was all show to get me, or whoever else, in bed. They, all the women there, it's been the same with all of them. I've never seen it."

"Hmm." She could tell him why, but the Holy Spirit clamped her mouth tighter than the lions' in the den with Daniel.

"Then, she started telling me all the things we'd do back at her place."

Just when she thought it wouldn't get any worse. Daisy definitely didn't want these details. Pushing her shoulders back, she steeled herself for what was bound to come next and prepared to shut him down.

"It was too much." He shook his head. "All I could see was you and me. How different our relationship was from what she was offering. No matter how perfect we were together, I can't have it back. But is the polar opposite all I can ask for? It's more glaring than night and day. And I never realized it."

Luke stood and paced again. Daisy kept silent, wasn't sure what she could say. It was a lot to take in on a few hours of less-than-restful sleep. He stopped in front of her.

"And what she said."

He closed his eyes. When he opened them, Daisy's heart broke seeing the wave of regret in his gaze.

"Every word, every phrase. Every. Single. Word. I'd said them to you just twenty-four hours ago. I've heard 'em before. But tonight, realizing I'd said the same to you, made me sick."

Daisy clenched her jaw. Tears burned. She wouldn't let them, focusing on the carpet at her feet. Her stomach churned. Luke dropped to his knees in front of her.

"Please."

What he wanted was clear. She bit her lip and met his gaze.

"I don't have any right. You've done more for me than anyone in my life. I never deserved it. And, despite my choice tonight, I still don't. But I have to ask. Daisy, can you forgive me for treating you that way? For all of it. Not just last night. Every stupid thing I've done?"

A mental checklist of offenses committed through the years scrolled through Daisy's mind. No, whether he'd asked or not, she'd forgiven those a long time ago. She refused to dredge them up again, though neither of them could ignore their existence. He'd done more thoughtless things than a single list could hold.

A sad chuckle escaped as Daisy wiped tears from her cheeks. "That's a lot of stupid."

"Yep." His smile held the hint of the Luke she loved behind the sadness. "I wish I could take every last instance back."

She frowned. "Why?"

Wariness replaced his smile. "What do you mean, why?"

"Why take every instance back?" She shrugged. "Why apologize? Are you cleaning the slate to make room for the future things? Being sorry you've hurt someone is different than taking steps to ensure it doesn't happen again."

A *V* formed between his brows. Defeat crept back into his expression.

"I forgive you. I always have, long before you asked." She

cupped his cheek, and his scruff against her palm was familiar, intensifying the pull of the past and her love, which had yet to fade. Though it tore through her to do so, she pulled her hand back. "But it doesn't mean my decision has changed. I can't keep coming back to this place. I can't keep watching this happen."

His hands closed around hers. The warmth they brought coursed through her.

God, why does this have to be so hard? No answer arrived as reinforcement for her tender heart. *Please, just take this ... this ... whatever this is between us. I can't do it. Show me what to do.*

"That's just it. I don't want this to happen again." He swallowed. "You're right. Every bad decision I've made started with drinking."

She cocked an eyebrow.

His head tilted to his shoulder in a half-shrug. "Okay. So not every bad decision, but enough of them even I can see the trend. This week alone, I lost you. My job. My phone."

"Your phone?"

He shook his head. "Story for another time. Point is, I'm tired of losing things. I know the man you see when you look at me, and it's not the one you want to see. The man you used to see. He's been gone a long time, but he can return."

"It can't be for me, Luke." Hope tempered with reality struggled to plant itself in her heart. "I'm not the pot of gold at the end of your rainbow."

"I understand." He nodded. "A future with you is gone. I've lost it. But we can be friends. If not, I still don't want to be the man I've become. The guy you've always seen in me? He's the one I want to find again."

Would he make the leap? Would he realize what change like that took? *Please, God. Let him see. He needs You if he wants to become that man again. You and cutting out the drinking for good.*

Luke stood from his crouched position in front of her. He

crossed to the window and stared out. "And," he continued without turning, "finding him starts with admitting I have a problem. Drinking has messed up the best things in my life and turned me into this guy I hate. It's time to let it go."

Hope bloomed and withered in the same moment. In the early years, right before and after their breakup, Luke had made declarations of committing to what was necessary to keep their love. This time, there wasn't a reward of love waiting for him if he succeeded. Could she trust this new revelation?

"Do you mean it?"

He turned. The look in his eyes was the same she'd seen every time someone told Luke Masters he couldn't. Determination. His chin lifted.

"Yes."

"It won't be easy."

"Nope."

"You'll face days when you'll want to go back."

"Yep."

"What will you do then? Find a group for accountability?"

He shook his head. "Don't need a group. It's my problem, and kicking it is on me, no one else."

"But …"

"No buts. I don't need any meetings. A friend or two might be nice, though. Someone to talk to when things are rough. But I don't need a group up in my business to lick this thing."

It wasn't a perfect plan, and he'd not mentioned God once, but it was a start. Maybe he was right and didn't need a group. As long as he knew it would be hard and had someone in his corner, maybe he could stay sober. She met him by the window.

"Do you have it? Someone to talk to when it's tough?"

"Not yet." He rubbed his hand across his jaw. "But I'll find somebody."

Somebody? Luke didn't have relatives, and he'd alienated the half of the town that wanted more for him. A pastor would be perfect, but Luke wasn't ready for God yet. Without stopping to consider the ramifications, Daisy grasped his hand.

"You do now."

"I can't ask you. You've made it clear, you don't want anything to do with me."

"No." She shook her head. "I don't want anything to do with the guy who refuses to see he's got a problem. The man standing in front of me not only acknowledges the problem but wants to purge it. I can offer him friendship and support. But"—she looked at him pointedly—"it's all I can offer him."

"It's enough." He squeezed her hand. "But are you sure? It doesn't have to be you."

She smirked. "Who else understands you enough to call you on it when you start justifying and excusing? Who else has seen you at your worst and has prayed for you to see it and want to change? Or better question, who haven't you run off acting like you haven't got any sense these last few years?"

He raised his hands in surrender. "All right. I agree. I've not been the most likable person lately."

"Only when you're drinking."

"But it's over. No more."

"Okay. Do we have a deal? I'll be your friend. You'll come to me instead of the bar when it gets tough? And you give me permission to be honest with you and call it like I see it, and you'll hear me out?"

He smiled and stuck out his hand. "Deal."

The breakthrough had her arms itching to pull Luke into a friendly hug to seal their deal. Instead, she let his hand swallow hers in an exaggerated shake. This wasn't going to be easy for either of them. Doubt popped up like weeds in her gardens. She yanked it out before it could take root. For the first time in years, a glimmer of light shone at the end of the tunnel. Luke was taking his first steps in coming home again.

But how was she going to help him arrive without taking any more damage to her battered heart?

Chapter Six

"I'll believe it when I see it." Bekah wiped the glass top of the rustic barn wood counter.

Daisy swallowed back the mean retort that sprang to mind. Bekah had reason to react as she did. But she hadn't seen Luke, hadn't heard the truth in his tone. "He admitted there's a problem. Doesn't that mean anything?"

"Sure." Bekah rolled her eyes. "It means he wants you back, and this is the way he's going to accomplish his goal."

Daisy huffed.

"You're not gullible, Daise." Bekah tossed the cleaning rag into the supply bucket and tucked it into a cabinet. "Luke's loved you since you were kids. You told him you loved him too. Then, not a day later, he has this epiphany about how what he's been chasing is empty and how he needs to stop drinking. Really? Seems a little too coincidental."

Again, Daisy couldn't blame Bekah. Daisy had wondered the same thing. If she hadn't witnessed the sincerity in his eyes as he spoke, she might have continued doubting. Even so, after Luke left, she'd spent the hours before work in prayer, asking God to confirm the truth. She'd left her house with a firm conviction that this was for real.

"I wish you could have been there." Daisy plunked herself down onto one of the stools at the high counter. "You wouldn't doubt it if you'd heard it from Luke. I've covered it with prayer, and I'll continue doing so. If I'm wrong, God will show me."

"Hopefully sooner rather than later."

"Bek."

"I just can't do it." Disappointment showed in Bekah's eyes as she shook her head. "I watched him destroy your heart once and then piece by piece chip off whatever was left. I can't watch him do it again."

"I broke up with him."

"Yeah. And it sucked out all your joy for a long time. It's been seven years. How many dates have you been on? It's not good, no matter how you look at it."

Daisy straightened her shoulders. "I don't date because I don't want to."

Bekah snorted. "You don't date because you forgot to take your heart back from Luke."

If Luke was going to succeed, he needed her support. If she was going to be there for him, Daisy needed her best friend. Why couldn't Bekah give him a chance?

Daisy drummed her fingernails against the counter. She didn't want to be at an impasse with Bekah. Their friendship spanned almost as many years as hers with Luke did. And it was void of the strain of drinking, unless she counted Luke's drinking. If his issues counted, their relationship had recently bent under the weight. Daisy didn't want to choose, but Bekah insisted on pushing her into a corner with no other way out.

"Trust me, please." Daisy's voice was calm and quiet. She didn't like the defeat present in her tone, but it remained. "Trust me. He's not doing it to win me back. I made it clear. A relationship is off the table. For the first time, Luke sees his drinking as a problem and wants to fix it. Can you give him a chance? Please."

Bekah's posture relaxed as her head tilted to the side, spilling her blonde hair over her shoulder. Resignation tinged her frown. "Fine. I'll try."

"It's all I ask." Daisy stood. "Now, if you've got things covered in here, I've got to check on the gardens. It's almost time for planting, and I've not done a thing to clean them out."

TEN AFTER NINE. Communi-TEA would be opening for the day. Luke should probably avoid Daisy's shop after their early morning discussion, but he needed a distraction. Instead of returning home to fall into bed and sleep away the morning, a strange, restless energy pulsed through every limb.

After attempting every sleeping position imaginable at least three times each, he'd given up. Thinking manual labor might help, Luke had purged his home of all alcohol and then scoured every cleanable surface in the house. His shower hadn't been this white since the day it was installed.

Still restless, he'd decided against another attempt at sleep. He needed out of the house. Without a job to keep him busy, he'd lose his mind before a week was up. He needed the distraction of physical labor.

"Communi-TEA it is." He snatched the keys to his Mustang and headed out.

Two cars waited in the lot, other than his. Daisy and Bekah. He was sure of it. Luke pressed the button on his fob. Two staccato honks assured him his baby was locked. While Daisy's tea shop-turned-crafter's haven was in a safe neighborhood, he refused to take an unnecessary risk.

Long strides made short work of the gravel parking lot and the paving stones leading to the heavy sliding barn doors framing the entry. Potential customers knew without turning into the lot if they'd arrived during off-hours. If the solid wood doors covered the coordinating glass-paned ones, Communi-TEA would be locked up tight every time.

"No tacky neon signs flashing open for Daisy." Luke grinned. Flashy was as far from Daisy as Earth from the next galaxy. Every detail of Communi-TEA, however, fit her like her favorite pair of cowboy boots.

Luke pulled the door open. Scents of Daisy's herbal teas blended with those of the polish she used to make the rustic wood surfaces gleam, and the fragrant essential oil-scented candles showcased in other vendors' spaces. What could have been a dark space was brightened by a few large windows and the Edison-style lighting strung from beams high overhead.

"Welcome to—" Bekah's words stopped short as she turned and realized it was him. "Luke."

Her voice couldn't be flatter if he ran over it with his pickup truck. He bit back one of his typical snappy retorts. In light of his recent self-discoveries, he might deserve more than her reticence.

"Hi, Bek." He made his way to the tea bar counter.

"Daisy's outside."

If her tone was any indication, the tea bar wouldn't run out of ice anytime soon. Cold didn't cover it. It was time to make amends. He sucked in a breath.

"I'll find her in a minute. First, there are a few things I need to say to you."

Her jaw tightened. One brow rose high. She didn't welcome conversation with him, but she didn't turn away from it either. It was something.

He cleared his throat. Tried but couldn't quite make eye contact. "I'm sorry."

"For?"

"Everything."

The granite in her voice had brought out his own. She snapped up the rag on the counter and started to turn. This was not going the way Luke wanted. He was trying to apologize, and she wasn't making it easy. Of course, if apologizing were easy, everyone would do it.

"Wait."

A pause.

"I mean it. Really. I've been an idiot."

She snorted. "Tell me something new."

"I can't." He swiped his cap off with one hand before running the other through his hair. "You've seen a lot of it, and I'm sure you've been filled in on the rest. I've hurt a lot of people, Daisy most of all. And I'm sorry. I'm sorry you've been left to pick up the pieces."

"Being sorry doesn't keep it from happening again."

"Nope. But laying off the drinking should help."

Bekah's chin lifted as her eyes narrowed with her appraisal. "Only on weekends? Or a few less than usual? Is that what you think is going to solve this?"

His palm stung as it slapped against his thigh. "Come on, Bek. I'm trying here. Cut me some slack."

Nothing but a tight-lipped glare.

"Fine. No. I don't mean I'm going to drink less. I mean, I'm not going to drink. I'm not going to lose anything else to drinking. I've lost too much already."

The door to his right swung open, admitting Lucy, the owner of By Sweet Design Bakery. Slight as she was, she pulled in a cart stuffed with individually wrapped baked goods behind her and managed to keep a bounce in her step even with the added weight. With a wave and a bright grin, she made a beeline for the tea bar.

"Hey, all. Just dropping off this week's baked goods." She moved behind the counter, opened the display case, and plopped the first muffin in its designated space. "Don't let me interrupt. I'll be out of here just as soon as I unload my stock."

"Great to see you, Lucy." Luke nodded. "I was just on my way to find Daisy. You take care."

He refused to acknowledge Bekah as he strode out the side door to the herb garden. Lucy, who immediately filled the silence left in his wake, had interrupted Bekah's response. Call him a chicken, but Luke wasn't sure he wanted her answer. Her opinions had rarely fallen in his favor, with or without reason.

Pulling his cap down to shield his eyes from the morning sun, Luke scanned the gardens beyond the fenced patio area dotted with wood-and-glass-topped barrel tables and rustic wooden chairs. Weather was still too chancy for customers to enjoy their tea bar drinks on the covered patio, but it was the perfect time for Daisy to prep the gardens.

Movement through the panes of the small greenhouse on the far side of the herb garden drew Luke's attention. Daisy. Ignoring the "No customers beyond this point" sign posted on the small picket fence, Luke raised the latch on the gate separating the patio from the gardens. Technically, he wasn't a customer, but he could only hope he'd be more welcome.

Before he could step through, a puff of white fur shot through the opening and wound itself around his legs. He bent to scratch the cat behind her ears.

"Hiya, Sage."

The cat purred a welcome.

"Care to tell me what mood Daisy's in today?"

The low rumble continued. Luke straightened and stepped around the unofficial mascot of the Communi-TEA Barn.

"Lotta help you are." He smirked as he latched the gate. "They may say you're a reformed stray, but, with your attitude, I'd be willing to bet Bek snuck you in."

Bereft of attention, Sage sauntered toward a shady patch of patio near the door. Once the door cracked open, the cat would escape inside, but why it would want to was lost on Luke. He breathed in the cool morning air. While it lacked the rich, earthy scents he'd expect after Daisy planted her herb gardens, outside was still better than the menagerie of scents swirling together within the confines of the barn.

"Candles, soaps, those stupid little baggie things women stuff in their underwear drawers." Luke shook his head. "Why does everything with women have to have a scent? It's too much."

Not that he'd tell Daisy. She made her living off the peculiarity of the fairer sex. Besides, he didn't mind it so much when Daisy used to snuggle in close enough for the scent of her shampoo to tease him.

He grinned. No strawberries and cream or coconut for Daisy. No, she'd blended her own shampoo with herbs from her garden and natural oils. Citrus and rosemary. At least, that's what she'd told him when he'd complimented it once. Paired with her springy, golden-brown curls, it made Luke think of sunshine. Made him think of Daisy.

As he pulled the greenhouse door open, Daisy turned. Her jade eyes were as cool as the stone itself. No one bothered her in her sanctuary. He should have waited, but it was too late now.

Chapter Seven

"What are you doing here?"

Doubt assaulted him. When had Daisy started being so surprised to see him that every conversation began this way? Never mind. The answer was obvious, and he didn't want to go there. Why did he allow himself to believe one late-night conversation about his regrets would take them back to the easy friendship they'd shared as kids? Better question. When had he gotten so dense? Yep. That was the million-dollar question.

Daisy's brows raised high, and Luke realized he had yet to answer. He shifted his weight to one foot and adjusted his ball cap. What *was* he doing there?

"I've got nowhere else to be."

The truth gut-punched him. No job. And no friends amounting to anything if he wanted to steer clear of the drinking crowd. Another thing his poor choices had cost him.

He shrugged. "Thought you could use some help around here or something. I owe you after last night. After more than last night, if we're shootin' straight about it."

Silent regard. He shifted his weight again. Swallowed.

"It's fine. Don't worry about it." He forced a smile. "I'm sure you've got things under control. You've never needed help getting things done. Talk to ya later. Okay?"

He turned toward the door. Humiliation and regret roosted heavily on his shoulders.

"Luke."

Her statement was barely above a whisper, the ache in it tangible. He paused but didn't turn. He wouldn't impose on her. She deserved better. So much better than him. But his whole being craved a return to their previous friendship. And all it took was that one spark of hope to freeze Luke in his escape.

"Luke."

It was stronger this time. He turned. Met her eyes. If only he could take away the confusion, the fear trapped inside them. Her full, shapely lips curved into a smile holding more sadness than joy.

"I *could* use your help."

Was that pity in her tone? The last thing Luke wanted was to intrude where he wasn't wanted.

"Listen, Daisy. I shouldn't have come …"

Her curls bounced with the shake of her head. "No."

"It won't happen again." He sighed. "It's too much."

She shook her head again. "That's not what I meant. I just. I agreed to be there for you. Support you in this. But—"

"But it doesn't mean you want me around all the time." He smiled as best he could. "Don't apologize or make excuses. It's a lot. And it's not your weight to carry."

Her jaw tightened as she swallowed hard. Emotions ran close to the surface. Luke recognized the signs. As lost as he was, he couldn't let his issues hurt Daisy any longer. It was time to step up. Be the friend she deserved.

"Aww, Daise." He stepped closer and opened his arms. She stepped into his embrace, burying her head in the curve of his shoulder. He cupped her head in his hand. "It's okay. Really. No worries."

Despite the situation, holding Daisy was like coming home. It'd been too long. No. That wasn't right. It couldn't be. His chest tightened as his mind wandered the path of the last several years. She'd held him up more times than he could count, with his arm draped over her shoulder and hers firmly around his waist. But each instance was to move him inside to sleep it off.

The last time they'd shared a real connection was after Pops died. Mom had retreated into herself worse than she had after finding out about his dad's cheating, and then his dad had reached out with a load of horse manure about wanting to be there for him in his time of need. Luke had laughed in his face. There was no way Luke would look for comfort from the man who'd broken up two families by having an affair with his best friend's wife. The fact his old man even tried showed how clueless he was.

No. He'd been alone, drowning. He'd held onto Daisy like his life depended on it. At least, until she wouldn't allow it anymore and walked out too. She blamed his drinking. He wouldn't hear it. Called it an excuse. Was it only last night he'd realized how wrong he'd been? And now, she was in his embrace once more, but the damage he'd inflicted was obvious. Was it possible to make things right?

Luke took a step back, severing the connection to her. With his fingertips, he lifted her chin to raise her eyes to his. "I never meant to upset you by coming here. I should've realized. There's a lot of hurt I've got to make up for. And it's new to both of us. Not to mention, neither of us got much sleep last night, thanks to me."

"I ..."

He shook his head. "No. Don't try to explain or apologize or whatever. I'll see you around. Take care of yourself."

It hurt worse than drawing out infection from a wound, but Luke dropped his hand and left without waiting for Daisy's response. He strode back through the garden. The last thing he needed was to face Bekah's scrutiny by exiting through the barn.

Instead, he jumped the thigh-high fence separating the patio from the parking lot. No matter what it felt like, he'd done nothing wrong this time. In fact, for the first time in far too long, he'd done the hard thing because it was the right thing.

DAISY STOOD FROZEN as Luke retreated. He'd come to her. Needed her. But when he realized it was too much too soon, he'd given her space. She'd always considered herself strong, but he was right. Between the lack of sleep, his acceptance of his problem, and his determination to overcome it, there was too much information to process so quickly.

It might not take long, but Daisy thrived on having time to work through the tough stuff. And this was the biggest situation she'd faced in a while. Though prepping the herb garden wasn't her favorite task, she'd opted for starting the chore over working in the barn, where customers, the renting crafters, and even Bekah would see her distraction. She'd only just begun working through the previous night's events when Luke showed up. His leaving added one more knot to her tangled thoughts.

Turning back to her workbench, Daisy scooped soil into plastic pots. Order might not be attainable in her mind, but she needed to accomplish something today. If she was going to have the plants she needed to create her teas, the seeds needed to be buried in the soil. Luke or no Luke, she had a job to do.

She grimaced as her elbow sent a filled pot crashing to the floor.

"You've got to be kidding." Daisy tossed her trowel onto the worktable and frowned at the mess at her feet. She righted the container and scooped as much soil as she could from the floor back into it. "Get your head in the game."

Breakage wasn't the issue. The wasted time, seeing how this was the third pot she'd knocked from the table in her distraction, was more irritating than the thorns on a rose bush. After adding an extra scoop of soil and reseeding it, Daisy set the pot with the others and pulled off her gardening gloves. There was no use in continuing if she couldn't concentrate enough to prevent careless mistakes.

Instead, she left the greenhouse and strolled along the pebbled paths between the raised garden beds to the dogwood tree in the middle of the space. Thankful she'd had the foresight to add a bench under the tree bordering a small decorative pond, Daisy plopped down on the wooden seat and let her gaze wander beyond the picket fence border of her garden. A gray fox trotted just outside the tree line edging her property. She closed her eyes and inhaled the cool, fresh air. Windchimes on the patio blended with the gurgle of water to massage away her stress and still her racing thoughts.

"Father, God." She breathed out the prayer. "Calm my mind. Remind me, convince me, I'm not responsible for Luke's sobriety or the issues he's having. I don't want to take on what's not mine. Show me how to be his friend and when to help. Give me words when he needs them. Lord, if he needs to keep busy, I pray You'd provide opportunity in a healthy way."

"Daisy." Bekah's voice carried from the patio doorway. "There's a lady here with a question about tonight's herb class."

"Coming."

She'd forgotten the class she scheduled on creative ways to use herbs. Most of her classes were repeats that she could teach on autopilot, but this one was new. She still needed to put the finishing touches on the projects. Her plants would have to wait for another day. While prepping the gardens was the least enjoyable part of the process, it was vital. It shouldn't have to be squeezed in between the things she wanted to do. But there was no helping it. Or was there?

Chapter Eight

"What're you doing here?" Mike asked as he crossed the parking lot toward Luke's pickup.

Maybe Luke should've driven the extra twenty minutes to the next closest landscaping and gardening supply store. Even the local hardware store's gardening center might have been easier, but Daisy liked to support the local mom-and-pop shops. So, he'd ignored the unease knotting his gut and headed toward Mike's Landscaping for the first time since he'd been canned. After he'd been going stir-crazy for nearly a week, Daisy reached out with something to occupy his time, and he was going to finish the project.

"I'm not giving you your job back." Mike stopped in front of him. "Might as well forget it, get back in your truck, and be on your way."

Luke held up his hands in surrender. "I don't need a job."

Mike huffed. "Haven't gotten it through your thick skull that your bad choices put you out of a job?"

Luke's neck muscles tightened. He might deserve Mike's antagonism, but it irritated like hot vinyl seats on bare legs in the middle of summer. He swallowed back a sharp retort. Picking a fight with Mike wasn't going to help convince anyone he was changing.

"My thick skull got it just fine." He tried for lighthearted, but humiliation weighed down the words. "I'm running an errand for Daisy. Sent me for some raised bed garden soil."

"How do you do it, man?" Mike shook his head.

"Do what?"

"How long'd ya work here? Three years? Four?"

Luke frowned. "Sounds right. What's your point?"

Mike led Luke to a row of flat carts and pulled one from the line. "How much does Daisy need?"

"Fifteen large ones. Wants name brand. Only the best for … that girl." He'd barely amended his comment to keep from saying my girl. Didn't need to add fuel to Mike's fire.

Even though he knew the layout, Luke followed as Mike led the way.

"That's what I mean." Mike tossed a look at him over his shoulder. "Daisy isn't one of the desperate women from the bar. She's got common sense, faith, and a strong work ethic."

Luke's jaw tightened. "What are you saying, Mike?"

"Don't get your hackles up. You know exactly what I'm getting at, and it's true. There's no reason for a girl like Daisy to stick by your side this long. You've told me every time she's picked you up, literally and figuratively. Now, you've lost your job, and she gives you a new one. It's insane."

If alcohol released inhibitions, Luke understood how he'd taken swings a few times at jerks in the bar. Because, at the moment, he was about to do the same without the aid of one too many beers.

"Not that it's your business," Luke paused so the truth could sink in, "but Daisy didn't hire me at first."

Mike stopped in front of a flat of bagged soil, dragged off the top one, and stacked it on the cart. "Then, why are you running her errands?"

"I'm hired now, at least temporarily. But originally, I needed something to do, and she had stuff for me to do." Luke hefted a bag onto the first one. He'd load them all himself if it meant Mike would leave him alone. "Keeping busy makes it easier to stay away from bad habits."

Mike stopped loading and stared at him. Luke continued working. It made Mike's appraisal less awkward.

"Bad habits? Drinking?"

Luke swallowed and lifted two bags. He needed the extra strain to work out the building frustration. Understanding where Mike was coming from didn't mean he liked it.

"Yeah. Decided it was time. Didn't like who I'd become or what I'd lost."

Mike continued his perusal before joining Luke in the work once more. "Good. Hope it sticks."

Other than necessary details like how much Luke owed for the soil, they worked in silence until the last bag was loaded into Luke's truck.

"It can't be easy, but I'm glad you're moving the right direction." Mike lifted the tailgate into position. "Give me a call if you need to talk or anything."

It wasn't lost on Luke, as he drove back to the CommuniTEA Barn, that Mike hadn't offered to give him his job back. But returning to his previous work wasn't why Luke opened up about the changes he was making. Luke hadn't verbalized regret over his actions, but it was there. Mike knew it, too. If he didn't, he wouldn't have offered the olive branch of a listening ear.

Their camaraderie was tentative, but it was a start. Facing Mike, owning the truth, felt less like a mountain to climb and more like an avalanche crashing into him. But it was the right choice. All he'd done was start reconciling with Daisy and Mike, but a weight Luke hadn't known he was carrying dissipated, leaving the hope he hadn't experienced in ages. His life was still a mess, but things were looking up.

"Daisy isn't here." Bekah barely glanced in Luke's direction from her place behind the tea bar's counter.

Patience. What was it Pops used to say? *You catch more flies with honey than vinegar.*

"Did she say when she was coming back?"

"No."

"Whether she wants me to start in the garden or wait?"

"Nope."

The bells attached to the front door jingled to announce a customer. Bekah's lips curved in a smile as she faced the newcomer. Of course, she could smile for the customers. They could have vices worse than his own, and she'd still smile. Their secrets weren't common knowledge, and his were all too apparent to her.

"Katie Phillips, where on earth have you been lately?" Bekah's friendly tone took any sting from her chiding as she raced around the counter to her friend. "And who is this?"

"Do you remember Erin and Paul?"

"Of course."

"This is their daughter, Joy. They're up to their necks in it, trying to inventory their two stores. So, Joy and Auntie Katie are having fun together while they work."

Luke's manners kicked in. He turned to greet Katie and stopped short when he spied one of those baby carrier things strapped to her front with a sleeping infant snuggled inside. He'd known Katie's husband, Nathan, from childhood, but Katie had left the area straight out of high school, only returning several years later. Luke had heard they'd ended up together, with Nathan filling the father role for Katie's son after her first husband died, but he didn't see either of them often, and the newest addition to their family was a surprise.

"Luke?" Katie spotted him around Bekah's hug. "I didn't expect to see you here."

"Seems to be a lot of that going around." He smiled and looked toward Bekah, who was just starting to loosen her death grip on Katie.

"It's good to see you." Luke nodded. "How's Nathan? Sammy? I had no clue about this new little one. Is this a little brother or sister for Sammy?"

"Sister. Angeline Ruth. Nathan and Sammy are doing well. They love spoiling this little one." She softly rubbed the mostly bald head peeking out from the top of the carrier. "Though Sammy insists he's Sam now. Says Sammy is for babies." Katie rolled her eyes. "They grow up too quickly."

Luke glanced down at the little girl he'd never met, holding tight to Katie's hand. He'd heard Erin and Paul adopted, but through his own choices, he'd had little contact with former friends. Luke moved closer and hunched low before the pig-tailed little girl. "And this little princess must be Joy?" She moved behind Auntie Katie's legs, but not before a shy smile peeked out.

Katie put a hand on the little girl's blonde head. "It's okay, Joy. This is one of mine, Uncle Nathan's, and Mommy's friends from when we were younger."

Luke smiled but didn't move closer. "Hello, Joy. I'm Luke."

The toddler stared, curiosity filling her eyes.

"How old are you, Joy?"

Cherub cheeks reduced Joy's eyes to slits as she smiled. She slid farther behind Katie.

"I don't think you're shy at all. I think you're faking." Without rising, he looked up at Katie for confirmation.

"There's only one time she's shy." Katie shook her head. "That's when she's flirting. Paul and Erin are hoping she grows out of it before the teen years. If not, she'll keep them on their toes, for sure."

"Aw, come on, now," Luke coaxed. "Are you three? Four?" He held up the corresponding number of fingers.

Joy's grin grew as she giggled. "Fwee." Three pudgy fingers clarified her announcement.

"Three?" Luke widened his eyes in mock surprise. "Wow. You're practically grown. It was nice meeting you, Joy. But now, I've got work to do."

"You're working here now?" Katie rubbed her lower back as Luke stretched back to full height. "I thought you were at the nursery."

"I was." Luke shifted his weight from one foot to the other. "But I'm out here for now."

"He's temporary." Bekah's voice wasn't as icy as when she spoke to him, but it left no room for argument either. "He's just helping Daisy with the herb garden."

Katie grinned. "The gardens always were her least favorite part of the job. She's a whiz with blending herbs. Loves to sit in the garden surrounded by the plants, but prepping, planting, and maintaining have always been a chore for her."

Either she didn't catch Bekah's tone, or she chose to ignore it. Either way, Luke would gladly accept it.

"Temporary or not," and Luke wasn't about to open a can of worms by pointing out that Daisy hadn't ever said temporary in regard to his hire, "I'd better get to it. Tell Nathan I said hello." He nodded to Katie before grinning at the little girl. "And it was nice to meet you, Joy. You'll have to visit when the garden's planted and see all the flowers."

He waved. Though still hiding, her pudgy fingers bent in acknowledgment. He glanced at Bekah. "Will you tell Daisy I'm in the garden when she gets back?"

"Sure."

It wasn't a hearty agreement, but at least she'd said yes. Maybe they needed to keep customers in the store 24/7 so she'd be a little friendlier toward him.

"Thanks."

He slipped out the garden patio door away from the women's chatter into the silence. At one time, a lack of sensory input would have been welcome. Lately, nothingness was short-lived as his mistakes came back to haunt and his temptations to taunt. Keeping active was only a small part. If he didn't distract his mind, he could end up down a dark path.

Pulling the new phone he'd splurged on and earbuds from his pocket, Luke opened a music app. Garth, Reba, and Alan filled the space between his ears to quiet his wayward thoughts as he hefted bags of soil from his truck bed over the low picket fence and onto the herb garden's walkway.

After depositing half his load, Luke swiped the back of his arm across his brow. It didn't do much good, seeing how his arms were just as sticky with sweat as the rest of him. He braced himself and hoisted another bag. A hand on his shoulder jarred him from his work. His grip on the heavy bag faltered, and before he could shift out of the way, it landed on his work boot-clad foot.

Pain radiated from toes to calf. He swore and jerked around to find Daisy, mouth pursed and brows high. Great. He ripped the earbuds from his ears.

"You can't be sneaking up on people." He narrowly kept the growl from becoming a shout.

"I called your name. Three times."

He held up the earbuds.

"Not my fault." Her voice held no responsibility.

He gaped at her. "Whose fault is it then? I'm out here minding my own business, or your business, or whatever, and you come up behind me without warning."

Daisy rolled her eyes. "You big baby. Did you huwt your wittle toes with the big old bag of diwt?"

"Really?" He retrieved the offending bag and tossed it onto a nearby pile. "I'm out here literally busting myself preparing your garden, and you're going to give me grief?"

"You bet I am."

In the old days, he would've kissed the sassy smirk right off her lips. He squashed the urge as quickly as it rose. Those days were so far in the past, he couldn't even see them in the rearview mirror.

"And don't pretend," she continued as her brows inched higher, "I didn't hear a bad word slip out either."

Luke laughed. "A bad word? What are we? Twelve?"

"Pops would've tanned your hide if we were."

He lifted his cap and ran his fingers through his hair before he thought better of it. Ugh. Sweaty. He replaced the cap. "One little ole word would've been the least of the things Pops would have issue with. I'm pretty sure, if he were here, he'd have given up by now."

"No." Daisy frowned. "Pops never would've given up on you."

He'd meant it half jokingly. Playing with her the same as she'd done with him. One truth was all it took for Daisy to kick any previous lightheartedness from the garden. Luke bent low and hefted the offending bag from the ground. If every easygoing moment was going to turn into a time of reflection on the sad state of his life, he was better off just doing his job, even if it wasn't paid.

Chapter Nine

Daisy sighed. Why couldn't she let a joke be a joke? Luke hadn't been serious about Pops. Giving up on his loved ones wasn't in Pops's nature. They both knew it.

Then again. Was it possible Luke wondered if he'd strayed too far for even his Pops's love?

As Luke tossed the bag of soil on top of the pile, Daisy tugged the next one from the truck. Lifting with her legs to keep from hurting her back, she positioned it in her arms and began waddling toward the pile.

Luke smirked. "Give me that before you hurt yourself."

The sudden loss of weight threatened to topple Daisy, but she fought it until she found her balance. Luke tossed the bag over his shoulder. Well-defined muscles tensed under the weight.

When his drinking started, Luke's almost-obsessive need to work out had seemed a contradiction to his lifestyle. His destructive habits and spiraling out of control didn't mesh with keeping himself in shape. Later, Daisy realized why. Physical strength was the only strength Luke could attain after Pops died. Everything else was irreparably broken.

Daisy leaned against the truck. She wouldn't share this new

bit of knowledge with him. Her blunder of venturing into the serious convinced her of the need to keep the atmosphere light.

"I feel bad standing here watching you work." She returned to discussing nothing of consequence. "I have unloaded soil a million times without your help."

Luke hefted another bag. "And probably suffered sore muscles for days afterward."

"Did not."

Doubt tinged the look he shot her. She fought to keep eye contact. When heat rose in her cheeks, their game of chicken ended. She looked away.

Luke laughed. "I thought so. Don't sweat it. I'm doing enough of that for the both of us." He removed his jacket and laid it on the side of the truck bed. "Hard to believe it isn't even summer yet."

"Barely spring."

"Right. Anyway, you relax. Let me do the heavy lifting. At least you'll be able to roll out of bed tomorrow morning without groaning."

As much as it irked her, she allowed Luke to unload the truck by himself. There would be plenty of work for both of them as they got the plants in the ground and coaxed them to maturity. Luke was right. She could still remember the stiffness she suffered the day after unloading the previous spring.

While Luke took the last bag from the truck, Daisy swung the tailgate into place. She could do at least that much. Turning, alarm zinged through her as she spotted a white fluff ball zoom around one of the retaining walls and straight into Luke's path.

"No! Sa—Luke!" It was as close to having the cat literally getting her tongue as Daisy had ever come. The words wouldn't come quickly enough or clearly enough to make sense before Sage found her way under Luke's boot. Luke jerked his foot away at the resulting yowl and hiss. Like slow motion in a movie, Daisy watched him fight for balance. Teetering one way, then the other, the battle was lost. Luke twisted. Bag and man crashed to the ground, finding the wooden garden walls on their way down.

Sage, offended at someone daring to step on her, shot across the garden path to hide under a bush. Leave it to the cat to sulk when she created the mess in the first place.

Certain all danger of making the situation worse had passed, Daisy rushed forward. Luke righted himself and rubbed his left shoulder with a groan. He glared at Sage, but kept his mouth firmly closed. Probably better. Daisy had no doubt the single word from earlier would've been mild compared to what his lips now held at bay.

"Is it just your shoulder? Or are there other injuries we should take care of first?"

"Hard to tell." He shoved the bag away with his foot before slowly standing. "Legs feel fine, but I think I might've done some damage to my ribs hitting the retaining wall."

"Come on." Daisy refrained from supporting him. After all, if it was his ribs, he should be able to walk without help. "I've got a first aid kit in the bathroom. Let's clean you up and size up the damage."

His lack of argument as he shuffled his way into the barn, favoring his injured side, was a testament to his discomfort. Bekah eyed them as they came through the door. Her frown begged for comment, but Daisy refrained. Surely, Bekah could see Luke was in pain.

Daisy snagged one of the stools they kept behind the counter and tried not to make eye contact with her friend. She'd get an earful later, but Daisy would give one right back. If Bekah had an issue with Daisy taking care of Luke after he'd been hurt in her garden, she'd have to get over it.

"Here." Daisy slid the stool into the small restroom behind Luke. "Have a seat. Let's see what we're up against."

She fished the first aid kit out from under the sink while

Luke settled on the seat. Tightness in his jaw told her more than his flat expression.

"Where's the worst of the pain?"

He grimaced as he reached his left hand toward the back of his right side. Whether the discomfort was coming from the shoulder he'd been massaging earlier, touching the wounded spot on his ribs, or both, Daisy couldn't tell. She moved behind him. The fabric was torn and its edges discolored with blood. Not good.

The wound needed a thorough cleaning and possibly stitches. Hoping for the former, she lifted the shirt as best she could. The cut was jagged, but she couldn't tell how deep. Holding his shirt up over the cut cast a shadow over the site, hampering her ability to assess and treat the wound.

"You've got a pretty nice gash there." Daisy moved back in front of him to set the first aid kit open on the sink. "I can't tell if you'll need stitches. Take off your shirt so I can see it better."

Despite his pain, Luke quirked an eyebrow. "If you wanted me out of my shirt, you didn't need to send your cat to attack me."

If not for the groan escaping his lips as he tried to do her bidding, Daisy would've responded. As it was, she stepped closer and helped him ease the torn material over his head before depositing it in the sink.

DAISY'S NEARNESS was as intoxicating as anything he'd ever drunk at the bar. Moving his arms to remove the shirt caused a sharp inhale of air scented with bright citrus and spicy herbs. Daisy's fragrance was almost enough to deaden the pain shooting through his shoulder and clamping down around his ribs.

If she noticed him looking up at her as she stood mere inches away, she didn't show it. All business. Some of the bands around his ribcage loosened when she moved around him to examine his back. Not the painful ones, but at least he could breathe easier.

"How's it look?" It was better to feign indifference to her proximity since Daisy gave no indication she was affected at all.

"Mangled, but you'll live."

"I'd hate the alternative."

Silence. He started to turn, despite the pain.

"I imagine at this point in your life, you might be right."

Her voice held no laughter. She believed him beyond wayward, probably outside her God's family. While she and Pops would spend eternity in the presence of God, she didn't have the same assurance for him. For the first time since Pops died, Luke considered the possibility of her belief being reality instead of making a wisecrack.

Man. Did life without the numbing stupor of alcohol have to be so grim?

"I'm sorry." Her voice was quiet behind him. "I shouldn't have joked."

He shrugged and immediately regretted the decision. A groan escaped as his shoulder throbbed. Her slender fingers probed the area, shooting a completely different sensation down his arm and through his chest.

"I'll give your shoulder a closer look as soon as I'm done with your back." Cool air replaced the warmth of her fingers. "I don't think it's going to need stitches, after all. But cleaning it might sting. Ready?"

He nodded, bracing himself for the unknown. "Go for it."

The sound of the spray bottle reached him right before the icy cold of the cleaner. His muscles twitched despite knowing it was coming.

"Sorry."

"It's fine." He straightened his shoulders as much as his injuries would allow, determined not to make a fool of himself any more than he already had. "I'm a big boy. I can handle cleaning a scrape."

She sprayed it again. "There, it's clean. Your shirt protected you some. I expected dirt and even splinters or mulch bits."

"Sorry to disappoint you."

A chill raced up his back and raised goosebumps on his arms as Daisy blew softly on the wound.

"What are you doing?" He sounded grumpy, but the last thing he needed was to clue Daisy in on what her breath on his skin was doing to him.

"Just drying the skin so the bandage will stick. You really are an awful patient. I've treated small children who were more tolerant."

Small mercies—she didn't have a clue.

Once the cuts were covered, Luke started to stand. Daisy's hands pushed down on his shoulders, bringing him back to his seat.

"I told you I need to look at the place by your neck."

He tilted his head to the right, feeling the muscles strain as he did. What she was looking for was beyond him. He'd not hit the spot in a way to cause another scrape. It was more about twisting or pulling the muscles.

He tightened his jaw as her fingers probed the area. She'd be done with her examination in seconds. Then, he could retreat to a safe distance.

"I don't think you did any real damage, but when we're done here, you're going home for the rest of the day. I don't want that gash opening up any more than it is." She didn't pull away with the pronouncement. Instead, her thumbs gently massaged the sore area.

"You don't have to do that." His voice held more gravel than he'd like.

She ignored him. "You were injured helping me. The least I can do is try to relieve some of the damage."

What about the damage her aid inflicted? Every cell in his body ignited and rampaged through his system as the memory of her slender fingers tracing across his shoulders and up his neck before their first kiss rushed in. In his haste to stand, the stool fell. As quickly as his aching body would allow, he righted it and snagged his shirt from the sink before depositing the ruined garment in the trash.

"Thanks again." He smiled, trying to erase some of the surprise on her face. "But I should probably go home and ice it. See you tomorrow."

He fled. Luckily, the main room was devoid of customers. Only Bekah, who stood behind the counter with her jaw practically hitting it, was present as he strode, bare-chested, across the room and out the door without so much as a word spoken between them. If his need to escape Daisy's ministrations wasn't so intense, he'd have found it hilarious.

How was he supposed to rekindle their friendship when every look and touch awakened deeper feelings he'd never managed to evict? It was enough to make a man want to drown out the day with a cold drink. But he couldn't do that anymore. Or could he?

Chapter Ten

Bekah cornered Daisy outside the restroom door.
"Mind explaining?"

Daisy shrugged. "I don't know what you mean."

Bekah took what Daisy long ago nicknamed her warrior's pose. Feet apart. Hands on hips. Chin raised and shoulders straight. It would've been intimidating if Bekah weren't the definition of petite. Oh, who was she kidding? Small frame or not, Bekah's tenacious, take-no-prisoners nature made her intimidating. But this time Daisy refused to be cowed.

"What?"

"Don't play with me, Daise." Bekah jerked her head in the direction of the door. "Luke all but ran out of this place half-naked not two minutes ago. Why?"

Daisy rolled her eyes. "Don't be so dramatic. Luke wasn't half-naked. It's not like men don't go shirtless all the time. No one thinks anything of it."

"Well, they don't do it in our shop. This is a first."

Deflection wasn't going to work. "Luke was hurt working in the garden. You saw us come in. He had a big gash on his back. I cleaned it. I covered it. The shirt couldn't be saved. End of story."

"So not the end of the story. The man ran out of here like something was chasing him."

Daisy shrugged. "I couldn't say why. I just took care of his injuries. That's all."

Bekah held up a hand. "Fine. Tell yourself whatever you want, but I know what I saw. Luke was running from something, and we both know where his running away leads."

Words of denial caught in Daisy's throat. The reminder that Luke was changing, committing to sobriety, ran through her mind, but wouldn't flow down to her mouth. Truth was, she didn't understand everything that could trigger an alcoholic to fall off the wagon. Stress for sure. Still, Luke wouldn't. Would he?

"I'll check on him later. He was probably just in a hurry to get home and rest. He got pretty banged up thanks to Sage. But we've got work to do. Luke can wait until I leave for the night."

Did her confident tone hide the quivering in her chest? Or was her doubt apparent? Daisy and Bekah went back to their work in silence, but the uproar in Daisy's mind was not so easily contained as she made her way upstairs to prep the area for the night's class.

If whatever caused Luke to leave also created the urge to drink, could checking on him wait until after work? Luke was an adult. She wasn't responsible for his choices. Was she? She did say she would stick beside him, help him any way she could. What did supporting him entail?

Daisy grabbed the broom from the utility closet and attacked the floor as if one speck of dust would bring the downfall of her business. If she couldn't rid her mind of these incessant questions, she could at least rid the space of unwanted dust. "What made me think I could help someone stay sober?"

The only things she knew about alcoholics and recovery

were the little she'd gleaned from internet searches. She couldn't even say for sure which websites were legit and which ones were simply people trying to make a name for themselves.

Daisy paused in her task as Sage wound around her legs, tracking through the pile of dust on her way to the balcony doors to lie in the sunshine.

"Evil cat." Daisy glared in the feline's direction. "I should've given you to the shelter when you first showed up on my doorstep."

Should have but didn't. Her soft spot for those in need had earned her a store mascot. At least with a cat, she wasn't woefully unqualified for the job. And if she had concerns, the local veterinary clinic was always happy to educate her.

Why couldn't she do the same with Luke?

"Not a veterinarian." She shook her head at the cat. "Don't be ridiculous." Though she spoke to Sage as if she was privy to her inner dialogue, the cat simply stretched out in the warmth of the sun and closed her eyes. "There has to be someone."

As she finished prepping the space, a plan of action took root. After work, she'd check on Luke. Then, she'd scour the internet once more, this time looking for a local recovery group. If she was lucky, they'd have resources to educate family and friends about alcoholics and recovery.

No. Luck would have nothing to do with it. She needed help, and she knew what her first stop should be. *Lord, I'm out of my depth here. I want to help Luke. He's serious and needs support, but I don't understand the first thing about this. Lead me to someone who can help us both.*

Daisy may have feigned indifference with Bekah, but something had been wrong with Luke's exit. She dropped into a chair. Sage didn't wait for an invitation to climb into her lap.

"Something happened." Daisy stroked Sage's fur. "Why am I petting you? This is all your fault. Tripping him like you did."

And something between his fall and her tending his injuries had set him off.

"But what?"

Sage purred her commentary on the subject.

Daisy walked through the events step-by-step in her mind. He obviously had reason to hurt. The cut had been ugly. Any deeper and she would have suggested a trip to the emergency room. His speed as he left, however, decimated the theory he'd rushed home because of his pain. The idea didn't hold water anyway. Luke wasn't one to whimper and whine when in discomfort.

He'd barely flinched when she applied the wound cleaner, even though experience told her the stuff was as cold as being doused with ice water. Never pleasant. No. The change happened after she bandaged his cut.

She'd seen him hit his shoulder hard. Contact like that always tightened muscles and made them sore. Other than applying a bandage, there was nothing she could do for the gash. But she could help ease whatever strain his muscles suffered.

"His shoulder was tight." Daisy continued stroking the cat.

Her fingers met resistance the moment they touched his muscles. Tight was an understatement.

"They were as solid as a marble statue."

Given time, she could have worked some of it out. The few seconds he allowed confirmed what she'd always believed to be true. Luke may have had a death wish with his drinking and loose morals, but he was in better shape as an adult than when they were dating. What was slim and toned back then was now strong and defined.

She'd seen it in the way his muscles moved as Luke had removed his shirt. Abs for days. Not what one would expect for a heavy drinker. She'd felt the strength in his shoulders under her fingers during her brief massage. Other than the obvious detriments, Luke had only improved with age.

Heat crept into her cheeks as awareness flickered. She was picturing Luke, shirtless, and finding the image as desirable as ever. She tamped down the fleeting urge to find him and finish massaging those shoulders, knowing the desire stemmed more from wanting to feel those muscles again rather than working out the stress residing there.

"Oh, no." Daisy's hand stilled on Sage's back. "Did he run because he felt it too or because he knew I did?"

Deep down, Daisy hungered for the answer but knew her curiosity would give in to starvation before she voiced the question. Neither answer led down a path they could travel. They'd covered it already. Yes, she still loved him. But even if he wanted her as much sober as he did when he was drunk, it could never happen. Their bridge burned ages ago, and neither of them had what it took to rebuild it.

"We've ignored it this long." Daisy lifted Sage from her lap and crossed the room to the stairs. "How hard could it be to keep pretending?"

Already back in the shaft of warm sunlight, sleeping, Sage offered no wisdom. Daisy flipped off the lights and headed down the stairs. Bekah was teaching the store's evening class tonight, freeing Daisy to find the answers to her questions. All except for the last query. If the heaviness taking residence in her stomach was any indication, that was one question she didn't want the answer to.

Chapter Eleven

Daisy stared through the windshield at Living Waters Church. Hers was a small country church on the eastern edge of Carbondale, but it didn't have a recovery support group. Neither did any of the other churches in town.

But the thirty-minute drive to Marion was nothing. People in southern Illinois expected a bit of a drive to get anywhere worth going. Unless her memory was faulty, Paul and Erin joined this congregation after moving back to the area. Nathan and Katie followed shortly after. The church had a strong reputation for loving others with Jesus's love in practical ways, evidenced not only in their attendance but also in the various ministries they hosted.

"Still," Daisy mumbled, "they don't know me from Adam. I doubt either of the couples I know is dealing with stuff like this."

Even if they were. Those couples were married. Katie wasn't a wife or sister or mother to someone struggling with an addiction. She was a friend, nothing more. Weren't these groups supposed to be for family support?

A knock on her window caused Daisy to jump. A woman smiled down at her with a small wave. Daisy frowned, trying to place the petite brunette with silver-gray highlights sprinkled throughout her long hair. Her wide smile and welcoming brown eyes were both framed with subtle lines. She had to be several years Daisy's senior.

Maybe the woman visited Communi-TEA Barn. That wasn't it. The woman was a complete stranger. Then again, Daisy was sitting in her car staring at a church she didn't belong to. The woman probably did and wondered who she was. Daisy pressed the button to lower the window.

"Hello." The lady held out her hand. "I'm Jill Bevins. Are you here for the support group meeting?"

Daisy quickly took the woman's hand, shook, and then dropped it. "Yes. But I don't think I'm supposed to be. I'll just be leaving. Nice meeting you."

"Please don't go." The woman's smile invited Daisy to belong. "Nerves are normal, hon, but we'd love for you to join us. We don't bite. I promise."

Daisy grinned politely at the standard but not really funny humor. "It's not that."

"Then what?"

"I don't belong here."

"Your life hasn't been turned upside-down because of addiction?"

"No." Daisy shook her head. "It has. But it's not the same."

"How so?"

Twenty questions in a parking lot with a woman she didn't know was not how Daisy intended to spend the evening. But Jill's expression was open and welcoming as she adjusted the purse on her shoulder and waited for Daisy to answer the question.

"I don't have a loved one struggling with addiction."

Jill's brows dipped low before rising again with the widening of her eyes as understanding hit. "Oh. You need the support group for those dealing with addiction personally. That's not a problem. It's the same place, same time. Mondays, Wednesdays, and Fridays." She rummaged in her purse and drew out a pen and crumpled receipt. "Here, I'll write the group leader's name and number down for you."

"No, no." Daisy reached out to her. "I'm not the one with the addiction. I meant, everyone else is probably a family member. I'm ... just a friend."

"Oh, honey." Understanding dawned. Jill commanded Daisy's complete attention with a single look. "First, there is no such thing as *just* a friend. Addiction is the companion that pushes people away quicker and farther than most. Maintaining healthy friendships is hard in everyday life. Add in addiction, and it sometimes feels like an impossible task."

Daisy nodded, but Jill wasn't finished.

"Second, if you haven't given up on this friend after what you've more than likely dealt with, then they *are* a loved one. Probably more than they realize. And you *do* belong here."

Hope tickled Daisy's insides. "How do you know? I don't want to intrude in a place not meant for people like me."

"I know because you're me." Jill moved away from the door, allowing Daisy to open it. "I've been coming here for five years. Ever since my best friend and business partner agreed she had a problem."

"I'm not trying to be nosy." Daisy waited for Jill's slight nod to encourage her to continue. "But I'm guessing your friend hasn't been able to stay clean since you're still coming here."

"She's not relapsed since those first few months." Jill tittered at what must have been open disbelief in Daisy's face. "I'm sorry, hon. I shouldn't have laughed. I remember what it's like starting out." She gathered her straight hair behind her and pulled it over one shoulder. "This road isn't always an easy one. People relapse, some after years without their preferred substance. It's a lot harder than making a choice and sticking with it. Those who haven't faced it may not understand. But my friend has been clean for four and a half years, and this program has helped her stay that way. It's helped both of us."

People relapse. Not the encouraging news Daisy wanted to hear. But false encouragement wouldn't help her deal with Luke. Truth and understanding were her only hope of aiding Luke in his fight for sobriety.

Daisy's truck honked as she hit the lock button on the fob. "I think you're right. This may be exactly what I need."

Jill looped her arm through Daisy's as if they'd been friends forever. "Then, come with me. The meeting's just getting ready to start."

Two hours later, Daisy walked beside Jill back out to the parking lot. In that time, she'd listened to and learned from others facing the same hurts she was. Though some of their situations sounded more grave than Daisy's, not one person made her feel like her story was unworthy of their time.

Each person she spoke with gifted her with a listening ear and understanding. A healthy dose of encouragement and wisdom accompanied those too.

"It's not going to be easy." Daisy had thought she understood that from experience, but hearing it from a group of loved ones facing the same battle every day sank the truth in deeper than before.

"No, it won't." Jill shook her head. "But you're not alone anymore. Don't you forget it."

Already, Daisy looked forward to the next meeting. While she never wanted for her life to include something like an addiction support group, most of these people were farther down the path, while she was at the start of it. Even this first group had infused her with strength and guidance for the journey, and it would provide her with the best tools to help Luke.

"I won't. I wish there were more than one a week, though." Daisy shoved a stray curl back from her face. "There's so much I don't understand. What if something happens tomorrow or the next day, and I handle it wrong?"

Jill pulled her phone from her purse and swiped the unlock code. "What's your phone number?"

Daisy rattled it off. In moments, her phone dinged from its place in her back pocket. Jill dropped hers back into her bag.

"There. Now you've got my number." Jill turned to go to her car but stopped and looked over her shoulder at Daisy. "Promise me that you'll use it. Day or night. Any time you need to talk."

"I will."

"Great." Jill waved. "Then I'll see you next week, if I don't hear from you first."

Daisy waved back and unlocked her truck. Jill had left by the time Daisy got settled and started her vehicle. A sense of overwhelm at her welcome and blessing at God's provision merged inside her. Overwhelmingly blessed. Daisy couldn't describe it any other way.

It didn't matter if Luke chose not to attend a group. She needed the help, and God provided. Not only was she now taking part in a ministry for people facing the same life obstacles she was, but God had also made it more personal. He'd gifted her with a new friend who wanted to be there for her, even outside the group.

"Thank You, God, for making me overwhelmingly blessed."

Chapter Twelve

Luke stared at the nondescript brick building out his windshield. How'd he even get here? After running out of the Communi-TEA Barn, he'd kept his word. He'd gone home to ice his sore shoulder. While it might have numbed his physical pain, the sensation of Daisy's fingers gently kneading them wasn't so easily dispelled.

Without so much as asking his approval, the stark white walls of his home played scene after bittersweet scene from his past with Daisy. All the laughter they'd shared buoyed his spirit. Every failure threatened to crush his ability to breathe. Too bad those were more plentiful.

He'd snatched his keys from the rack by the door and headed out. A drive to clear his head. No destination. Instinct was his only navigator. He stopped at each traffic light, or at least, he hoped so. He couldn't really remember any, though he knew each one's location. While he tried to corral his thoughts, years of running led him down a familiar road. Quik Stop Liquor. Another failure to add to his tally.

His mouth watered as surely as a dog's hearing Pavlov's bell.

The promise of silence in place of painful memories filled his cab. He gripped the steering wheel until his knuckles paled. This wasn't good. Not good at all.

"God, I can't." It wasn't a prayer. He'd given up on the God who didn't care ages ago. It was simply the deepest cry of his soul pulled free from the prison of his lips. Then again, wouldn't Daisy declare those the sincerest of prayers?

Pfft. Way too much angst for one day if he was thinking on the theological.

A knock on the driver's side window jerked him from his thoughts. Dread instantly weighed down his insides, but Luke pasted on what he hoped was a friendly smile as he pressed the button to lower his window.

While his expression hid his desire to tell Lisa to go away, hers promised to stay with him forever. Or at least until a good time was had by all.

"Luke Masters, this is my lucky day."

"Lisa." Luke nodded his greeting. "Nice to see you, but I can't stop and chat. Gotta be somewhere."

She looked past him to the vacant seat beside him. "Doesn't even look like you've gotten what you came for yet. We could catch up while we shop."

"Didn't come for anything." Technically, it was true. "Just a pitstop to figure out my next destination."

Disappointment pulled her mouth into a pout. "Are you sure you have to go? Seems to me, you could use a break. How about it? You can come to my place for lunch, and we'll see where we go from there."

There was no question where they'd end up. Luke had taken her up on her offers a time or two, and the game was always the same. Food rarely made an appearance, but drinks flowed as plentiful as a freshwater spring. Why they even kept up the pretense was beyond his uninebriated mind. It always ended with him mumbling something about needing to go as he found his clothes and beat a hasty retreat while the emptiness chased him out the door.

That was the crux of it all. He could join Lisa. He could empty every shelf in the liquor store and fill himself with the contents of each bottle. But in the end, the alcohol-induced numbness faded. Even the shame and regret he'd experienced early on stopped hounding him, leaving Luke as empty as he started.

"Sorry, Lisa." He softened the rejection with a smile. "I can't. Gotta get going. See ya later."

"Your loss." A sassy shrug failed to hide her disappointment. "Maybe next time."

Luke prayed there wouldn't be a next time. How had things gotten bad enough that he'd even think of speaking with God not once but twice in less than thirty minutes? Man, a drink sounded better every second. If this was the battle he faced at every turn, how would he ever stay sober?

"Yeah, next time." He nodded and rolled up the window.

Lisa stepped back as he started up the truck and shifted into gear. He had to find a safe place until the urge passed. His current safe place landed him in the liquor store parking lot. Which made Daisy about as safe as a field pockmarked with landmines. He needed a peaceful place, but not one that urged him into the deep end of his thoughts.

He pulled out of the parking lot and turned toward Giant City State Park. As much as his muscles might consider it unjust punishment, a hike, even a light one, might clear his head. Quicker than the speed limit allowed, he pulled into one of the gravel parking areas near the head of one of the easier trails.

Luke crossed the narrow road to the sign displaying a map of the trail. He didn't need the instruction. He'd roamed these trails as long as he could remember. They weren't as well-kept as they were when he was a kid or even a teenager, but they were peaceful. Exactly what he needed. Still, he couldn't seem to make his feet move past the wooden posts and onto the well-worn path.

"Luke?" The familiar voice blended with the clop of hooves against asphalt.

Luke turned. "Hey, Nathan." He greeted his high school friend with a smile. They'd not stayed close, but even after everything, Nathan always greeted Luke as a friend when they ran into each other in town, and Luke knew Nathan owned a place on the southwest side of town. He nodded at Nathan's horse. "What are you doing out here? Don't you have enough trails to ride out at your place?"

Nathan shrugged. "Sometimes, a guy needs a change of scenery. Besides, the youth group had a picnic out here today. I brought Buck to let the kids have a quick ride, tethered, of course. Most of them have never even been on a horse. Figured I owed Buck a trail ride after he worked so patiently."

Luke stroked the horse's velvety muzzle. "Seems like a good horse."

"Yep." Nathan patted the dun-colored withers. "And Buck here has just enough age to make him gentle and predictable with the kids."

"Well." Luke nodded. "I guess I should leave you to it. Great seeing you, Nathan."

He moved onto the trail.

"Hey, Luke."

He stopped. Turned. "Yeah?"

Nathan dismounted and walked toward him, leading Buck. "My trailer's just over at the next shelter. What do you say I take Buck back so you and I can catch up? It's been a while."

"Why?" Luke hadn't meant to voice his curiosity. He didn't have anything against Nathan, but they hadn't hung out since graduation. Nathan might have come to Pops's funeral, but the day was such a blur that Luke couldn't remember clearly.

Nathan frowned. "I don't mean to speak out of turn, but you

seem like a man with a lot on his mind. You might want someone to talk to."

Blowing off Nathan would be easy. Luke could politely tell him to mind his own business. But Nathan had never been the type to worm his way into other people's lives or gossip about others. If Nathan was offering, he meant it. Somehow, he sensed Luke's need and wanted to help. How he knew was anyone's guess. As long as Luke had known him, Nathan seemed to have a sixth sense about things.

"Sure." Luke shrugged.

"Great. I'll be right back."

"It's all right. I'll join you."

Companionable silence filled the short walk down the road and around the bend to Nathan's horse trailer. As they approached, the truck door swung open. Katie hopped out of the truck and waved.

"Didn't expect Nathan to bring back strays." Katie's smile was warm as she joked, inviting him into their space.

"Didn't expect to see you again so soon."

"Nor I you." She glanced at her husband. "I finished packing up. Everything's ready to go, but I figured I'd wait for you."

"Change of plans, if it's okay." Nathan led Buck to the back of the trailer and opened the door. The horse moved inside without being coaxed. "Luke's invited me to join him on a hike. Would you mind taking the truck and trailer? I'll bring the Jeep later."

Katie's head angled to the side as her chin raised. Mischief twinkled in her eyes. "I might be talked into your plan. But since I'm going to have to do the work of unloading …"

Nathan's snort cut off her thought. "Work? The second Buck realizes he's home, he'll back himself out of the trailer and head straight for his stall. He's easier to take places than Sam."

Katie pursed her lips. "Humor me."

"What's the price?"

"Dinner. JT's pizza."

Luke couldn't fault her choice. He'd enjoyed the food truck many times. It only took minutes for JT to make the best pizzas in his wood-fired pizza oven that Luke had ever eaten .

"The usual?"

Seemed a favorite of the Phillips family as well.

"Yes. And don't forget the cream soda."

"Wouldn't dream of it."

Luke wandered closer to the picnic shelter, giving the couple privacy. Plopped on one of the wooden tabletops, he tried not to watch them but found it difficult. The way Katie looked up at her husband drew him. Nathan's tenderness as he ran his hand down her arm and leaned in for a goodbye kiss turned Luke reflective.

He and Daisy shared the same kind of relationship once. Little touches. Secret smiles. He could almost feel her fingers kneading his muscles again and convince himself happiness was possible. Craved it more than anything. But no. He'd messed it up.

The only woman he'd ever loved was out of reach. She might love him, but there was no way she'd take him back. They were friends, but Luke wanted more in his life. He wanted someone to bribe him into bringing pizza home. He craved sharing the day while sharing a slice or two. Nothing sounded more perfect.

But if finding a decent girl who'd give him the time of day was possible, he'd lose Daisy. His dad destroyed their family selfishly seeking more than life and family shared with the woman he said he loved. His dad's betrayal shattered his mom, leaving a shadow person to raise him. She tried her best but never moved beyond it. Luke had turned to Pops. His mom hadn't had anyone.

No. Luke determined then that he'd never cross that line. Even emotionally. Married women were off the table. He couldn't do to another family what his father had done to theirs. Marrying someone else while his heart clung to Daisy wouldn't be any better, even if he wasn't physical with her.

Single for life. It was his fate. He'd better get used to the idea, because losing Daisy was out of the question. Even if it meant forgoing the dream of a relationship as good as Nathan's.

Chapter Thirteen

Nathan stopped where the trail opened onto a solid rock bed. He claimed a boulder several feet from the cliff's edge as a seat. Luke dropped onto another nearby.

"What's going on?"

Luke shrugged.

"Seriously. I can tell something's eating you. You agreed to talk. So, talk."

"I don't know."

"Sure, you do."

Luke rubbed a hand over his jawline. "I'm not sure where to begin. Life's a mess."

"Heard you're not at the garden center anymore."

Luke jerked his head up. Frustration mounted in his chest. "How?" His clenched teeth shaped the word into a growl. "Did that—"

Nathan raised a hand to cut him off and shook his head. "Nothing like that. News travels fast in small towns. But I didn't hear it through the grapevine. I don't put stock in rumors. I stopped by the garden center and wanted to say hi. Mike told me you weren't working there."

"He tell you why?"

"Didn't ask."

"But you're curious or you wouldn't bring it up."

Nathan grinned. "I only mentioned it 'cause a big change can create some of the mess you were talking about. Thought it might give you a place to start talking."

"Fair enough." Luke nodded. "You're right. It's a part, but I'm thinking it's not what started it all. Least, not really."

"What did?"

"Drinking." There it was out there. "But I'm sure, as you said, you already know that, seeing how we're in a small town."

"I'd heard. But like I said, I don't listen to the rumor mill."

Luke picked up a twig from beside his foot and tossed it out over the cliff. "Well, it's true. Never thought it was a problem. But now?" He shook his head. "I'm done with it. I've lost too much."

"No matter the reason, being out of work hurts. Knowing why is a start, though. Any leads on a new job?"

Luke frowned. "I'm surprised Katie didn't tell you."

Nathan shook his head. "Tell me what?"

"About The Communi-TEA Barn."

"She said she ran into you there. Told me you were good with Erin's little one. Nothing else."

"She's a charmer. Joy, I mean." Luke grinned. "Erin and her husband are going to have to keep an eye on her."

Nathan chuckled. "I'm positive Erin and Paul have already started. But back to you. Are you working for Daisy now?"

"Started off just helping her for something to do. Easier than trying to occupy myself without getting into trouble."

"Makes sense."

"But, yeah, she hired me to help with her herb garden and stuff."

Nathan didn't say anything. Didn't nod. Just regarded him.

Luke tried not to squirm as he tried to figure out what Nathan saw in him.

The silence was unnerving.

"What?"

"How's it work? You guys were a serious couple in high school and college. Then, it ended."

Luke raised his chin. "It ended because of my drinking. I'm done with that now. Besides, we never stopped being friends."

Nathan raised his hands in surrender. "Okay. Didn't mean anything. Sometimes it's hard to work with an ex, is all. Dredges up old feelings and stuff."

"Can I level with you?" How could his insides be tied in knots and excited to share his load at the same time?

"It's why we're here."

"After Pops died, drinking was the only way to not feel. Not even losing Daisy stopped it, and life without her hurt almost as bad as losing Pops. Now, I have this chance." Internal energy pulled Luke to his feet to pace. "Not for a relationship with her, but for our friendship. Only, I've still got these feelings. But I need this job. I've got bills, and a guy's got to eat. Besides, I can't just quit on her. And she's why I even realized I needed to get sober. But how am I supposed to work with her knowing my feelings aren't going anywhere, without wanting to head back out to the bar and drink the voices quiet?"

"Do you really want an answer?" Nathan's tone demanded respect for whatever response he gave.

Luke nodded.

"Daisy isn't enough."

A storm whipped up inside Luke. He glared. Daisy was more than enough, and Nathan better watch himself.

Nathan put up a hand to stave off any onslaught of Luke's ire. "Simmer down. I'm not insulting Daisy. She's a great girl and a loyal friend. Anyone can see the truth. But you need someone else to turn to. Someone not Daisy. Someone you can be honest with, and they'll be honest right back. Someone you don't love."

Luke never said he loved her, just had feelings for her. Of course, it wouldn't take a rocket scientist to figure it out. No sense denying it. "Because I love her, she can't help me?"

"No." Nathan shook his head. "She can still help you. You can still be friends and work together. But if your feelings for her trigger your desire to drink, you need another, safe outlet. Maybe …"

Luke waited for him to finish. He needed the answer. "Maybe?"

"My church …"

"No. God and I aren't on speaking terms. He got me into this in the first place."

Nathan looked like he wanted to argue. Luke almost hoped he would. He was amped up and ready for a fight.

"I'm not suggesting going to church. But my church hosts a Celebrate Recovery group. It would be a safe, private place full of people going through what you're going through. It's run by a buddy of mine, a licensed counselor. I help where I can, but it's his group."

"Nope. Don't need one of those self-help groups. If I did, it wouldn't be a faith-based one. And to my understanding, all of them want you to pay homage to a higher power." Luke shook his head. "But I wouldn't mind it if I could call you every now and then when the idea starts tugging at me."

Resignation drew down Nathan's shoulders. "I don't think I'm the answer, at least not permanently. But sure. I'll be your sounding board until you decide you're ready. I'm honored."

Nathan's comment didn't sound like a joke, but it couldn't be anything else. Luke snorted. "A real honor. Sure. If the rumor mill is half correct, you've just agreed to babysit one of the town drunks. Real honor there."

"I've told you I don't put stock in people's talk." Nathan's tone left no room for argument. "And it's time for a dose of truth. You have a problem with alcoholism, but it is not your entirety. You're going to see the truth if it's the only thing we accomplish."

And there was the problem. Nathan was bound to be disappointed, because Luke knew the truth, and it was nothing like Nathan believed.

Chapter Fourteen

"Let me help you." Luke lifted the large box from Bekah's arms. "Where do you want it?"

"Upstairs in the storage closet."

She eyed him with as much distrust as an antelope spotting a lion in the brush. He wasn't the sum of his mistakes. How many times had he reminded himself in the month since his talk with Nathan? Well, his first talk. In the two days following, he'd realized the wisdom in Nathan's advice about seeking an outside source of help, and he'd come to tentatively accept that truth Nathan wanted him to understand. Though they'd slowed down to a couple times a week, the guy was probably regretting his decision to be Luke's secondary sounding board.

Working at the Communi-Tea Barn, despite providing needed income, didn't come cheap. His commitment to sobriety was sorely tested, especially when dealing with Bekah, who still didn't want to give him a chance.

"Got it." He tipped his head toward her and headed to the stairs at the back of the room.

Upstairs, he stowed the box on one of the closet shelves. He wasn't ready to head back into the ring for round two with

Bekah. Instead, he crossed the room to the balcony. The cool spring air did nothing to release the heat of his irritation.

Four weeks. Thirty-six days to be exact. Not one drop of alcohol in just over a month. Why couldn't she see he'd changed?

It shouldn't matter, but next to him, Bekah was Daisy's best friend. If she wouldn't give him a fair shake, his welcome in Daisy's life might wear thin.

"Ridiculous."

But which was more absurd? Thinking Daisy would cut him loose, or believing she still considered him a better friend to her than Bekah? With the exception of the last month, his friendship with Daisy revolved around her picking him up off the ground when he was too drunk to even care. Guilt gnawed at his stomach.

"No more." A new resolve joined his dedication to sobriety. He'd pull his weight in their friendship. He'd be someone Daisy could count on.

"What in the world is taking you so long?"

Bekah's impatient question pulled Luke from his thoughts. He turned. A raised brow taunted him with a silent reprimand, slacker.

"Daisy needs help with a customer. Think you can pull yourself away from whatever it is you're not doing and manage that?"

He'd not been gone that long, but of course, she wouldn't see it that way. His moment trying to calm his mind was one more nail in the coffin Bekah was fashioning for him. He was worthless to her, and in her mind, to Daisy too.

He wrestled back the sharp retort begging to be freed to fly and moved past Bekah. "I'll head right down."

"Hmph."

Luke kept his eyes forward. The lack of footsteps on the stairs let him know she hadn't followed him down. A moment of quiet. He'd take it. Biting his tongue to keep the peace was creating tension not even the best workout could eliminate.

"Bek told me you have a task for me." He stopped next to the customer who waited at Daisy's counter.

"Mrs. Elliott bought one of the wishing wells. Will you please load it in her car?" Daisy motioned to the half dozen yard decorations of various sizes in the woodworking booth.

"No problem." He turned to the petite, gray-haired lady next to him. No bigger than a minute. It was no wonder she needed someone to haul the thing for her. "Mrs. Elliot, why don't you show me which one you bought, and I'll tote it out to your car for you."

"It's right over there." Mrs. Elliott pointed in the general direction. "The one with the little wooden gnome next to it."

Luke sauntered over to pick up the well. More solid and heavier than it looked. There was no way a fragile elderly lady would be able to manage it.

"Mrs. Elliott?" Luke carried the well over to the counter. "Do you have someone available to help you unload this at home?"

A sheepish look crossed her face. "Well, not exactly. I'm hoping my Matthew, my boy, will drop by. Until then, I'll just leave it in the car."

"That's not going to work for me." Luke glanced at Daisy. "Would it be all right if I delivered Mrs. Elliott's well? I hate to think she's at the mercy of her son's visit to display this thing."

Mrs. Elliott laid a weathered hand on his arm. "Oh, no. Please, don't go to any trouble for me."

"It's no trouble at all," Luke spoke for Daisy.

His conscience pricked him with the reminder that the shop was not his and he was far from a place of decision-making. But still. She was an elderly lady on her own. He flashed Daisy his best pleading smile. Her own smile eased the needling in his mind.

"Luke's right. We can't have this beautiful piece stuck in

your car until your son decides to visit. Of course, he'll deliver and set it up." She turned to Luke. "Did you bring your truck today? If not, take mine. I can't imagine wrangling it into the backseat of a car."

Luke nodded. "I've got mine. Now, Mrs. Elliott, if you'll lead the way, I'll follow you out and take care of this for you in no time."

The woman's smile would brighten the day of the grumpiest grump. Such a little thing to make a difference.

"You are just the sweetest thing. Someone raised you right, no denying it." She waved to Daisy. "You better be sure if anyone asks about your place, you'll get a positive word from me. Going above and beyond. So rare nowadays."

THE SWEETEST THING. Daisy grinned as the door closed behind the pair. Mrs. Elliott was smitten with Luke, for sure. Despite knowing she shouldn't be, Daisy couldn't deny she was getting more distracted by him every day.

Over the last month, he'd been more the man she fell in love with. She supposed he'd always been there, but she'd witnessed it so rarely in the past few years. Instead, she got to see his self-destructive side.

"Thank You, Jesus." The praise came easily. Whether Luke realized it or not, faith played a part in his change. So what if it was her faith instead of his. It was real and powerful all the same. And his would come. She prayed every day to see his return. She didn't doubt she'd see it come to fruition too.

It was too late for them as a couple. There was too much water under the bridge. She snorted. There was a whole ocean to their past, and the bridge had long since been overtaken. But Daisy didn't care. If Luke could accept the Savior he once claimed, it would be worth every tear.

"Surprise. Surprise." Bekah strolled toward Daisy with a roll of her eyes. "Luke is flaking out yet again. When are you going to learn and cut him loose?"

Daisy frowned. "What are you talking about?"

She jerked her thumb toward the front door. "I was upstairs setting up for tonight's workshop when his truck pulled out of the lot. Should have known he couldn't cut it after I found him standing around on the balcony before I sent him down here to you. He's dead weight, and you're going to have to deal with it."

Heat swirled in Daisy's chest. Her jaw tightened. She flattened her friend with a glare. "Enough, Bek."

"I can't believe you're taking his side. I know you've still got a thing for him, but this is ridiculous."

"I said, enough. You don't know anything about what's going on." Daisy quickly scanned the room to make sure they were alone. They needed to have this discussion, but she'd never sacrifice her professional reputation doing so. "Luke wasn't slacking."

"Please." Another roll of her eyes. "I watched him leave."

"Yes. You did. He was following Mrs. Elliott to her house to deliver a wishing well she bought." Daisy flattened her palms against the countertop and leaned closer to Bekah. "When he learned she would have to wait for her son to come visit before setting it up, he immediately offered to take care of it for her."

"Fine. One time the guy was nice. It doesn't make him a knight in shining armor."

Rage surged, but Daisy held it back. "No. It doesn't make him a hero. But despite the problems he's had, including the ones he's created in his life, he's not a villain either."

"Well, he's certainly ..."

"Stop."

Daisy raised one hand. Before continuing, she closed her eyes and sucked in a breath. Bekah's attitude was understandable but out of hand. However, releasing her temper on her friend would only make Daisy's situation worse.

"Bek, I love you." She paused to make sure her friend was listening. "You've seen a lot of stuff between me and Luke. Much of it wasn't happy. You've always been there for me. I don't doubt that my pain hurt you too. But what Luke did, he did to himself, and he did it to me."

"Yeah, he did it. And I wish you wouldn't gloss over it."

"I'm not glossing over it, and I'm not forgetting." Daisy smiled, hoping to infuse her words with the reassurance Bekah needed. "Luke is trying to change. Rid himself of the demons he's palled around with for the last few years. What I'm choosing is forgiveness and a belief that recovery and redemption are possible. As much as I value your support, our friendship, I don't need you holding grudges for me."

Bekah threw her hands in the air. "How am I supposed to forget all the times he's hurt you?"

"You don't. But you do need to forgive or they're going to eat you up inside." Daisy sighed. "I want better for you. We share the same faith. You know how this works. Forgiveness and redemption are what it's all about."

"He's not coming to God."

Despite the tension in Bekah's jaw, Daisy knew she was taking in every word of the conversation. Sometimes, it took her a little time to admit the truths she wrestled with. And she had a point. So far, Luke hadn't wanted anything to do with God, only sobriety.

"You're right." No matter what she felt, she couldn't argue. Besides, her agreement would help Bekah understand that Daisy was being objective. "I'm praying, believing the day will come when Luke returns to God. But perhaps the desire to stay sober is where his path to faith starts. If it is, I don't want to discourage him or make the path rougher than it's already going to be."

Bekah gnawed on her bottom lip and slowly shook her head.

"I'm not sure, Daise. I've watched him destroy you time and again. But what you're saying has merit too. I'll think about it. Good enough?"

"Yeah, good enough."

Daisy came around the counter and drew her friend into a hug. "I never want to lose you."

Bekah returned her embrace before pulling back. "No matter what, it's not going to happen."

"Even if you don't agree with me?" Daisy raised a brow.

Bekah laughed. "I don't agree with you most of the time. I've not left yet."

Daisy jerked her back into the hug, laughing with her. "I love you, Bek."

"Right back at you." Bekah held her just as tightly.

"Should I come back later?" Luke's voice interrupted from the doorway. "Don't want to break into your little love fest or anything."

Daisy shook her head, stepping away from Bekah. The previous joy on Bekah's face fell away. Her shoulders squared. Disappointment weighted Daisy's. Had her words meant so little?

Bekah inched toward Luke. "No. Come in. I've got something to say to you."

Nerves skittered up Daisy's arms. She fought the urge to reach out and hold Bekah off. The wariness in Luke's eyes as he nodded his ascent to Bekah left Daisy's throat tight. If the two people she loved most in the world couldn't manage cordiality, where did it leave her?

"The other day, you had your say." Bekah stopped short in front of Luke. "I didn't have anything to answer then. I do now."

Luke swallowed. "Okay."

"I don't like how often you've treated my friend so horribly. You know you've hurt her, but she's not shared half of how deeply those wounds go. Wounds you caused. If she had, and you cared at all, you wouldn't think of coming around." She raised her chin.

Her pause allowed Luke time to argue his case. When he didn't, Bekah continued. "But you're here, and you're trying to overcome a lot. I hope you succeed. And while I hope you do it for you, I want it even more for Daisy. She doesn't deserve more hurt."

"I don't want her hurt either." Luke's voice was barely audible under the layer of guilt and shame covering it.

Bekah regarded him, eyes narrowed, before a curt nod. "I believe you. But I don't know if it's possible. I hope so. But as has been pointed out, I'm not Daisy's guard dog, and it isn't my responsibility to keep her safe."

"Okay." Luke's brows dipped as low as his frown.

"You need to understand where I'm coming from before I say what I really have to say."

"Sure. I get it."

Bekah's jaw worked, betraying her emotion despite the strong front she presented. "A few weeks ago, you apologized to me. Told me you were trying to get it together. I didn't cut you any slack then, and I haven't since then."

Luke nodded but kept silent.

"I was wrong." Bekah sighed. "I may never have done the things you've done, but I've made mistakes. I wanted others to forgive me, but I refused you the same grace. It ends today. I forgive you, Luke, for every time you've hurt Daisy and messed up her life. And I pray this change in you sticks. Daisy isn't the only victim of your choices, and I don't want to see you hurt yourself any more than you already have."

He fidgeted with the bill of his cap before settling it back in place. Luke's throat worked. "Thank you." There was enough gravel in his voice to pave her driveway.

Bekah regarded him a moment before turning to Daisy. "I

need to head upstairs and set up for tonight. You got things covered down here?"

Daisy nodded.

"Great. I'll get to it then."

The air settled as heavy as a down blanket between Luke and her as Bekah made her way up the stairs. Daisy's chest couldn't hurt any more if someone had punched her. Luke's green eyes darkened with the storm swirling inside. Daisy only wished she knew which emotions were crashing in waves over his soul.

Luke's eyes flicked to the clock on the wall. "It's nearly closing time." He cleared his throat again. "Mind if I take off early today?"

Yes, she minded. What damage could Luke inflict upon himself in his current emotional state? Would it tempt him to find peace in a bottle?

No. Daisy could not go down this road. Just like Bekah wasn't responsible for keeping her from life's hurts, Daisy wasn't Luke's defense against poor choices. He had to choose on his own, despite the fear spiraling through her. And she had to give those anxious thoughts to the One who promised to guard her heart.

"Sure. It's been a long day."

"Thanks, Daisy. I'll talk to you later."

She grinned as if she didn't have a care in the world. "You better."

Chapter Fifteen

Luke stared unseeing out the windshield of his truck. Thoughts swirled in an unstoppable vortex, leaving him unable to unravel the tangle of emotions created by the conversation with Bekah.

He resisted the urge to drive aimlessly, having learned a lack of direction left him at the doorstep of temptation. Last time it was the liquor store. This time it could be the bar. He wouldn't fare well at either.

Outside the window, Highway 51 invited him to pick a direction, north or south. Giant City Park wasn't far to the south. And while he knew he wasn't lucky enough to run into Nathan this time, could the park still provide a haven for him to work out this internal struggle?

He wasn't sure. But at least it wouldn't add temptation on top of everything else.

In minutes, Luke pulled into a parking spot next to a large shelter and playground. Signs indicated two hiking trails. Not having frequented the park since high school, he left the decision to chance. Crossing the narrow blacktop road running in front of the shelter to wind around countless curves farther along, Luke stepped onto the mouth of the trail.

Despite the downright cold evenings of spring, scattered dogwood and redwood trees showed the early signs of life. Their buds had yet to burst into bloom, but hope was there. Could Luke say the same for his own circumstances?

The bare branches of trees and bushes gave way to an outcropping of rock. Large and flat, the area wasn't the steep drop-off of some of the bluffs in the park, but it still sat above the treetops. A large boulder sat at the back of the area, nature's invitation to all passers to have a seat and take it all in.

"Don't mind if I do." Luke lowered himself onto the hard chair, only tensing for a moment as the cold of the stone seeped through the fabric of his jeans. While he might have wished for a warmer welcome, at least the cold meant he could rest assured he wasn't trespassing on the sunning spot of any reptiles.

Luke stared beyond the treetops at nothing in particular. The occasional chirp of birds, eager for the warmth of spring and the rustle of crisp, brown leaves that had forgotten to fall, were the only interruptions to the silence.

If only it were as easy to find stillness to replace the noise of his mind. Luke inhaled a deep breath, lungs welcoming the coolness as it proved he wasn't as numb as he feared.

What disturbed him about Bekah's apology? Shouldn't he feel relief? No more having to prove himself or guard every word when he was around her. With the impenetrable wall of hatred removed, their workplace could become cordial, even relatively friendly.

"That's a good thing, right?" Luke posed the question and was met with silence. Nature might provide a place of solitude, but it wasn't a great counselor.

Daisy would've told him if he sought the answers from the Creator instead of the creation, he might get farther. Too bad he didn't subscribe to the plan anymore. When he had, it hadn't done him any good. He did better on his own.

Did he really, though? Bekah's words haunted him. *Daisy's not shared half of how deeply she's been wounded by your actions.* Luke's stomach churned. He'd piled a mountain of hurt and disappointment on Daisy. More than anyone should have to face, especially from a friend.

If Bekah was to be believed, those hurts were only the tip of the iceberg. And he didn't have reason to doubt her assessment. In fact, after Bekah said it, he'd seen the way Daisy's gaze darted to the floor as he looked to her for confirmation. Truth hit hard, knocking the breath from him.

Daisy, his best friend. The woman he loved. If any other man treated her the way he had, Luke would've been first in line to smash a fist into his face. Nobody could treat Daisy so badly and get away with it. No one but him.

If you cared at all, you wouldn't think of coming around. Wasn't that Bekah's other assertion? But Luke did. Every time. And at his worst, Daisy had shown up to pull him out of the mess. When was the last time she'd shown up to simply be his friend? He scoured his mind trying to locate the distant memory.

A smile formed as he found one. Daisy in his kitchen, a cup of coffee in each hand, one held out to him with a "Good morning, Sunshine."

Nausea replaced his smile as the rest of the scene cleared. There'd been another woman at his house that morning, and she wasn't dressed for company as she joined them in the kitchen. Daisy hightailed it out of there before he had a chance to do damage control.

From that morning on, Daisy only witnessed the aftermath of his choices when he went home alone. And only when his drunken mind convinced him that calling her was somehow right. When he needed someone, and instinct stronger than the alcohol reminded him she was the only one he could call.

"Daisy, what have I done?" He rubbed a hand over his stubbled cheek. Regret stabbed him with each remembered failure. "Is Bek right? Should I ..."

He choked on the rest of the thought, though it echoed in his mind. *Should I leave and not come back?* It was the honorable choice. But he'd as soon cut off his right arm than sever his relationship with Daisy, however wrong it might be.

I forgive you, Luke, for all the times you've hurt Daisy and messed up her life. Bekah's words humbled and embarrassed him. No, he'd not offended Bekah directly, but still. If their roles were reversed, if Bekah had hurt Daisy, would he be man enough to offer a second chance? Probably not. Yet, Bekah did. Daisy did too.

Unworthy. The judgment echoed in every rustle of wind. Luke was defenseless against the onslaught. A chill beyond the temperature seeped into every pore and burrowed deep into his soul. Unworthy. Even his refusal to walk away taunted him with the judgment.

His choices played judge and jury against him. Were there none to speak in his defense? Nothing to counter the condemnation?

Fear snaked through him. There had to be something, someone, to stick up for him. To declare these voices wrong.

"Pops."

The memory brought with it the sting of tears. At seventeen, Luke's impulsiveness earned him a trip to the principal's office for fighting. Though it wasn't really a fight. The guy went down after Luke's first swing.

With Luke's anger still surging, he'd sat opposite Pops in the living room.

"Why?" Pops broke the silence.

One word. Not angry. Not disappointed. A simple request for information. The anger and defensiveness drained from Luke in that moment.

"He shouldn't treat her that way." Luke's jaw had tightened as he voiced the reason.

"Who shouldn't treat who what way?"

Luke shook his head. "He was telling everybody. Even if it had happened, you don't go around blabbing it."

Understanding lit in Pops's eyes. It was the encouragement Luke needed.

"April didn't do what he said." Luke looked away from Pops's level gaze. "Cam got a little … pushy … on their date, but April put a stop to it. Made him take her home. I was there when she called Daisy crying and spilled everything. He had no right to go around school talking about how easy April is and lying about what all they did."

Pops worked his jaw. "You were defending her."

It wasn't a question, but it was.

"Yes, sir."

"Luke, I want you to listen to me and listen well." Pops waited until Luke gave him his complete attention. "I can't condone fighting. There's almost always another way to solve your problems."

"Yes, sir."

He held up a hand. "But I can't fault your reasoning. A friend was hurting, and you stood up for her when no one else was. When she didn't feel she could. Standing up for the truth is admirable. So is sticking up for the underdog. You showed loyalty, truth, and compassion. Those are the makings of an honorable man. Don't ever forget they're a part of you. I'm proud of you, son."

Tears flowed with the memory. When had Luke lost his way? When had he stopped being the man Pops would be proud of? Luke spiraled out of control after Pops died. But the man Pops commended was still inside Luke. He'd peeked out at various points through the years, more so since Luke decided to put down the bottle.

Hope budded like the dogwoods promising spring. The man Pops admired was still in him. Luke couldn't deny the man he'd become was unworthy, but it wasn't who he really was. Those times were over. Free of the addictions he'd nursed over the years, Luke was able to reclaim the man Pops saw. Finally, Luke was worthy.

∼

"You're not going to regret this, Daisy." The pleading in his tone willed her to believe. "Wait and see. I don't deserve your friendship or forgiveness, but you've given it anyway. And I'm not going to let you down."

"We've been over this before." Daisy sat next to him on the porch swing. "I've already forgiven you, and you've never lost my friendship. Where is this coming from?"

Daisy knew Bekah's little speech at the shop had unsettled him. Did it make him question the completeness of her forgiveness? She revisited the conversation in her mind, but it still made no sense. Bekah hadn't mentioned Daisy's forgiveness of him, only her own.

"Why do you doubt I've forgiven you?"

"I don't."

"Then …"

She didn't fight it when Luke angled toward her and snuggled her hands in his, drawing them onto his lap. "I know you've forgiven me. I need you to understand that from now on, I'm going to do everything to deserve it."

"You don't have to earn my forgiveness."

His thumb brushed the back of her hand. "Still. Bek's words made me angry at first. But then I realized, I'd have killed anyone else if they'd even thought to treat you the way I have. Makes me sick, how much I've taken advantage of your friendship."

Daisy believed nothing could make her happier than Luke understanding he had a problem and determining to beat it. But now, with him acknowledging the depth of what he'd put her through and showing real regret for it, the last brick in the wall keeping their friendship at a safe distance tumbled down.

Any complaint she might have voiced when he let go of her hand fled when he brushed the back of his fingers down her cheek. The butterfly touch drew her eyes to close. When his lips warmed a spot by her temple, a sigh escaped.

"Daisy." He rested his forehead against hers. "I'm a different man. And from this day on, I will always be worthy of your friendship. I promise."

Chapter Sixteen

"Be careful."

At Bekah's caution, Daisy rolled her eyes. "I don't know what you're talking about."

"Sure you don't." Bekah snorted as she sorted tea containers on the shelf behind the tea bar. "You're playing with fire, and fire burns."

"If you're talking about me and Luke, don't worry. It's just a movie. Friends go to the movies all the time. Besides, I thought you forgave him, giving him a second chance and all that."

Bekah shot her a reproving look. "Don't pull that with me. I've forgiven him. Since I did, I can see where he's changing. But this isn't about him."

"Then what's the issue?"

"You love the man." Bekah sighed. "And while the change in him is drastic, there's one important aspect he's not accepted."

Faith. Bekah didn't need to voice it. Luke's disinterest in all things God weighed on her too. Three weeks ago, when he'd declared he would be worthy of her friendship, she'd held out hope God might enter the equation. Since then, the Luke she'd known since childhood reappeared without failure. God, however, was still *persona non grata*. Luke was determined to beat his addiction and prove his worth on his own.

"I know." Daisy nodded. "Don't worry. We're friends. That's it."

Bekah chewed her bottom lip and nodded. "Remind your heart on occasion. Okay?"

"I'm aware of my limits." Daisy offered a reassuring smile.

The bell signaling a customer's entrance ended the conversation. Bekah's concern was understandable, but she didn't understand. She and Luke were always close, even before they dated. Grabbing a bite to eat or going to a movie didn't signal a return to romance. Her heart was as safe as ever.

WHEN DAISY NUDGED him with her shoulder in the theater parking lot, Luke casually draped his arm over her shoulders and tugged her closer. The familiar camaraderie after such a bitter absence was sweeter than ever. Why'd he ever give this up in favor of everything else he'd chased?

No. He wouldn't go there. Not tonight, when their evening was reminiscent of Luke and Daisy, the early years.

"Popcorn?" Luke directed the question to Daisy as he accepted his ticket from the greeter. They'd purchased their own tickets, but with the price of concessions, sharing made sense.

She scrunched her face comically. "Do you need to ask? Movie theater popcorn is not to be missed."

"My treat, this time." He stepped into the line. "You can have next go around."

"Sounds fair. I'll go find our seats." She turned back after only a couple of steps. "And in case you've forgotten, absolutely no butter. I've never understood why people take perfectly good popcorn and then make it all soggy with butter. Yuck."

Luke laughed as she trounced toward theater three. Even

without her reminder, he'd have forgone the butter. The memory of twelve-year-old Daisy pouting through a two-hour movie because he'd not known her aversion to anything other than salt on her popcorn was seared into his brain. Never again would he make that mistake.

Snack and drinks in hand, Luke plopped into the seat next to Daisy. She took the drinks from him, allowing him freedom to press the button to raise his feet and lean his head back. With the perfect viewing position, he balanced the tub of popcorn on the thigh closest to Daisy and kept it steady with one hand as the lights faded and the previews began.

With his focus on the superpowered heroes on the screen, Luke dropped his hand into the bucket for another handful of popcorn. When his fingers brushed across Daisy's, Luke captured hers in his grasp and leaned close.

"You've more than eaten your half." His whisper was for her ears alone.

She jerked her hand from his and shot a glare at him before retrieving her snack and shoving the kernels in her mouth with a victorious grin.

"Tsk. Tsk." He shook his head before leaning next to her ear once more. "Now you owe me."

Daisy huffed and turned back to the screen. Her chin raised with her complete dismissal. Luke stifled a chuckle. He'd forgotten there was a better perk to sharing a tub of popcorn than saving a few bucks. He'd gladly pay for ten buckets to keep enjoying the quick little touches and flirty attitude they'd shared since their preteen years, even if she wouldn't ever allow their relationship to move beyond the bounds of friendship.

DAISY STOOD as the post-movie credit scene ended and the theater lights brightened. The straw gurgled as she sucked the last dregs from her drink. Luke nicked the cup from her hand and dropped it into the equally empty popcorn tub where he'd already deposited his. With their trash contained, Luke claimed her hand with his free one.

Contentment wove through her. It awakened when Luke's fingers brushed hers during the movie or his arm rested over her shoulders when walking in. Should she remove her hand from his? Would it give him the wrong idea about her intentions?

As friends, she and Luke had always shared what others considered a flirty relationship. It wasn't until later that those actions ushered in kisses and whispered terms of endearment.

Thinking about his lips against hers was almost enough to prompt Daisy to tug her hand free. Then again—could they return to the innocence of friendly flirting without risking their hearts? They were adults, capable of keeping a firm rein on their hearts. They weren't hormonal teenagers.

"Whatcha thinkin' about?" Luke swung their hands between them as they walked. "And don't say the movie. It was a superhero flick. It wasn't deep."

Daisy shrugged. Luke's grin left no doubt. She wasn't being truthful, and he knew it. Still, he didn't push. He opened the Mustang's door and allowed her to slide in before shutting it for her.

Silence filled the interior from the time Luke started the car until they'd pulled out of the parking lot and through the first main intersection. Daisy sighed. Luke was giving her space. But could their newly revived friendship survive if they weren't up-front with each other? There was already so much stacked against them.

"I think we need to talk."

Luke's focus remained on the road ahead. Streetlights illuminated the interior enough for Daisy to see his Adam's apple dip as he swallowed.

"Okay."

She closed her eyes and took a breath. Time to let the trapeze swing free and hope there was a net beneath her. She opened her eyes and focused on Luke's profile. If he decided to clam up, his body language would be her only clue to his reaction.

"Do you think we should be touching each other?"

Luke's laugh wasn't what Daisy expected.

"I'm serious, Luke."

He schooled his features and cleared his throat. "I'm so sorry."

"Yeah, right."

"No. Seriously. I'm sorry."

If the car weren't swathed in shadow, his glance in her direction might have shown his sincerity. As it was, Daisy decided to let it slide.

"Fine. Back to the question."

His shoulders dropped. "Now, don't go gettin' mad. It's the way you said it. Sounded a whole lot more serious than holding hands and the occasional hug. It left me wondering if you were talking to the right guy or if I needed to have a talk with whoever that guy was."

Luke had a point, even if she wouldn't agree with him out loud. No need to encourage him. She couldn't help the awkwardness in their situation. When had she ever dealt with trying to rewind a friendship that had grown into more? It was like trying to put the proverbial genie back in the bottle. It might not be impossible, but it sure was beyond her skill set.

Luke's hands twisted around the steering wheel. "I get it, Daisy. I do. This whole mess I've made is as uncomfortable as a metal slide in the middle of summer. As for touching and stuff, I don't see any harm. Holding hands, an occasional hug. It's friends being friendly. Nothing more. We're both adult enough to understand that."

His glance slid her way. Hers darted out the windshield. He sighed, and it didn't take a peek in his direction for Daisy to envision the expression on his face. Eyes focused while his jaw worked to prep his mouth for what he was about to say. She'd seen it many times before.

"But if you'd rather we didn't, I'll respect your decision." He ran his fingers through his hair, short enough the nervous action didn't leave a trace, before resting on the console between them. "I don't deserve the chance you're giving me. I'm not taking that for granted."

Humility was a rarity in Luke, who always knew he had life figured out and under control, even when he was dead wrong. His willingness to abide by her wishes, rather than trying to sway her, loosened the yarn of doubt tangled up in her mind.

"No. You're right." Daisy placed her hand over his. "We're friends. Whatever else, we always have been and always will be."

Her heart would have to accept the truth and move on.

Chapter Seventeen

"How's that working for ya?" Nathan shifted the reins against his horse's neck, guiding the animal to the right. "I imagine it's a mighty fine line you're walkin'."

Luke nudged his mount in the same direction. "We're doing all right."

The look Nathan gave him from under the brim of his cowboy hat screamed his doubt, though his demeanor stayed unruffled as always. The steady calm Nathan exuded was one of the reasons Luke not only continued but looked forward to their weekly check-ins. Nathan's commitment to speaking only the truth was another. While insisting on being up-front could've turned Luke off, Luke knew Nathan only wanted the best for him and was learning to heed Nathan's words.

"Fine." Luke adjusted the bill of his cap. "I won't deny there are some bumps in the road. Some of Daisy's looks have me half hoping friendship isn't the end of things for us."

"You're not the man she fell in love with."

"Am I so different?"

Nathan's hat raised with his eyebrows.

"What? Since I've quit drinking, I'm the old Luke again."

"Nope."

The meaning didn't need verbalization. Luke knew the issue Nathan referred to.

"That don't make a hill of beans difference."

Nathan reined in his horse at the creek, forcing Luke to do likewise or pass him by. After dismounting, Nathan allowed the horse a drink from the stream and then to graze on the grassy banks. Though historically the move was a harbinger of deeper conversations, which never turned in Luke's favor, the alternative was leaving Nathan and riding back to the ranch on his own. Not exactly a friendly move. Besides, there was something about sitting in the woods with water gurgling and a chill in the air that made the heavy topics a little easier to stomach.

Once Luke's horse joined the other one, Luke plopped down on a fallen log. Nathan perched on a flat-topped rock a shade closer to the creek's edge.

"Get on with it, then."

Nathan eyed him. "You know what I'm gonna say."

"Yep. But that don't mean you're not going to put it out there."

"Daisy's faith isn't a small thing. Not to her." Nathan plucked a stem of barnyard grass and picked at the seedheads at the top. "Her faith makes her who she is."

"I'm aware. Doesn't mean I have to subscribe."

"You also can't ask her to split her loyalties."

"I'd never even suggest it."

Nathan's grin was tinged with sadness. "Not in so many words. But it happens. You won't mean to, but she'll have to decide between you and her faith. You remember those verses about being unequally yoked? Daisy doesn't play with her faith. Those words mean she's called to something more than just falling in love with anybody. She needs a man who will support her beliefs because he believes too."

"I wouldn't make her give up her faith." Luke toed the dirt beneath his shoe.

"No?" Nathan tossed the grass aside. "What about being a godly example for her kids? Or being the head of the relationship, she can trust to listen and lead in whatever direction God leads?"

Luke raised his hands in front of him. "Whoa. Slow down, buddy. We're not even dating and already you've got us married with kids?"

"You're missing my point. Daisy doesn't date for the fun of dating. She sees it as a way of vetting relationships to find the one God wants her to share her life with." He pointed at Luke. "And you can't be him, because asking Daisy to commit to you without you being a believer is asking her to choose between you and her faith. And you said it's a line you wouldn't cross."

"Why are we talkin' about this?" Luke stood, trying to give vent to some of the frustration buzzing through him without it seeping into his words. "Daisy and I are friends. End of story. No marriage. And definitely no kids to worry about."

Nathan meandered over to his horse and mounted. "Then I'm wrong. There's nothing at all to worry about."

"Right." Luke's curt nod closed the door on the topic, at least in the conversation between him and Nathan.

Nathan wouldn't push. He'd said his piece and would leave it alone. He always did, and even if they disagreed, it didn't strain their easy camaraderie.

Luke shifted in the saddle. If only stifling Nathan's words were as easy once they'd left his mouth and lodged in Luke's head. Luke spent the return ride internally arguing all the reasons Nathan was wrong this time.

He could love Daisy and leave her faith intact.

Didn't matter, though. He and Daisy were friends. Nothing more.

Daisy should be thankful Bekah had moved on from the whole Luke-is-evil schtick, but her "guard your heart" mantra wasn't much easier to hear day in and day out. In the weeks since Daisy and Luke went to the movie, they'd continued to hang out, friends only. A dinner or two, a trip to the garden store (which was more business than an outing), coffee and pastries at By Sweet Design, and a *Psych* marathon at her house did not mean they were dating.

"Friends spend time together." Daisy swiped the cleaning rag over the counter. "You, Katie, and I went for manicures last week. And if I remember correctly, we even stopped for lunch on the way home. Doesn't mean we're dating."

Bekah angled the broom to avoid hitting Sage, who slept in a shaft of sunlight coming through the window, before rolling her eyes. "Don't pretend the three of us have the same relationship you and Luke have."

"We're friends, Bek. Nothing more."

"I see the way you two look at each other when the other isn't looking."

"Oh, please." Daisy snorted. "We do no such thing."

Bekah rolled her eyes. "Whatever. I'm just asking you to be careful."

"And I love you for it." Daisy turned the lock on the door and flipped the sign to open. "I just wish you'd ask it a little less often. Every day is a bit much."

"Fine. Unless I see you two marching down the aisle, I'll keep it to myself from now on."

"Put away the pout."

Daisy tilted her head to the side, allowing her to glance out the window overlooking the patio and herb garden. Luke milled in between the plants. Time for work.

"You've got things covered in here, right? I need to help put the new plants in the ground."

"Of course."

Bekah didn't try to stifle her sigh as Daisy moved around her and out the door toward Luke.

Chapter Eighteen

"What about this one?" Luke held up what looked like a small container of chocolate mint. "Want it here with the rest?"

Daisy shook her head. "No. That one spreads like wildfire. I've got a little garden for it right over there." She used her trowel to indicate. "The one close to the fence where there's plenty of sunshine."

Luke moved to follow her instructions, exactly as he had the other two days of planting. She sat on the wide brick rim of the raised garden circling the silver dollar gum tree she planted to provide protection for shade-loving herbs and as an addition to her tea-and-herbal-infusion-making repertoire.

After placing the sweet violet in its space and gently pushing the dirt back in around it, Daisy surveyed the garden. In three days, she and Luke managed to finish what would have taken a week and a half working alone. Hiring him had been a good idea.

"And," she reasoned, looking down as Sage wound between her feet, "it hasn't proven the disaster Bekah keeps declaring is right around the corner."

Not once had Luke stepped beyond the bounds of friendship.

It felt good, right even, for Daisy to have her friend back. Though Luke remained committed to sobriety and was holding his own, a caution remained in Daisy's spirit. Luke's only support system was her and Nathan, and only one of them had ever dealt with a problem like Luke's. It was working now, but one day Luke might need more.

"Maybe if I tell him I've been attending a group meant to help family members, he'd consider it. They've helped me understand it better."

The cat glanced up as if she understood every word Daisy spoke and meowed.

"You're right. Best to keep that to myself for now."

"Keep what to yourself?"

Daisy started, flicking rich dark soil from the bed onto Luke's light tan work boot.

"You've done it now." Luke's eyes took on a mischievous grin that brought Daisy to her feet. "This is my good pair and now you've gone and got them dirty."

Daisy tucked her bottom lip between her teeth, refusing to smile. She glanced at his feet. "I think you're mistaken. They're so dirty, my little trowel-full didn't make it any worse."

"Where? Where are they dirty?" Luke exaggerated a wave toward his shoes. "These were clean before you got hold of them."

"Really?" Daisy lifted her chin. "I see a bunch of dirt. Right there."

A sly movement dumped another scoop of soil directly on the top of his boot. Daisy giggled and clasped the trowel in both hands behind her back. Luke glanced from his dirt-covered footwear to Daisy. She grinned and raised her shoulder to her cheek.

"Oops."

Luke's eyes narrowed in mock outrage. "You're in for it

now." He ran his hand through the unplanted soil and came up with a handful. "I'd run if I were you."

Trowel tossed in the bed, Daisy warded him off with her outstretched hands. "Now, Luke, let's be reasonable. You don't want to do anything you'll regret."

A full smile drew his dimples out of hiding. "I guarantee, I'm not going to regret anything."

One step in her direction sent Daisy running down the brick pathways, weaving through the maze of flower beds. Luke followed close behind. A momentary lapse in direction ended the chase. Daisy had run herself into the corner where the edge of the greenhouse met the bordering fence. She turned to face her assailant.

"Please. You don't want to do this."

Luke regarded her, the wicked gleam still visible in his eyes. She pulled a pout, complete with puppy dog eyes.

"Please."

Luke let the soil slip from his fingers. "Fine."

Thinking the battle over, she let her guard down, stepping toward him. Too late, she realized the glint was still there. His arms swooped around her, enclosing her and lifting her from the ground in a bear hug.

"What are you doing?" She laughed despite knowing she'd been had.

He swung her around before placing her feet back on the path. "Just giving you what you deserve." He loosened his hold on her only to wipe his dirt-covered hands down the back of her sweatshirt.

"Lu-uke." She contorted herself to assess the damage. "Ugh. How bad is it?"

She spun around to give him her back. The pause stretched out longer than necessary to figure out if her shirt was headed for the washer or the wastebasket, and she looked at him over her shoulder.

"Well?"

His gaze dipped for the briefest moment before finding hers again. His rogue's smile tipped his lips as one brow raised. "Looks perfect to me."

Daisy's breath caught at his meaning. She leveled him with a scowl. "My shirt, Luke. How does my shirt look?"

The man went from pirate to innocent boy next door in one second flat. "That looks fine too."

With a wink, Luke turned away and wandered back over the garden paths, picking up their discarded tools along the way. Daisy fanned her cheeks. They were warm from the chase, that was all. If only she could as easily explain away how her heart had tripped when she realized Luke was checking out her backside.

Daisy strode across the garden and headed straight for her office once inside. She pulled the sweatshirt over her head. A quick once-over proved it salvageable. She tossed the garment aside and straightened the Communi-TEA Barn T-shirt she'd worn under it. A comb through her hair, and she'd be ready to join Bekah up front.

Physically maybe. But Bekah would instantly sense something had happened. But nothing had. Not really. Right? She couldn't deal with Bekah's questions if she couldn't find the answers here in the silence of her office.

"I can't talk to Bek, though." Daisy pulled her hair back into a low ponytail. "She already doesn't understand. But maybe Jill. That would be great. I'll meet her after work if she's able."

Daisy pulled her cell phone from the top desk drawer and quickly shot off a text to the woman from the support group meetings who had taken Daisy under her wings. An answer pinged before she'd set the phone down. Jill would meet her at By Sweet Design for coffee as soon as Daisy locked up for the evening.

The only thing left was for Daisy to survive the next three hours under Bekah's watchful eye.

∼

"Are you positive it's not manipulation, hon?" Jill sipped her latte.

Daisy let her attention wander from Jill to the tabletop and out By Sweet Design's front window, which overlooked their table. She'd experienced Luke at his most manipulative. Every time he played off his drinking. Each day after, as he tried to prove he was still a good friend to her. Still the man she'd always known and loved. This was different.

"I'm sure." Daisy picked at her triple chocolate fudge brownie. It wasn't right to pick at something as decadent as Lucy's brownies, but there was too much on Daisy's mind to enjoy it. "I'm not saying he would never try, because he has on many occasions. But this is different."

"Is he drinking again? Even socially, do you think?"

God, don't let that be the case. "I've not recognized any of the signs. He's open about his struggles. On time to work. Hasn't had bloodshot eyes since his decision. He doesn't stay out late. And I've not seen anything in his house the few times I've been over there."

"You're sure?"

Daisy nodded. "I'm sure."

Why did Jill's questions hit differently than the same ones from Bekah? Clarity came as soon as the question formed. Jill asked from a place of understanding and truth-seeking. Bekah's, while Daisy didn't doubt she cared, always seemed to come from a place of judgment. Until their recent ceasefire and Bekah's change of heart, Bekah, at worst, had seen Luke as the evil to be extricated from Daisy's life and, at best, an impossible fixer-upper project. Neither attitude moved past the addiction to the person underneath it all.

Jill stared into her cup. "Hmm." She glanced up. "There's one other issue we may need to consider."

"Yeah?"

"You've mentioned a time or two that you're just friends. But is it possible Luke's falling in love with you?"

Daisy laughed. "To fall in love implies he ever stopped in the first place. Luke and I have a complicated history."

"As does nearly everyone dealing with addiction." Jill brushed a lock of her long, brown hair out of her face and tucked it behind her ear. "You told me early on about your friendship growing to love and then losing it all due to his drinking. You're both determined to recapture the friendship part. I get that you understand a romantic relationship with Luke is impossible. But is it out of the realm of possibilities for Luke?"

Daisy popped an edge of brownie into her mouth to buy some time before answering. In all fairness, the question was the one prompting her to meet today. If they'd shared the same thought, did that give it merit?

"He knows we can't go there again."

"I didn't ask if he knew it. I asked if his heart isn't listening to his head."

Daisy snorted. "Wouldn't be the first time. But even if he was struggling with it, I don't think he's going to risk us this time."

"Do me a favor." Jill tipped her cup to drain the last of its contents. "Be careful, hon. Okay?"

"You've got it." Daisy wiped her hands on her napkin and tossed the wad onto the ceramic saucer now devoid of its brownie. She'd gotten used to guarding her heart around Luke, but doing so didn't always stop the rush of feelings his presence ushered in. She willed the decisiveness she'd answered with to become her reality.

"And call me if you get into trouble."

"Of course." Reaching out to her friend was much easier to guarantee than safeguarding her heart against the love for Luke she'd never quite purged.

Chapter Nineteen

"Hey, Bek. Have you seen Sage?" Daisy scanned the cat's favorite hiding places in the storefront.

"Nope. Not this morning." The question didn't interrupt Bekah's task of arranging their products on the shelves behind the tea counter. "Have you tried setting out food?"

"That's what made me wonder." Daisy lifted the tablecloth over one of the displays to peek beneath. "Usually when I pop the top of the can, she comes running."

"Check outside?"

"That's my next stop." Daisy checked a couple more nooks and crannies. With full run of the inside of the shop and several opportunities to sneak out the door into the garden every day, Sage could be anywhere. But she knew the schedule and never missed breakfast.

"Spring's finally decided to stay awhile. She's probably outside sunning herself." Bekah sighed. "I'm almost jealous."

"I know what ya mean." Daisy stopped with her hand on the doorknob. Luke knelt on the ground in the garden, but he wasn't near one of the raised beds. With his back to her, Daisy couldn't see what he was doing, and his positioning gave no clue.

She stepped out. "Hey, Luke. Whatcha doing?"

Without turning, Luke swung one arm behind his back, warding her away. "Stay there."

Her steps paused only momentarily. What had gotten into him? Bossing her around in her own garden. "What in the world are you doing?"

"I mean it, Daisy." His voice was tight and commanding. "It's Sage, and you don't need to see this."

"See what?" Fear glued her in place as cold seeped into her veins. "What's happened to Sage?"

Luke wrapped what looked like a sweatshirt around what must be their cat. He awkwardly pushed himself to his feet with Sage bundled up and held close to his chest. He thrust his chin toward the barn.

"Go get one of the small boxes out of the storage room and take it to my truck."

"What happened to Sage?" She shouldn't shout, but Luke still hadn't answered her question, leaving her mind to race through the worst.

Luke's shoulders dropped. "Looks like she was attacked by something. Could be a coon. Or a coyote."

"Is she …"

He shook his head. "No. But we need to take her to the vet. Now. Please, go grab the box."

"No." The intensity of her headshake would likely leave her with a headache. She didn't care. "I'm coming with you." She started for him with her arms outstretched to relieve him of his load. She paused. "But Bek's teaching a class. Can you watch the store? No. That won't work. You can't make the drinks. But you could … No. I'll … Maybe I should just close."

"Daisy," Luke called her from the cyclone of indecision. "I can handle this. You take care of the store. I'll take Sage to the vet, but I'm not going to lie. She's not in good shape here. I've got to hurry. Now, go get the box."

Luke's eyes were pleading. Sage needed care. Daisy fled for the shop.

"What's lit your tail on fire?" Bekah asked as Daisy stormed through the store.

There wasn't time to explain. Daisy rushed around displays to the back room. She snatched an empty box from the stack and sprinted back through the store, out the front door. Luke waited in his truck, Sage still cuddled in his arms. Daisy yanked open the passenger door and placed the box next to Luke on the bench seat.

With more gentleness than any man should possess, Luke laid the sweatshirt-bundled cat in the box for safety as he drove. "I'll call as soon as the vet tells me anything."

Daisy nodded and backed out of the truck. She swung the door shut and watched until Luke's truck disappeared from sight. The Communi-TEA Barn didn't set out to have a mascot, and a cat wouldn't have been the one Daisy chose. But in the years since she'd shown up outside their door, rail-thin and cold, Sage had become one of them.

"Please God, let her be okay." Daisy's voice caught. "Please."

LUKE SMACKED his hand against his steering wheel. For once, why couldn't he be the bearer of good news? The good Lord knew he'd brought enough bad, causing most of that himself.

Not that he wanted God having anything to do with him. As much mess as he'd made of things, he was better off on his own than paying homage to a God who didn't play fair. Besides, Luke had proven he could do just fine without God. He'd given up drinking without any help from the Almighty.

Still, he'd almost bend the knee to keep from hurting Daisy one more time. He stared at the small, covered box the vet provided. There was no way around it, but despite what he'd told her when he left, he wasn't going to deliver this news over the phone.

Before he'd steeled himself for the task at hand, Luke pulled into the parking lot. Daisy was in the herb garden. He scanned the garden porch. No customers milled about sipping drinks and discussing weather. Good. They didn't need any prying eyes for this one.

With a weighted sigh, Luke gingerly picked up the box and headed toward the garden fence. Daisy caught sight of him as he stepped over the wooden slats. Her brow pulled in confusion. He'd promised to call. He read the judgment in her face.

Her gaze dropped to the white box cradled in the crook of his arm and then back up to his face. Her eyes widened, and Luke detected the sheen of tears.

"No."

The single whispered word cut like a knife.

Luke stepped close and took her hand in his. She allowed him to lead her to the bench under a tree in the far corner of the garden, where they'd have privacy from all but those who might wander outside to the garden porch.

Daisy dropped to the cold, unforgiving stone. Luke lowered himself next to her.

"I'm so sorry, Daisy." He handed her the box. When she moved to lift the lid, he stayed the movement with a hand over hers. "Trust me. You don't want to remember Sage like that. She got messed up. It's not pretty."

Silent tears coursed down Daisy's cheeks. Her hand brushed over the top of the box.

"There was nothing the vet could do." Luke choked back his own emotion. Daisy needed to know. "Sage was gone before I got her in the door."

She covered her mouth with her hand. Luke blinked and swallowed hard as Daisy's shoulders shook with her tears.

Despite all the grumbling he'd heard about Sage this and Sage that, Daisy loved the animal to distraction.

"Thought you'd want her buried out front, under the dogwood. I've seen her lounging there more often than I can count. Might be a proper final resting place."

"Yeah." The answer was hoarse.

"I'll take care of it." Luke stood. "You don't have to worry about a thing."

Slowly, she relinquished the box to him. He took it with the reverence of accepting a treasure. She glanced from the box to stare at nothing in the distance.

"Want me to stay or take care of things?"

Her gaze flicked to him. "I'm fine." She cleared her throat. "Take care of Sage."

Torn, Luke moved to do her bidding. By the time he finished, Bekah and Daisy had canceled their evening class and posted a sign declaring the store closed for the rest of the day. He couldn't blame them. He didn't rightly want to deal with people, either, and Sage wasn't even his cat.

Bekah sniffed and pushed her purse up on her shoulder. "Thanks for everything, Luke."

"No problem." Luke nodded. "You good to drive home?"

"I'm fine."

"You take care of yourself."

"Sure." She turned to Daisy. "See you tomorrow."

"Yeah. Tomorrow."

Once Bekah left, silence enveloped the room. Daisy shuffled items around on the counter and shelves, only to put them back where they'd started. When her arms dropped to her sides with a sigh, Luke knew she needed to leave.

"Everything's done." He retrieved her purse and handed it to her. "Time to go."

Her lack of argument would've been alarming if her emotions weren't teetering close to the edge of a cliff at the moment. Daisy almost always breathed fire when he tried to boss her around and sometimes when she only thought he was.

"I want to see the spot." Daisy finished locking the door and pocketed the keys.

Luke didn't answer, just walked beside her to the dogwood tree. Daisy's surprised gasp as she surveyed his work made the extra care he'd taken worth it. Not only had he buried Sage, he'd constructed a raised bed to surround the tree and planted hostas interspersed with bleeding hearts. Arced concrete benches circled the garden, making a practical yet decorative wall.

"Oh, Luke." His name came out as a breath. "It's beautiful."

"I figured you'd want Sage to have a special place." Luke grasped her hand and led her to one of the benches.

"What's this for?" Daisy fingered a shepherd's crook, too small to hold flowers, which stood sentry between the plants.

Luke sat and urged Daisy to the bench beside him. "It's to mark the exact spot where Sage is buried."

Daisy tucked her quivering bottom lip between her teeth and sucked a deep breath through her nose. Pools of emotion filled her eyes. Luke cleared his throat. If she kept looking so broken, it'd be nearly impossible for him to get through the rest. He pulled a flat, round ornament from his jacket pocket and offered it to Daisy.

Hesitantly, she accepted the gift and turned it over in her palm. Seeing Sage's name painted in pale green and her pawprint pressed into the dried clay, the dam broke. Luke was helpless as rivers of hurt flowed. She held the disc to her chest and looked up at him with the saddest smile Luke had ever witnessed.

"It's perfect." She brushed her fingers over it once more before hanging it from the hook. "Thank you for everything. I don't think I … could have handled it on my own."

As her voice broke, Luke pulled her into his embrace and laid his cheek against her soft hair. "You don't ever have to worry about that. I'll always be there for you. Whatever you need."

"I'm being silly. Sage was just a pet." Her breath, as she mumbled against his chest, spread warmth across his chest.

"Pet, yes. Just, not a chance." He tightened his arms around her. The scent of freshly laid earth and plants mingled with the herbal aroma of her shampoo. Luke breathed it in deep. "It's understandable to be upset."

Daisy leaned from his embrace, searching his face. For what, he couldn't guess. Whatever it was, she must have found it as her lips curved in a wistful smile that was incongruous with the tears marring her cheek. Luke gently wiped the moisture away with his thumb. Daisy's eyes slid shut. Her hand covered his. She turned her face until her lips brushed across his palm with a feather-light kiss before she lowered both their hands to her lap.

"Just the same, thank you. You were my knight in shining armor today."

The words, meant as lighthearted, stood in contrast to the hurt seeping from every pore of Daisy's body. Luke's heart pounded as he watched emotions play across her features. He'd done so little to ease her pain. A garden and a little decoration.

What was that? Time, sweat, and a little bit of cash. Daisy might appreciate it in days to come, said she did now. But it didn't do anything to take her hurt or bring her peace. An overwhelming urge to draw the pain from her like poison from a wound urged Luke to take her into his embrace once more. Even holding her in his arms while she cried didn't dull the ache.

He framed her face with his hands. Her skin was soft and warm against his work-roughened hands. He gazed into her eyes and saw everything. Her pain. Her love for him. A yearning he thought he'd never see again. It called to him.

Slowly, he dipped his head in answer. The moment his lips grazed hers, he paused. She deserved a moment to stop what he meant to do. Her gentle lean into him was her answer. It was one Luke couldn't refuse.

Like their renewed friendship, the kiss started tentative and soft. The sweetness of her mouth against his released the torrent of feelings he'd kept contained behind the dam of friendship only. Her arms encircled him. His echoed her movement. He slid one hand up into her full, thick hair and deepened their kiss. She moaned and responded, mirroring his actions this time.

When all tension had melted from her shoulders and all hesitancy had fallen away, Luke forced himself to break the contact. The distance did nothing to douse the fire her touch had released inside, but she'd allowed him to take some of her grief in this intimacy. He refused to take advantage of her by asking for more. They'd both be sorry for it if he did.

As it was, the rounding of her eyes as she realized what they'd done sent the message loud and clear. Like it or not, Daisy was already toeing the line of regret. With speed he'd never have guessed, she shot up from the bench.

"We can't. I shouldn't. This was—"

"It was a friend comforting another friend." Luke ran a hand through his hair. Would she accept his explanation? It was the truth. Whether it got his heart pumping was beside the point. "It's not going to happen again."

"No." Daisy shook her head and started pacing in front of him. "No. It can't. It shouldn't have happened now. I don't know what I was thinking."

"You weren't thinkin'." He tried to grasp Daisy's hand on her next pass by, but she yanked it away. He dropped his to his lap. "You were feeling. There's nothing wrong with that."

"But we can't."

Everything Luke felt for her rushed over him, leaving him with the need to release the steam of his frustration. "Why not, Daisy? Would it be so wrong?" He stood in front of her, barring her path without touching her. "You love me. I love you. Drink's not an issue anymore. Why can't we just go back to where we were? Second chances happen all the time."

A flash of desire lit in Daisy's eyes. She wanted it too. Couldn't deny it. Just as quickly, the wanting faded. Luke clenched his jaw. Regret. He had his answer, and she'd not yet spoken a word.

"I won't try to deny it."

Daisy held his hand in hers. Luke had the urge to yank it back as she'd done him. But her touch meant more to him than venting in that moment.

"I love you, Luke. Probably always will."

"Then …"

"No."

Cold hit his skin as she dropped his hand.

"We can't go there. I made it clear from the beginning. It wasn't all about your drinking."

"God." Luke spoke it as fact, but his tone dripped with derision.

Daisy's smile was the patient one a parent offered a disappointed child. "Yes. God. I won't be in a relationship with someone who doesn't share my faith." She held up a hand. "And before you suggest it, no, faking it isn't enough."

"What if that isn't enough for me? What if I can't settle for being friends?"

It wasn't exactly an ultimatum, but Luke considered reneging on it just the same. No. He couldn't. He might not have understood how true it was when he spoke the words, but he wasn't sure he could shove his love back into the box again. Wasn't sure he wanted to. Surely, Daisy could see how much she meant to him. Make this small exception. It wasn't like she didn't love him too.

"Then we have to end this." Daisy blinked back a new onslaught of tears. "You've got a job until you can find a new one, but I think it's best you start looking."

"What?"

"It wasn't supposed to go this way. But I can't give what you're wanting." She took a step back. "As much as I love you, God comes first. I can't compromise my faith and be who I know I am."

"You don't mean it."

"I do." She pulled her keys from her pocket. "Goodbye, Luke."

Chapter Twenty

Luke's feet were as rooted to the ground as the dogwood tree beside him. Helpless to pursue Daisy, he watched her retreat until she pulled out of the parking lot without Luke so much as calling after her. How could he have made such a phenomenal mistake? All he wanted was to offer comfort, not lose Daisy forever.

"She loves me."

Every incredible moment of their kiss replayed through his mind. Nothing stood between them as he offered comfort in the most natural way he knew. Their past, his issues, their differences all melted away as the stress drained from the muscles he'd massaged under his fingertips.

All it took was the memory of Daisy in his arms to draw a groan from deep in his core. Her response told him everything. Daisy loved him. She'd told him as much when his drinking was a barrier to her feelings. Any remaining doubt was annihilated as she molded to his arms once more.

Of course, God had to step in and ruin everything. He'd conquered his demons without God's help, and God couldn't stand for that.

"You've never helped me." The old anger churned in his gut. "All You've done is take. My parents' marriage. Pops. Daisy."

And now, after dangling hope in front of him, letting him enjoy renewed friendship with Daisy, God interceded once again to yank the rug out from under his feet. God would never let him have anything good in his life. He'd written off Luke the first time he'd taken a drink.

"Two can play that game, God."

Luke yanked open the door to his truck and threw himself inside. Slammed the door and tore out of the parking lot. The urge to drink had become a less familiar companion over the past few months. Held at bay against its will, with this new opportunity, desire flared to life like a fire through dry prairie grasses.

Abstinence was overrated. There was nothing wrong with wanting a drink every now and then. He'd proven he could tackle the demons. Drinking didn't have power over him anymore. Maybe it never did.

"It was everyone else with the problem." Luke lifted his chin. "They just didn't approve of my choices. Well, too bad for them."

He was a grown man in complete control. If he wanted a beer, why shouldn't he have one? One drink didn't mean he'd get fall-down-stupid drunk. He would stop long before that point. Show Mike and Bekah and Daisy and everybody else how wrong they were. He wouldn't even get buzzed. Luke was in control.

DAISY GULPED air and swiped the heel of her hand across her wet cheeks. "I'm not sure how it happened. And then Luke was … he … was broken when I told him what we'd done was wrong."

When clarity of thought returned, Daisy would probably kick herself for storming Jill's house. To this point, they'd met at the church during support group meetings and a couple of times in public places or over the phone. But when Daisy had called her incoherent and frantic after her failure with Luke, Jill insisted that being in public was the last thing Daisy needed.

By the time Daisy arrived, Jill had arranged two cups of coffee on the end table. A sweet gesture, but they cooled untouched. Liquid comfort waited inside those cups, but Daisy couldn't think of seeking comfort until she'd worked through the depth of her mistake.

Liquid comfort. Is that how Luke viewed alcohol? Was he falling into its snare even as she sat there bawling in front of Jill? Had she driven him to it?

"What if he goes to the bar? I hurt him so much." A new batch of tears replaced the ones she'd wiped away. "That's a trigger, right? I mean, we've talked about triggers in the group. Did I just push him too far?"

Jill's demeanor remained calm despite Daisy's spiral out of verbal control. Unhurried, she picked up her cup and took a long, slow sip. Daisy's skin crawled with the need for answers, but without intending to, she found her breathing mirroring Jill's. Anxiousness melted away into the silence.

"It's good you're listening and picking up the terminology." Jill took another sip. "From what you've told me about Luke's situation, he could very well see this as another abandonment. And abandonment sounds like a big trigger for him."

"Noo." Daisy moaned as her head fell against the back of the sofa.

"I'm not finished." Jill waited until Daisy made eye contact. "Triggers are those things that bring back the familiar urges and call those in recovery back to patterns of behavior, regardless of how destructive those habits are. But," she paused, pinning Daisy to her seat with a look, "triggers do not mean the person is going to fail. It's a temptation. A strong one, but deniable nonetheless."

"If he doesn't ..."

"If Luke gives in to the temptation, it isn't on you, hon." Jill reached across the space between them and covered Daisy's hand with her own. "It. Isn't. On. You."

"But …"

Jill shook her head and sat back. "You can't take that on yourself. Recognizing and avoiding triggers is a big part of recovery, but not every trigger is avoidable."

"Failure is inevitable?"

"Not at all. Situations that push that urge into a person's day might not be avoidable, but the person still has a choice. They develop coping mechanisms to help them make the healthy choice, even in the face of heightened temptation."

Daisy blew out a sigh of relief. "He'll be okay then."

Jill's smile was sad. "I didn't say that either. Even those in recovery for what seems like most of their lives can slip back into those old habits if the temptation hits just right."

"But if I can't trust Luke to make the right choice, what hope is there?"

"Our hope isn't in people to make right choices. It's in God's ability to work in the person even when they fail."

Daisy rubbed her temples. "Luke doesn't believe in God."

"Then his battle is harder. The self is a poor regulator of our choices. We're all fickle and given to following our changing emotions." Jill motioned between them. "All of us. It's just his fight's a little bigger than some. But God can still work in and around Luke. Plus, you know where your prayers need to focus."

"It's all so much."

"Keep it simple. Your hope is in God. Trust Him to bring you through, whether Luke rises above or hits hard in the fall."

Chapter Twenty-One

"It's good to have you back, buddy." Tim clapped Luke on the shoulder. "Thought we'd lost you."

Luke harrumphed. His eyes didn't shift from the amber drink in front of him. The empties had already been removed by the waitress. Out of sight, out of mind.

"Pool table's open." Tim jerked his head in the direction of the game. Tyler and Jessica were wrapped around each other by the cue rack.

The shake of Luke's head was barely discernible. "Not tonight."

Tim laughed. "Gotta break back in slowly, huh?"

"Something like that."

"We're here, if you change your mind."

Tim sauntered away. If he expected Luke to change his mind, he'd be disappointed. The night wasn't about hanging out with his old crew.

What is it about?

Luke's head jerked up, eyes scanning the immediate vicinity. No one.

What are you doing here?

They sounded like Daisy's words or at least what she'd more than likely say if she ever darkened the door of a place like this. But it wasn't her voice invading his mind.

"No law against being here." He lowered his head as he mumbled. No need for everyone to think he'd drunk himself into hearing things. He'd only had a couple. He wasn't even properly buzzed.

You sure about that? How many have you had?

Luke tried to picture the times the waitress had stopped by the table. Once. Twice. Oh, who cared? Luke motioned the waitress to bring another. See how the voice likes that.

The silence was as disturbing as the voice.

"Compliments of the woman in the blue tank top." The waitress slid his refill onto the table.

Luke glanced where the waitress indicated. The blue tank top was easy enough to find. Luke lifted the glass from the table and nodded in her direction, questioning if he knew his benefactor.

She stood from the bar and sashayed toward him. He downed half the beer in one gulp as he watched her approach over the edge of the clear glass. Long, straight bottle-blonde hair swayed in movement with her hips. Hips covered with one of the shortest skirts he'd ever seen. Even he knew that was saying a lot, considering where he was sitting. Long, tan legs stretched from the bottom of the skirt, ending at an impossibly high pair of heeled sandals.

His gaze made its way back up. Was that a tattoo peeking out on the right side where the material of the tank top didn't quite meet that of the skirt? He tilted his head. A scarlet rose. Generic. Slightly disappointing. But a few more inches north, there wasn't a thing to be disappointed about. He had no idea how the scant material contained the ample flesh, but he wasn't one to complain.

The red-glossed smirk waiting as he continued his perusal left no doubt that his reaction was carefully planned for. Black mascara framed eyes the same deep blue as the shirt. Eyes that promised not to demand Luke be more than what he was, a man sitting at a table in a bar. He could handle that.

"Are you going to invite me to sit down?" Full lips gave a tiny pout.

Luke pushed out the chair next to him with his foot and nodded. "By all means. I could use the company."

"I could too." Her eyes narrowed as she grinned seductively. "And I promise, I'll be good company."

LUKE GROANED and turned his face into his pillow. Unfamiliar, stiff material rubbed against his cheek. He shifted. Nothing was familiar, not even the mattress. He scrubbed a hand over his eyes and forced them open.

A motel room? Noises from what he assumed was the bathroom drew his attention. The previous night came flooding back. The bar. The beer. The woman who'd come on to him stronger with each drink they'd shared.

What have you done?

Didn't Luke shut that voice up once and for all last night? No. Well, he'd see to it this morning. The previous night's escapades seemed to work pretty well. Time for a repeat performance.

He edged the pillows against the headboard and sat up against them. He scratched a hand over his bare chest. He might not look his best first thing in the morning, before the last remnants of sleep escaped. Then again, neither would she.

Luke's eyes widened as the woman came from the bathroom. Where had she found the long black pencil skirt and professional but feminine white blouse? Was this her hotel room?

Details were sketchy but there. She was in town for work. Heading back today. A one-night stand, no strings attached arrangement. Last night, it sounded perfect. Still didn't sound too bad.

"Morning." Luke caught her attention before adopting a flirtatious grin and patting the mattress. "Didn't need to get all dressed up for me."

"I didn't." She tilted her head to the side and inserted a small gold hoop into her earlobe, eyeing him in the mirror as she did. "I need to head back."

Luke slid from the bed and huddled up behind her, slipping his arms around her waist. He nudged her hair away from her neck and left a trail of kisses up the soft skin. Her head fell back with a moan, allowing him to continue. "Can't play hooky for one day? Tell your boss you're not feeling well?"

"I'm my own boss." She stepped from his embrace as if she hadn't almost turned to putty in his hands.

He reached for her again. "Then there's no problem."

She avoided his attempt at an embrace, slid her purse onto her shoulder, and stepped toward the door. "My boss won't mind. But my husband might. I promised I'd be home in time to pick up the kids from school. If I don't leave now, I'll miss my flight." The smile she flashed him was tinted with disappointment and pity in place of the red lipstick from the night before. "Bye, Luke. Maybe we'll see each other again, next time I'm in town."

The door clicked closed behind her without a word from Luke. Guilt glued his bare feet to the floor. Married. Had he known she was married? He scrounged through still hazy memories of the night before. Allison, at least he was fairly confident that was her name, was here on business. She bought him a drink. They talked. They drank some more. Those details didn't change.

Try as he might, he couldn't remember a ring. He always

checked. Nothing in their conversation indicated she might be married. With kids.

Luke hightailed it to the bathroom and dove for the toilet just in time.

Images assaulted him, each one clenching his insides. Twelve-year-old Luke cowering on his bed as his parents' voices echoed through the house after Mom caught Dad with his best friend's wife. Mom throwing his "aunt" out of the house when she came offering meaningless apologies while admitting they were in love and couldn't help themselves. Mom, despite it all, begging Dad to work things out. Dad, suitcase in hand, walking out, never to return.

Mom's broken cries when she thought Luke couldn't hear. Pops stepping into the mess and pulling Luke free with the offer of a place to stay. Pops showering pre-teen Luke with the love and support he'd never received from his parents.

He'd sworn, no matter what, he'd never be that person. Luke Masters wouldn't destroy another's childhood the way his father had stolen his. Did Allison's children even have a Pops in their lives to temper the blow?

Over and over, he purged himself of everything except the guilt. In all the years he'd sought solace in alcohol, Luke had never been so careless. Never so much as toed the uncrossable line. How did it happen this time? Had Allison lied to him? Told him she was single when she wasn't?

He groaned. The idea made no sense. She'd been more than forthcoming this morning. Didn't seem fazed by their hooking up at all. Luke couldn't imagine he'd been drunk enough to ignore a mention of kids and husband. They must not have been mentioned.

Does it matter?

"Yes, it matters." Luke rubbed his hand over his face as reality hit. "No. No, it doesn't."

Luke steeled himself as his body made another attempt to purge the shame. It was useless. Nothing would ever clean Luke of the truth. How could he have let this happen? Luke had become his father.

Chapter Twenty-Two

"I wasn't sure you'd show up today." Daisy didn't have to look up to recognize Luke's shadow as it fell over her. She carefully grasped a weed close to the dirt and pulled it without dislodging the mint vines it was tangled in. She tossed it aside and glanced at her watch. "I guess you almost didn't."

"Still work to do."

Fatigue weighted each word. Defeat clung to his usually confident frame. Daisy dropped her head. Blinking, she stemmed the onslaught of tears. The years had honed her response until it became a sick sort of muscle memory—the unwanted friend she'd hoped they'd sent packing.

She glanced up. Luke's strong arms were crossed over his chest. His jaw set. His eyes, ringed with his lack of rest, held a silent challenge, along with a telltale redness. He wasn't going to offer information freely. He would ignore the bottle between them and make her ask the questions he knew she didn't want the answers to.

She focused on the dirt.

Should she play his stupid game? The last couple of months

had dangled hope like a carrot on a stick, only to yank it away. Jill warned her it could happen. Daisy's mind had accepted the probability. Her heart had warred against the idea and won. She'd held that sliver of hope like a lifeline.

How did one phrase tear away the small buoy she clung to, leaving her to drift in the rough waters on her own? She swallowed the disappointment lodged in her throat. Daisy bit her lip against the tears trying to escape. She couldn't deal with this today.

She raised her gaze, but only to the landscape. She refused to look at Luke again. Letting him in even that much was a mistake. He crumbled her defenses every time.

"Go home, Luke."

"There's still plenty of daylight left." Though he tried for the same old easy-going Luke, need carved a path through his voice. He dropped to his knees beside her. "Scoot over. I'll do this. You go tend to things inside."

Insanity. Doing the same stuff but expecting different results. Daisy didn't know where the phrase came from, but if her life could be summed up with a few words, these topped the list. It was past time to correct course.

"I told you, go home."

He stilled beside her. "You don't mean it."

"How bad was the hangover this morning?"

Silence.

Daisy nodded. "That's all the answer I need. Go home, Luke."

He slowly pulled himself from where he had knelt on the ground. She steeled herself against glancing up at Luke when his shadow remained still beside her. He would not sway her. She wouldn't allow it.

"Fine." The blown-out breath carried an unmistakable yet unspoken curse. "I'll see you tomorrow."

"No."

"What do you mean no? I'll be fine tomorrow."

This wasn't a discussion to have while playing in the dirt like a child. Daisy braced her hands against the top bricks of the retaining wall and pushed herself up. *Father God, give me strength.*

She paused after the silent plea. The strength of Samson didn't fall from heaven to infuse her with supernatural resolve. Still, Daisy forced her body to turn, face Luke head-on. He had to see for himself how earnest she was. Wouldn't believe her any other way.

"I can't keep doing this." Her voice held more steel than she believed possible. A trickle of courage steeled her spine. "You can't come back tomorrow. This isn't working."

With one hand, Luke reached out to her. Daisy stepped back. His palm slapped against denim as his arm fell to his side.

"Don't do this."

His eyes were nearly her undoing. Like sunlight through the forest canopy when he smiled, now, filled with his plea, they resembled a stormy sea pulling her in and holding her under. Daisy swallowed as his silent urging begged her to reconsider.

He licked his lips. "It was one time. It's not going to happen again."

"Don't make promises you can't keep."

"You don't think I have what it takes to abstain?"

Need covered him as thickly as caramel on an apple at the state fair. All it would take was one touch. The briefest of contact to find herself mired in the sticky mess. If she gave in, it would contaminate every other part of her life.

She'd allowed it for years. This time, she couldn't do it. She wouldn't do it.

"No."

Luke swallowed hard. Though his jaw tightened, his eyes

held the traitorous sheen of tears. Angry Luke was one thing. She'd dealt with him countless times.

Broken Luke? He was an entirely different story. His loss and longing called to her. And they threatened to shatter her into pieces right alongside him.

"I messed up." His husky voice willed her to reconsider. "I'm sorry. And I won't let it happen again. But I need you. You make me want to be better."

She shook her head. "Don't put that on me. You can't do it on your own, and I'm not the kind of support you need. I can't be your reason to stay sober. That's not my weight to carry."

"You're abandoning me?" He scoffed. "What would Pops think?"

All possibility of acquiescence fled in the face of red-hot rage. Daisy's hands dropped to her hips. "Do not use Pops against me. You don't have the right."

In the face of her vehemence, Luke straightened for the slightest moment before lifting his chin. Daisy knew he was about to fling a retort her direction. But her anger hadn't been expelled yet. She speared him with a look that locked his answer behind his closed lips.

"Not now. Not ever."

"He's not your Pops." Luke aimed a finger in her direction. "You don't get a say."

Daisy's body vibrated with her anger. "And neither should you. Pops always fought for you. He'd still be fighting for you if he were here, but not because you deserve it. You've taken everything Pops taught you, everything he believed in, and tossed it out the window when he died. You might as well have spit in his face."

"Then God shouldn't have taken him from me." Pain infused Luke's yell. "Following a God who would take the only good thing a person has going for them is stupid. Person would have to be weak as water or crazy to follow a god like that."

"I follow that God." Daisy's disappointment softened her tone. "So did Pops. And no one could find a stronger, wiser, or more loving man than him."

Luke's jaw worked as he stabbed his fingers through his hair. "Y'all are different."

"No." Daisy shook her head. "You can't butter your bread on both sides, Luke. Either God's worthy or we're weak and ignorant. You can't claim faith is a badge of weakness or insanity, then turn around and say it isn't so for those believers you respect. Simple as that."

Luke's gaze was as skittish as an unbroken colt. Daisy waited, keeping her demeanor soft for those times his attention momentarily flitted to her. He was wrestling with the truth, but she wasn't under the illusion he'd let truth win the gold. Still, she'd not give Luke a hand in the fight by remaining closed off to him.

Luke hooked his thumbs in his jeans pockets. His square jaw lifted. The door was closed. Daisy'd said all she'd be allowed to on the subject. Whether he'd heard a word of it or not remained to be seen.

"All that's neither here nor there." He jerked his head to the side to indicate the flower gardens. "You gonna give me another chance with the job or not?"

Regret burrowed into her stomach and settled in.

"No."

"Guess I'll see you when I see you then." Luke turned and stalked from the garden.

The invisible thread that had tied them together through the years stretched taut between them, pulling at Daisy's chest, begging her to follow him.

God, help me. The urge was more powerful than any she'd ever known.

As Luke's tires spat gravel and kicked up a cloud of dust in the parking lot, Daisy trudged through the garden and into the shop. Bekah looked up from her place behind the counter.

"Daisy?" She frowned before scanning the store. "What happened?"

All the starch she'd forced into her demeanor in dealing with Luke fled in the face of her friend's concern. Without so much as a warning, her tears flowed, restricting her ability to answer.

Bekah's expression turned dark. She glared past Daisy into the garden and moved from behind the counter.

"Where is he?" The growl in her voice warned that her bite would be even worse than her bark.

As Bekah moved to push past her, Daisy laid a restraining hand on her friend's arm. Bekah's warning glare didn't prompt Daisy to remove the restriction. Staring at one another, Daisy saw the moment Bekah's look softened in response to her pain. Pity reined in rage. Daisy released her hold.

"He's gone."

Good riddance. The thought wasn't verbalized, but it hung between them. Daisy steeled herself against the friction. Though Bekah was her best friend, the understanding Daisy needed wasn't going to be found in their relationship. It hadn't been present in any of the previous years, and it wasn't going to be there now.

The knowledge didn't bring the frustration and helplessness it used to. Bekah would always be her best friend, but God witnessed her need for understanding and provided. She wasn't left to navigate this path unaided. Jill told her to call any time, day or night.

"Can you …" A hiccup stole Daisy's words.

"I've got this covered." A pity-filled smile. "Go."

Bekah didn't need to tell her twice. In only the time it took to grab her purse and keys, Daisy was out the door and dialing the one person that, in His mercy and wisdom, God had placed in her life for just this moment.

LUKE WASN'T EXACTLY clear on how he ended up in the driveway of Nathan's ranch or even when he'd settled on it as his destination. Pops would've said it was heavenly orchestration. If Luke believed, he'd agree. He was half tempted to anyway.

But just because he'd landed there by whatever power, be it heaven or luck, didn't mean he should be there. Nathan was a busy man. He had a thriving ranch where he trained horses and their riders, some for pleasure, others in preparation for the rodeo.

Luke glanced at the house beyond the paddock and barn. A physical representation of Nathan's additional responsibilities. Katie and the kids. Nathan wouldn't call them responsibilities. Blessings, more likely. Whatever he wanted to call them, they needed Nathan's time and attention.

"What am I doing here?" Luke didn't move to unlatch his seatbelt. "Nathan's got enough on his plate without babysitting a drunk."

He decided to leave a minute too late. Luke recognized Nathan's purposeful stride as he made his way through the pasture toward him, but was too far to judge whether he recognized Luke's truck.

Luke swiped his sweaty palms across his thighs. As difficult as his conversation with Daisy was, the one looming before him now promised to be worse. He'd not broached any specifics with Daisy. He wouldn't get off quite so lucky with Nathan. He was sure of it.

The man in question raised his hand in welcome, his strides quickening with his recognition of his visitor. All Luke could manage was a half-hearted nod and wave in return.

"Luke Masters." Nathan's grin warmed his words. "What are you doing in my neck of the woods?"

Spill it or keep his failures to himself? It was now or never, and Luke was leaning heavily into the never camp.

"Nothing, really." Luke dug up the best, easy-going smile he could muster and chose to lie through his teeth. "Just passin' by and thought I'd say hi."

Nathan's grin fell into a non-committal flat line. He adjusted his cap and cleared his throat. "Wanna try again? The truth works better for me. You might try it."

The challenge didn't rile Luke the way it should have. Maybe because he knew he'd been playing a losing hand before he'd opened his mouth. Nathan Phillips had a way of knowing what was going on in a person's mind almost before they knew it themselves. He'd found it humorous before. Directed at him, not so much.

"Just some stuff goin' on." He shrugged. "Doesn't matter. I'll let you get back to it."

"You're already here." Nathan stepped back. "Might as well stay a spell."

Luke clicked the latch on his seatbelt and opened the door. Leaving now would be an insult, and he didn't have such a stockpile of friends that he could afford to waste this one on careless insults.

"Ya sure?" Luke pushed the truck door closed. "This one could take more than a spell."

"I'm fixin' to check the fence in the north pasture." Nathan pointed to his destination with the hammer Luke hadn't noticed in his hand. "Walk with me, and you can have all the spells you want."

Luke fell in step beside Nathan, matching his long, easy strides across the grass-covered pasture. Wispy clouds covered the sun, taking the edge off summer's heat. Luke inhaled the scents of summer—rich soil, freshly mowed grass, and honeysuckle. A feeling of peaceful simplicity hung in the air, beckoning or taunting him. Luke couldn't be sure which.

When more distance stretched behind them to the barn than in front of them to the fenced boundary of the pasture, Luke realized he'd yet to utter a single word, much less unburden himself. But Nathan let the silence be.

Luke glanced in his direction. Just as at ease as any other time. Had to hand it to him, Nathan's feathers didn't ruffle much. He was a solid guy and about the only friend Luke could claim at the moment. Why he'd given him the time of day was beyond Luke.

"Why'd you do it?" The question slipped out before Luke thought out the ramifications.

"Depends on what you're talking about."

In for a penny, I guess. Luke met Nathan's gaze. "You're a real stand-up guy. Successful business, great family, and a great reputation to go with it. I've screwed up everything I've touched since high school, maybe before that."

Nathan examined a stretch of fence, found a couple of nails that had worked themselves out of place, and drove them back in with a quick swing of his hammer. "Still don't hear a question."

Pathetic. That's how he would sound to Nathan. Still, something in Luke demanded the answer.

"You've got everything going for ya. I've got less than nothing." Luke busied himself fiddling with the fence like he was there to help. "Why'd you bother with me? No one else does, least of all men like you."

"Hmm." Nathan adjusted the faded cap he wore and stared off in the distance. "Reckon I never thought about it like that."

Every second that passed ratcheted up Luke's nerves, but Nathan wasn't in a rush to answer, moving instead to the next section of fencing. Hadn't Luke just been admiring the trait that now wore on him like sandpaper? He took a deep breath and followed along, forcing his mouth to keep quiet.

Nathan drove in a couple more nails. "None of us is perfect."

"You're way closer than I am."

Nathan chuckled. "That's what you see. Truth is, I've had my own struggles. Some that people see. Some they don't."

"Everybody sees mine." Luke toed the dirt beneath his boot. "Act like they don't to my face, but they do. I hear what's said behind my back. Think I'm a big bunch of wasted potential. A disappointment, but none of 'em tell me to my face."

Luke scratched over his ear. "Nope. That's not entirely true. Bek, that friend of Daisy's, she tells me straight up. No doubt what she thinks of me, and it isn't good. Much as she hates me, I should return the favor. But ya know what? I don't. I can respect her stickin' to her guns. Least she's being honest."

Nathan leaned against a fence post and crossed his arms over his chest. "That how you see me? You think I'm being nice to your face and badmouthing you the minute you're gone?"

Luke eyed him a moment before shaking his head. "Nah. Not you. And I can't figure it out. What do you see that no one else does?"

"I see a man who doesn't understand how loved and wanted he is by the One who created him."

It sounded so much like Pops that any smart-aleck retort died in Luke's throat. In the times he was completely honest with himself, which were few and far between, Luke knew God was real, just the way Pops taught him. Pops lived his faith every day. The difference was obvious. Luke had felt its truth.

But knowing the Creator existed and believing that same Creator loved and wanted a relationship with Luke were two very different things. Stubborn. Loser. Drunk. Homewrecker. All those things could be added under his photo in the yearbook of life.

What he wouldn't give for "loved" to replace each one.

He might as well hope to find that million-dollar winner symbol on his next scratch-off. Odds weren't in his favor, even if his chest ached with the need.

"God doesn't want anything to do with the likes of me."

Nathan pushed off from the post. "That's where you're wrong. God sees the real Luke Masters, and He loves him all the way to the cross."

A sick feeling settled in Luke's stomach. "I could've believed that before, but not now. Not after what I've done."

Chapter Twenty-Three

Daisy shifted from foot to foot, willing herself not to march back to her car. Seeking solace from Jill sounded great until she stood on the porch of the simple ranch-style house. Calling ahead now seemed like the most appropriate course of action. "Call anytime" was not synonymous with "drop by my house unannounced."

Maybe a carton of Rocky Road would be the better option.

The heavy click of the bolt lock broke her silence and destroyed Daisy's last chance to escape unnoticed. Jill's eyes widened a moment before her brows dipped into a low V.

"Oh no, hon. What happened?"

It wasn't until tears filled Daisy's eyes and Jill ushered her inside that Daisy noticed a large paintbrush in Jill's hand. She'd not only dropped in unannounced but also interrupted a home improvement project in the process.

"You're busy." She swiped her fingers over her cheeks. "I shouldn't have interrupted. I'm sorry."

She was stopped mid-turn toward the door by Jill's hand around her wrist.

"Please. Stay."

Jill's expression was sincere. Daisy could almost believe her arrival really wasn't an inconvenience. Still, her friend was obviously in the middle of something.

"Please." Jill motioned down a nearby hallway with the brush in her hand. "I'm just painting my new hobby room now that the last bird has finally left the nest. I could use the company."

Daisy nodded. Jill released her hold and led the way down the hall. Daisy glimpsed photos of Jill and her family of three along the walls. Happy faces. Joyful memories. A family. All the things Daisy dreamed for herself but never realized. Her feelings for Luke always stood in the way, barring anyone who might attempt it from finding their way into her heart.

Pathetic. How many years had she prayed for God's intervention? Begged Him to bring back the Luke she loved or free her from her feelings for him? God heard her cries, understood her pain and confusion. His silence on the matter didn't rock her faith, but she wished she could comprehend why answers to both appeared to be resounding nos.

"Is Luke my thorn in the flesh?"

Jill tossed a quizzical glance her way as she dipped her brush in a can of mossy green paint. Daisy grimaced. How was Jill to know the conversation Daisy'd been having in her mind? Probably sounded like an insane person.

"It's so hard." Daisy cleared her throat. "Do you have another brush? I can help if you'd like."

Jill nodded toward painting supplies in the opposite corner. "There's a roller over there. I've edged those two walls. You can start on those, if you like. Now, as for Luke, why don't you start with what's happened, and we'll work our way back to the thorn in the flesh thing."

"He arrived at work at one o'clock today. Five hours late and sporting all the signs of a hangover." Jill filled a paint tray, finding unexpected calm in the way the thick liquid ribboned into the plastic holder. "He tried to play it off. I told him to leave and not come back."

"At all?" Jill's brush paused midway to the wall.

"Yep." Daisy could hardly believe it herself. "And I'm not sure how, but we got into an argument about God. He can't believe in a God that would take Pops from him. Faith is for the weak and stupid. Well, except for me and Pops, apparently. But I told him he can't have it both ways."

"How did he react to your logic?"

Daisy pushed the spongy roller into the color in the tray. "Ignored it completely. His only concern was about losing his job. He wasn't ready to hear the truth. I'm beginning to wonder if he ever will be."

"Do you really believe that?"

"Who knows?" Daisy shrugged and pushed the roller across the wall with zig-zagging motions. "I want to believe God's not finished with Luke. Maybe it's just wishful thinking. I want it so much, maybe I'm blind to the truth. Luke's gone, and he's not coming back."

"Hmm."

Daisy itched to ask the meaning of the short, little sound. So innocent on the surface, but it had to be rife with meaning. Did Jill agree with her assessment? Was she in doubt? If so, why didn't she come out and say it?

"So, why's he your thorn in the flesh?"

Jill's question cut through the rhythmic swish of brush and roller against the walls. Daisy, still caught in her own musings, took a moment to switch gears before answering. Jill just kept painting.

"I can't help it." Daisy sighed. "Despite everything, I love him."

Jill's shoulders fell. Her brush hesitated before continuing its journey across the wall. It was just as well. Daisy didn't want to read pity in her friend's eyes.

Jill paused once more. "Is that wrong?"

The quiet question released a storm inside Daisy. *Yes* had a million reasons backing it. *No* had a million more. If she knew the correct answer, she'd run with it and not look back. But if God had a preference, He was keeping it to Himself.

"Honestly? I'm not sure anymore."

"I take it, from your words about the thorn in the flesh, that you've asked God to make what you feel for Luke to fade?"

"Asked? More like begged and bartered and anything else I think may help."

"And have your feelings changed?"

Daisy worried her lip. "Not a bit. I can't seem to purge the man from my system."

"You can't purge what you won't step away from."

Defensiveness shot straight from Daisy's heart and spilled over in words. "Luke is my friend. You don't walk away from friends because things are tough."

"No." Jill glanced over her shoulder at Daisy. "But there also comes a time, and I'm not saying this is that time, when a person may have to put space between themselves and their friend. When friendship is detrimental to their spiritual or emotional well-being, it may be the wisest option. It's not easy. And when romance muddies the waters, it's harder."

"He needs to remember the faith from his past. To realize God's love for him."

"His return to faith isn't any more your responsibility than his continued sobriety. Both must begin from something in him or they won't do him any good."

Daisy finished her wall with one last swipe and moved to the next. As she pushed the first streak of color over the stark white, she released her frustration with it. Walk away. Break all ties. What had kept her from it all this time?

"If I walk away, there's no one left to help him find his way back."

Jill wrapped her wet brush in a plastic bag, grabbed the painter's tape, and moved to frame a window on the last untouched wall. "Isn't your God big enough to bring Philip to Luke?"

"Philip? Who in the world is Philip?"

"From the Bible. When the Ethiopian was out in the middle of nowhere, God didn't leave him to fend for himself. Philip was sent down the least expected path for the sole purpose of meeting the Ethiopian's need. God will bring Luke his Philip when the time is right."

A flicker of rebellion flared in opposition to Jill's words. "I'm right there. He's my friend. No Philip needed."

"Perhaps. But maybe it's not your task. You've asked God to bring Luke to a place of acceptance. Trust it will happen in God's timing and in His way, with or without you."

After all they'd been through together, the idea that God might not want her to play a role in Luke's return to faith grated. A deep inhale steadied her racing thoughts, and she continued her painting. Jill's words, as irritating as they were to hear, might hold merit.

While Daisy regularly prayed for deliverance from her feelings, every moment she glimpsed the compassionate, fun, or loving Luke of the past, her heart secured itself to him a little more. Was staying so closely bound to him like asking God to deliver her from the temptation to cheat on a test while refusing to look away from the answer sheet? Sure, God might miraculously make the answers disappear, but God asked her to walk in wisdom and flee from temptation. That meant walking away from the answer key, and it might mean walking away from Luke too.

Lord, prepare the one You will use to show Luke the way. Give them the words and the perfect timing to bring him back to You.

The silent prayer flowed from her heart. A weight she'd

grown so accustomed to carrying that she didn't realize it was there lifted from her shoulders. Freeing. Yet it didn't offer relief to her bruised heart. The idea of exorcizing Luke from her life was enough to steal her breath. A spasm tightened her chest.

Life without Luke. Life without drunk dialed calls and lewd suggestions. Life without his misplaced anger that deemed his problems the fault of everyone but him. Perfect if not for one thing.

Life without Luke.

Chapter Twenty-Four

"It can't be that easy." Luke huffed. "Nothing in life is that easy."

Nathan drained the remains of a cold cup of coffee down the sink before disposing of the cup in the garbage. "Why do you think it's easy?"

Luke shook his head and scanned the now-empty room. Many of the chairs had been filled only thirty minutes ago. The group had welcomed him without question, and he appreciated that. But some things were too good to be true.

"Some of those guys struggled with addictions to things a lot stronger than alcohol."

"Yeah."

"They lost everything."

"True."

"But they just gave it over to God and He magically made it disappear?"

Nathan turned from the sink to face Luke. One brow rose high. "Who said that?"

"All of them." Luke's upturned hand swung in front of him

to include the entire room. "They all say God helps them stay clean. He gives them the strength. He gives them the reason."

"Just because God helps and strengthens and even provides a reason, doesn't mean their addictions have disappeared." Nathan grinned. "If that were the case, none of them would be here. There'd be no need for a support group because there'd be nothing to support."

"Then what's the good of having God, if He isn't going to make it go away?"

Nathan swiped a damp rag across the counter and folded it over the division of the sink compartments. His squinted eyes told Luke he wasn't being ignored. So, Luke didn't push for the answer, no matter how much everything might hinge on what Nathan would say.

Nathan took a seat at one of the tables bordering the chairs that had been set up for the meeting. He motioned to the one across from him. Luke plopped down.

"I've been listening to this group's stories for several years now." Nathan folded his hands together in front of him. "Each one is as different as each person doing the telling. Some would say pain brought out their addiction. Others would credit it to making stupid choices in their younger days. Peer pressure. Learned behaviors from parents and caregivers. It's a never-ending list of possibilities. You heard some of them tonight."

Luke shrugged. "Yeah."

"No matter the start, no one set out to become an addict. No one wanted to lose their jobs, homes, relationships, or health. For some, the spiral into addiction happened over a relatively long time. For others, it happened quickly, even with that first drink or hit. Whatever their reason was, no matter whether they became addicted quickly or slowly, their choices led to something much bigger than they could control."

Luke worked his jaw. "You saying no one can move past their addictions without God?"

"Nope. There are some who choose to give it up, and they do. I can't say if they weren't that far into it or if something else was at play in their ability to do so. Doesn't really matter." Nathan nodded toward the empty chairs. "These people, they've lost a lot. Some have lost everything. They didn't set out to implode their lives, and they sure didn't want it that way. But it happened, and still, they'd find themselves using, even knowing they'd still be in the same sorry shape after the high passed."

Relatable. How much had Luke lost over the years? How many times had he told himself no more, only to find himself right back where he said he'd never go again?

"I was closer this time. Really thought it would be different." Luke rubbed his hands down the denim of his jeans. "It was for a while."

Nathan nodded. "You did manage sobriety for longer than you'd done before. But what happened when you fell?"

There was no judgment in Nathan's question, but the sick feeling in the pit of Luke's stomach flared up again. Truthfully, it hadn't completely gone away since he woke up in that hotel room to find he'd been with a married woman. Even sharing the sordid details with Nathan earlier hadn't purged the feeling as he'd hoped it would. Nothing was going to put him to rights after this mistake. He'd better get used to it.

"I don't want to mislead you." Nathan licked his lips. "Some of the people in this group came to get sober and clean, nothing more. Some came because they already realized there was more to their addictions than substance abuse and their substance of choice wasn't taking care of the problem but making it worse. Some, like you, came with the misconception that God is some kind of spiritual suboxone to cut the cravings and enable success."

"They must all think He is and it's working, or they wouldn't come back."

Nathan nodded. "I can see why you might think that, but

you'd be wrong. Don't misunderstand, God is a big part of their recovery. He does give strength to overcome the temptation. But God is not waving a wand over them and making the addiction disappear. A magic pill won't erase the issues that ushered in the addiction in the first place. Not even those with an opioid addiction who use suboxone have guaranteed success. The pill cuts the physical withdrawal, but it doesn't fix the root problem. It doesn't erase the triggers from the addict's life so they never face the craving again. Thinking so is the equivalent of slapping a bandage on an infected wound and considering it healed."

Had Luke been using a Band-Aid when he needed an antibiotic? Once he admitted a problem, he had not thought beyond his drinking being the issue. If Nathan was correct, and that was a big if, his drinking was the symptom. An out-of-control symptom that caused a whole new issue, but just the same, a signal that something bigger was happening.

In Luke's experience, Nathan was a straight shooter. He didn't beat people up with the truth, but he didn't shy away from sharing it either. Working off the premise that Nathan was correct, what was Luke trying to medicate through drinking?

Luke shook his head. There was a lot to unpack in what Nathan said. More than Luke could handle in one sitting. And Nathan still hadn't touched on his first question.

"If God's not going to take it away, what good is He? Why are the people in the group singing His praises for helping them make it one more day?"

"As much as God wants to see each addict free from their addiction, He's more concerned with what caused it in the first place. Find and deal with the root, and the addiction is easier to put in its place. Not easy, but easier." Nathan toyed with a crumb they'd missed in cleaning the white plastic tables. "I've personally heard the stories from most of those who shared tonight. I've seen 'em wrestle with and come to the truth that God loves them. He loves the man who was abused as a kid by one meant to protect him. He loves the one who never could seem to live up to their potential. And He loves the one who has committed sins they feel are unforgivable."

"Love doesn't make those things go away."

"Nope. But knowing God sees their worst and loves them anyway is a powerful step in the right direction. He offers healing for the hurts, grace for the failures, and forgiveness for their sins. Once a person experiences those, working through the issues is less daunting, less impossible, because they know God is right there with 'em every step of the way."

"Pray for forgiveness, and it all goes away? Seems far-fetched to me."

"That's not how it works. A relationship with God doesn't necessarily mean the addiction suddenly loses its hold on a person. Trauma or loss or whatever doesn't disappear."

Luke frowned. "Then what's the use?"

"Knowing God means they have someone bigger than themselves to lean on. He gives strength and holds them through the rough patches as they keep taking one day at a time. God celebrates each success with them, picks 'em up after their failures, and comforts when they take steps to deal with deeper issues, whether that's admitting the issues or seeking counseling to help gain understanding and coping tools."

When Luke didn't say anything, Nathan didn't push. Instead, he stood and started stacking chairs against the wall. Luke joined him, allowing the physical activity to help his mind process everything Nathan said.

"That's what I like about our recovery group here." Nathan paused and glanced over at him. "When the deep issues come out, and believe me, they can come out with a bang, we offer them the hope of God, but we also have someone at each meeting trained to deal with those psychological and emotional issues from a mental health perspective. It's not required as a program host, but I've seen it add more success in the group. We steer them in the right direction for the counseling they need, while offering them foremost the relationship with God they were created for."

Created for a relationship with God. It sounded nice, but Luke knew the ugly underbelly of trusting God. He'd traveled that route and learned sometimes God couldn't be trusted.

"What about when God fails?"

"What d'ya mean?"

"Like when someone trusts God, but He doesn't come through?"

Nathan put the last chair on its stack. "Never seen it happen. But I've seen how the wrong perspective makes it seem that way."

"God doesn't fail? We just think He does because we're wrong?"

"Pretty much." Nathan shrugged. "There are times when we want to see God like a genie waiting to grant our wishes. He's God and can do anything. Miracles are another day in the office for Him. We forget, He's allowed us free choice. In our rush to think we're as smart as God, we mess things up. The junk we put up with in life isn't easy, but it's of our own making as people. Sin ushered in all the brokenness, pain, and evil we experience. God doesn't always take it away, but He promises to be with us in it. That's why forgiveness and a relationship with Him are most important to Him. The bad isn't going away until He comes again, but we don't have to wade through the muck on our own."

"Still sounds like a cheap way out."

"Maybe. But have you ever considered what would happen if God gave everyone what they want all the time?"

"Yeah. People would love Him and want Him around."

Nathan laughed. "You'd think so. But that's only loving what someone can do for you. Using someone. If you give kids everything they want, they don't love you more. They become spoiled and want more. We're no different. If God gave us everything, we'd never reach the end of what we'd wish for. We'd never love Him for being Him. Only use Him to live our selfish dream."

Luke plucked his jacket from the coat rack and slid it on before grabbing his cap. "I know you want me to drop to my knees right now and give my heart to Jesus or something."

"Might be nice," Nathan smirked. "But it's gotta be real. Doesn't do you any good otherwise."

"You've given me a lot to chew on." Luke could admit that much, anyway. Nathan would probably say the ache in his chest was God talking, but Luke wasn't so sure. Some of his questions were still rattling around in his head without satisfying answers. "Thanks."

Nathan nodded at him. "Any time. I'll be praying for you."

Luke reached for the doorknob.

"One word of caution." Nathan's voice stopped him. "If we demand every question be completely answered before we can believe, there's no need for faith. Seeking is great. It's how we get to know God, but there are some things we may not understand for a while, maybe not until Jesus returns."

Luke looked over his shoulder. "Thanks again."

For a moment, once Luke reached his truck, he sat staring out the windshield. What he'd seen, the conversations he and Nathan had, and his questions about God rolled around in his head. As much as Luke didn't want to admit it, he could sense the truth of Nathan's words, both about his addiction and his non-existent faith. That left one glaring question.

What am I going to do about it?

Chapter Twenty-Five

Daisy watched Katie unwrap the chocolate cupcake with chai-spiced buttercream frosting. "How did you manage to sneak away without the kiddos?"

Katie took a bite of the sweet and moaned. "Kiddos? What kiddos?" She took another bite and swiped excess frosting from her lip with her tongue. "Seriously. These are good enough to make someone forget all their responsibilities and half their troubles too."

"Lucy always does a great job." Daisy laughed. "This time she knocked it out of the park, creating a treat that not only complements but uses a tea flavor."

"Once upon a time, I thought no one had as much baking talent as Austin." She swiped her finger through the frosting like a child before licking it clean. "I can admit when I'm wrong."

Daisy laid a hand on Katie's forearm. "Austin would be over-the-moon happy you found someone as talented as Lucy to take over his bakery."

"He would." A wistful smile curved her lips. "He mentored her, and she understands the history of By Sweet Design. That's the icing on the cupcake."

Daisy groaned. "Great sentiment, but did you really have to go there?"

"Fine." Katie laughed and shoved the last bite in her mouth.

"Do you visit there much?"

"The bakery?"

Daisy nodded.

"Not really." Katie shrugged. "When I need my sugar fix, I can find my craving killer here. I love Lucy, and I'm glad she's such a success. But sometimes staring the past in the face doesn't leave room for the present. And I've got a pretty great present."

Daisy gathered the cupcake wrapper and wadded-up napkin to dispose of them. "I get it. The past has a way of weighing you down until you don't recognize it's happening. Then, when you finally let go, you can't help wondering how you were living carrying it all around every day."

"Something like that, though it's less about carrying a weight in my situation and more about being fully invested in the here and now." Katie stood from the high stool. "Don't get me wrong, Austin is part of my life. Nathan accepts that. He's aware he isn't my first love but is secure enough in our love that Austin's memory can be part of the here and now. Besides, Sammy needs to know his dad."

Katie's head tilted to the side. "But I get what you're saying, and I sense you've got a story to go along with your epiphany."

"She finally cut the dead weight, once and for all." Bekah butted into their conversation with her two cents as she walked behind Daisy to stock the shelf.

Daisy clenched her jaw and sucked in a deep breath through her nose, letting it release slowly through barely parted lips. Katie's grin betrayed her discomfort as she glanced between Daisy and Bekah before turning her attention to the wall of windows leading out to the garden patio.

"Your garden is always gorgeous." Katie's smile relaxed.

"I'd love to take a closer look now that it's green. Maybe I'll see a blossom or two."

"You good in here, Bek?" Daisy funneled every ounce of patience she possessed into the question. Frankly, she didn't really care if Bekah was good or not at the moment.

"All under control here. Go ahead."

Bekah's easy grin as she continued stocking the shelves gave clue to her lack of understanding. Luke being out of their lives didn't mean Daisy was happy about it. With Bekah focused on her task, Daisy shook her head and followed Katie out the door.

As soon as the door closed behind them, Katie swung around to face Daisy. "I hope I didn't overstep in there. I had a feeling we wouldn't get much talking done with Bek around."

Daisy harrumphed. "That's the understatement of the century. Bek's never been a fan of Luke. She chilled out a little when he was sober, but now, she's not cutting him any slack."

"Is it true?"

"You mean that Luke's out of my life?" Daisy let her fingers brush over some of the taller plants as they walked the brick-lined path between the garden beds. "Yeah."

"A lot of weight in that one little word."

Daisy dropped to the built-up wall of edging stones and began carefully pulling weeds from between the plants. "I wasn't lying. Hard as it was, letting Luke go took a weight I'd gotten so used to I didn't realize it was there."

"But?"

Daisy shrugged. "I miss him."

"So, why cut him loose?"

Daisy sighed and scooped up the uprooted weeds to deposit in her compost bin. "It's not what you're thinking."

"And what is that?"

"That he showed up hungover, and I sent him packing."

"Isn't that what happened?"

"No." Daisy sighed. "Yes, but it wasn't about that. Not really."

"Then what?"

Daisy opened the compost bin and dumped the handful of weeds inside. "I was proud of Luke for staying sober. He hadn't lasted that long in ages." She dusted her hands off on the rag she hung on the side of the bin. "But alcoholics slip, sometimes even after years of sobriety. It's more about what prompted his fall and how much I was struggling with slipping myself."

Katie frowned. "I'm sorry. I didn't know you fought that battle too."

"No." Daisy smiled and shook her head. "I don't. Never. Not after seeing what it did to Luke. Mine was a more personal struggle."

Katie regarded her in silence. Though she'd asked God's forgiveness a million times in the weeks since that day, shame and regret were diligent taskmasters. The memory still brought the familiar, heavy burn in her chest.

"I kissed him, Katie." Daisy blinked against a sudden urge to cry. "He was comforting me about Sage, and he'd been so sweet. So much like the Luke I've always loved. And he'd been that way for a while. And it just sort of happened. I told him it was a mistake. We couldn't be together."

Katie simply nodded. Daisy wished she could tell what she was thinking. But her poker face kept it hidden behind a mask of blandness. Was Katie calling Daisy every name in the book for being so stupid? Daisy deserved it. She'd called herself a host of unkind names since that day.

"When Luke showed up hungover the next day, I'm sure he thought I was letting him go because he failed."

"That isn't what happened?"

"No." Daisy shook her head. "I mean, we did have words about his drinking. But it was more for self-preservation." Daisy swiped a tear from her cheek. "I love Luke. So much." She gulped. "I always have, and if God doesn't help me, I always will. But Luke's off limits. He walked away from God."

Katie sat on one of the garden benches and waited for Daisy to join her.

"I drew that line and said I'd never cross it." Daisy swiped at more tears. "But in that moment, standing there in Luke's arms, accepting his kiss like there wasn't a whole ocean under that bridge, I knew I would cross that line. It wouldn't be that day, but it would happen."

Compassion reflected in Katie's eyes. "Losing Austin hurt more than anything I've ever experienced. But he was taken from me. There was nothing I could do about it." She sniffed and rubbed her lips together, fighting her own tears. "I can't imagine experiencing a forever kind of love and having to choose to walk away. I'm so sorry."

Daisy tried to smile, though it came out more like a grimace. "In some ways, it has been freeing. I'm not always wondering when the next shoe will drop or trying to figure out if it's going to be a slipper or a stiletto. And I don't have to guard myself around him to stay on the right side of the line. Now, if my heart will stop bleeding so much every time I think of him, I'll be set."

"Really?"

"Okay. Maybe not set, but better. I don't think I'll ever be fully set. I may have let him go, but I pray every night that Luke's slip-up was a one-time thing and that he's not plummeted back into that life. Not after all the progress he made."

Katie lifted one shoulder. "If it's any comfort, he's looked good the last few times he's been out at the house."

A frisson of interest pinged against Daisy's ribcage. While not an official sponsor, because Luke refused the idea that he might need a group, Nathan had been a friend to Luke through all this. He was Luke's Jill. If Luke was still meeting with him ...

"Then, they're still getting together? How's it going? Has he mentioned the way we left things between us?"

Katie held up a hand. "Oh, no. First of all, when Nathan or I meet with someone, we don't break that confidence unless it's a protection thing. I couldn't tell you what they talk about. Second, even with specifics, I wouldn't break the confidence."

Daisy accepted the gentle rebuke. "You're right. I'm sorry I asked."

"No need. Anyone would be tempted to ask. I can tell you, Luke's eaten supper with us a few times, and he's seemed in decent spirits." Katie's smile was so wistful, Daisy would've thought she had feelings for Luke if she didn't know better. "He's great with the kids. Sam eats up the extra attention from a man other than Nathan. And the baby lights up when he plays with her."

That explained it. Katie had a soft spot for anyone who adored her kids as much as she did. Luke had always been good with kids. One day, he'd make a great dad. A prick in the area of Daisy's heart accompanied the image of a little boy with Luke's smile and her auburn hair.

Daisy sighed. As hard as letting Luke go had been, purging him from her heart once and for all was proving impossible.

Chapter Twenty-Six

Daisy pulled into the parking lot of Mike's Landscaping. As soon as Mike called to tell her the geraniums and organic fertilizer she had ordered had arrived, she texted Bekah to let her know she'd be late for work and rerouted to pick up her plants.

"Where's my phone?" She stepped out of the truck for a better look. It should have been on the seat next to her. She glanced at the floorboards. Found it. The thing must have slid off on that last turn into the parking lot.

She opened the notes app as she locked and shut the door. "I need lemongrass, but what else was on my list?"

She scrolled to the correct note. Lemongrass. Mint plants. Hopefully, Mike had them in stock. Planting season was passing swiftly. If Mike didn't have them, she'd have to look elsewhere. She'd run out of time.

She swiped the app closed and, with a little huff, stowed the phone in her jacket pocket. Time. It hadn't seemed like such a precious commodity until she let Luke go. Why hadn't she realized how much time he saved her with his work in the garden?

"Hey, Mike." Daisy greeted the man behind the counter. "I'm here for my geraniums and fertilizer. And I have a few other things I need while I'm here."

Mike looked up from the register with a smile. "Gather up whatever you need. I'll have the rest waiting for you whenever you're ready."

Daisy moved through the building and grabbed one of the small flat push carts out the back door. Large wheels allowed her to move it over the gravel pathways between carefully organized rows of plants and keep her eyes open for the ones she needed.

The mint, lemongrass, and an extra cinnamon basil that looked healthy were placed on the cart in no time. Daisy steered her purchases back into the shop and up to the counter, ringing the bell for service when she reached it.

"Hi, welcome to Mike's Landscaping."

No. It couldn't be.

"How can I—" Luke froze halfway through the door directly behind the counter. The one marked Employees Only. "Daisy. I … it's good to see you."

Daisy's mouth felt stuffed with cotton. Though somehow a boulder had made it past the cotton to lodge in her throat, blocking words and air.

She swallowed hard and gasped, "You're back."

It was a dumb observation, even to her own ears. Of course Luke was back. Otherwise, he wouldn't be coming out of the employee's back room looking … No. She wouldn't think about how good he looked, with that five o'clock shadow that started long before noon. Or those hazel eyes that were free of the fog she'd seen last time she looked into them. Eyes that still held the desperation of a man drowning and confidence that she was the lifeline he was looking for.

She ripped her attention away, landing on her special order flat behind him. Much safer. "Mike left my order right there."

Daisy pointed while hoping she didn't sound as breathless to Luke as she did to herself. "And I've got a few extras to add to it."

When he didn't answer, she dared another glance in his direction. The intensity threatened her reasoning abilities. *Please,* she begged silently, *please just let me finish my purchase and go.*

After a second that seemed to stretch for decades, the tug lessened. His shoulders dropped almost imperceptibly. He grabbed the pricing gun and, without a word, scanned each plant on the flat behind him before moving to those on her cart.

"One hundred eighty-five dollars and sixty-two cents." His voice was all business as he read the total off the register.

Daisy tapped her business card against the reader and punched in her four-digit PIN. Luke handed her the receipt as soon as the machine spat it out.

"If you'll hand me the geraniums, I can add them to the cart." She nodded to the plants behind him. "Then, I'll load them and come back for the fertilizer."

Luke moved the plants in question to the counter in front of her. "No need to come back in. I'll carry the bags out for you."

Daisy plopped the last pot on the cart with less care than she'd usually exhibit and spun back around. "Oh, no. I can't ask you to do that. I can come back. No problem."

His jaw twitched. "Just the same, I'd like to keep my job."

Maybe he didn't mean it as a barb, but it still stung.

"Mike expects all customers to receive the best service." He hefted one of the bags. "That includes helping them with their purchases." He added the second bag. "I assume you're in the truck?"

"Yes." Her quiet answer was all she could manage as Luke walked past her and out the door. She didn't want special treatment. Didn't want him to care. So, why did knowing he'd carry the load for any of his customers leave her deflated?

Daisy would have to unpack that later. She pushed the cart out the door after him. If she valued her emotional stability, there was only one thing she needed to focus on. Loading her truck and getting away from the yearning in Luke's eyes as quickly as possible.

"Leave already." Mike shook his head as the clock moved to five o'clock. "Go take care of things with Daisy and come back tomorrow with your head on straight."

Luke knew the words were offered as a friend and not his boss. Mike had seen the aftermath of Daisy's visit. Claimed Luke looked like he'd seen a ghost before realizing the special-order flat was gone. Once Mike realized what had happened, he apologized. He knew where the chips had fallen in that relationship, and he'd meant to be there when Daisy showed up.

Distraction may have been a reasonable side-effect, but Luke knew Mike was right. He and Daisy lived in a small town. They'd only avoided running into each other since she'd fired him because he steered clear of places she liked to frequent. But Mike's offer of a job had been a God-send Luke knew he couldn't pass up, even as he knew it would bring Daisy back into his solar system.

"I'm not sure how to fix things." Luke adjusted his cap and fished his keys from his pocket. "But I'm gonna try."

Mike frowned. "Call me, okay? If things go wrong—well, just call."

Luke didn't need it spelled out. And as much as he'd like to take offense, Mike's worry wasn't misplaced. In fact, it spoke volumes to the restoration of their friendship. "I won't go there, Mike."

"But if you need to ..."

"I'll call." Luke gave a short nod.

It was all Mike needed. His concerned scowl relaxed into a neutral expression.

"See you tomorrow," Luke called over his shoulder and headed out the door to his truck and an uncertain welcome.

Luke hit end on his phone and pulled into Daisy's driveway. Nathan's prayers couldn't stop the onslaught of nerves he'd experienced from the moment he'd walked out of the breakroom to find her standing at the counter.

He gripped the steering wheel. "It's just Daisy."

He scoffed at his own reassurance. That was the problem. It was Daisy. But, to Luke, Daisy had never been *just* anything.

"God, help me." It was the closest to a coherent prayer Luke could manage with his thoughts playing pinball in his brain. Hopefully, Nathan was right, and God knew the prayer in his heart.

The front door opened. Even from the driver's seat of the truck, Luke could see Daisy's irritation. Maybe coming had been a bad idea. Leaving now, without talking to her, would be a disaster of epic proportions. Daisy left her porch and stalked toward his truck. Luke steeled himself at her approach. He opened the door and stepped out before she could trap him inside the cab.

"What are you doing here?"

Anger fueled each word, but hurt lay just beneath her ire. He scuffed the gravel with the toe of his work boot as he contemplated the answer least likely to result in his expulsion from her property.

"The truth, Luke."

Of course, as intimately as he knew her, Daisy knew him too. She'd know he was searching for something to pacify her and buy him time. Whether it would earn him another glare or the full force of her ire, Luke couldn't stop the slow tipping of his mouth into a one-sided grin.

Daisy's eyes narrowed before she sighed and let her shoulders drop. "Luke, it's been a long day. What do you want?"

"We need to talk." He lifted his chin. She wanted the truth. He delivered it in the simplest of forms.

"No. We don't."

"Listen, this isn't some half-baked attempt to make an inroad with you." He adjusted his cap. "It's just, after seeing you at Mike's, how uncomfortable this thing"—he waved his hand between them—"has become, we need to clear the air."

One brow raised. "My air is pristine. Not a bit of smog in sight."

Luke clenched his jaw. Did she think he was blind to her reaction to him at the shop? They were encased in pollution. "You said the truth. Or did that only apply to me?"

"Fine." Her shoulders were ramrod straight. "Let's go inside where we can avoid being the topic of gossip over tomorrow morning's coffee and doughnuts."

Without waiting for so much as an agreement, she spun on her heel and marched back inside. Luckily, Luke's long legs kept stride with her. Otherwise, he wasn't convinced she wouldn't have changed her mind and slammed the door in his face.

Daisy dropped onto the couch and swung her feet onto the cushions in one swift movement, cutting off any possibility of his joining her. Like he would have in her current mood. Who was he kidding? Angry, happy, sad, ready to throw him out on his ear—Luke didn't care. He still wanted nothing more than to be close to her. But now was not the time for entertaining those desires. Instead, Luke smiled and took the recliner.

Luke shifted his cap before removing it to run a hand through his hair. "It may not be Mayberry, but this area is small enough for the locals that we're going to run into each other sooner or later. And with me working at Mike's again, it's gonna be sooner and more often."

"Yeah. So?"

Laughing at her tough-girl act would only make matters worse. Luke kept his expression matter-of-fact. "So, we need to figure out a way to make that happen without causing discomfort for each other and everyone else within a five-mile radius."

"How do you suggest we do that?"

Luke shrugged. "I'm not totally sure. But it begins with an apology."

"I've listened to more than enough of your apologies." Daisy's eyes softened. "I'm not saying you don't mean them when you give them. Only that they lose their potency with alarming speed."

Arguing the fairness of her statement would cause those shutters on her gaze to slam back shut. If Daisy was really going to hear him out, she had to stay open. He weighed his next words carefully.

"You're right. This last time was the most I've let my regret prompt me to better choices. And I failed again." More than she knew. Luke pushed down the prick of unease. Now was not the time to take the deep dive into his latest and greatest failure.

"And now you're sorry again."

"Yes." He leaned forward, resting his forearms on his knees and looking up at her. "But it's different this time."

Daisy rolled her eyes. "Because you're going to make it work this time? You can't promise that."

Luke's head dropped for a moment as he offered a silent prayer for strength and took a deep breath. "You're right." He captured her gaze again. "I can't promise I won't ever fail again. As much as it sickens me, the temptation can strike at any time. It's not different this time because I won't be tempted or fail. It's different because this time, I'm not fighting on my own."

Daisy shifted her feet to the floor, making her view of Luke more direct. She licked her lips before shaking her head. "You had Nathan on your side before, and you still went back to the bar. You showed up at work with a hangover. Even if Nathan somehow convinced you to join a group—and don't misunderstand me, I hope he did—it's not enough. They aren't with you twenty-four seven, keeping that bottle out of your hands."

"They aren't." Luke met her eyes and held her gaze. "But God is."

Daisy sat back, staring like she'd never seen Luke before. "Don't play, Luke."

With his arms still resting on his legs, Luke turned his hands palm up. "I'm not playing. I wouldn't. Not about this."

"You? You and God?"

Luke nodded. "We're on speaking terms and then some."

"When? How?"

"It was a process for sure. When I finally hit rock bottom and just kept falling, I knew I needed help. Took Nathan up on going to one of his groups. All that talking he did about drinking being the symptom started making sense." Luke stood and paced to keep his restless energy in check. "I knew I had to work on the issues that drove me to it in the first place. I'd always thought it was losing Pops. Come to find out, that loss was only an excuse. I'd been angry at God for quite a while."

"And now?" Daisy's voice was a whisper.

"I'm not angry anymore." Luke took a chance and sat on the sofa, allowing a cushion between them. "It took a few man-to-man talks with Nathan and a lot of soul searching, but God got my attention. My parents, Pops, and every time God didn't answer my prayers the way I thought He should, it put another nail in the coffin of my belief. Mostly, it was loss when God could've done something about it."

Daisy reached across the space between them to take his hand in hers. "I'm sorry you've lost so much."

Luke allowed the warmth to soothe his frayed emotions. He

nodded and swallowed against the knot in his throat. "Everybody loses people and things they love. But it's a hard lesson for a kid and harder still when it's reinforced as a teenager. My faith was tenuous at best until Pops died. No matter how much I doubted God's care, he assured me it was true. Promised that God allowing my parents to die instead of saving them wasn't a sign that God didn't love me or that my faith wasn't good enough or that God really wasn't as in control as everyone always said He was."

Daisy blinked several times. "And with Pops gone, you didn't have anyone reassuring you of the truth anymore."

Luke shook his head. "No. I had people. You were one of them. I just couldn't believe it anymore. God failed one too many times to be of use. That's what I had to deal with. After some hard talks with Nathan, it started to make sense. I'd only wanted God when I believed He could be used like some all-powerful genie in a bottle, doing what I believed to be best. I let my pain fester and become angry disappointment."

As much as he took comfort in her touch, Luke freed his hand and stood to pace. "Nathan, and the rest of the group, helped me see I couldn't be as angry as I was with God if I didn't believe He was there in the first place. I just needed to deal with the pain of loss and accept God as He is, not how I thought He should be." He chuckled. "Just. Like it was something easy. Took a while and a lot of prayers. But God's forgiven me, and my faith is more real and grounded in truth than it's ever been."

"And the anger?"

"I still struggle with why God allowed me to lose so many of those I love, but I refuse to hold it against Him. If I need the answer, He'll make it clear."

The sight of tears flowing down Daisy's cheeks shattered his heart like a hammer on glass. After all the prayers she'd prayed for him, Luke knew they were tears of relief and joy. But with the love they'd lost—the love he'd destroyed—there were some tears of regret in the mix. While she would be happy about his return to faith, it didn't put him on solid ground in their relationship. As much as his arms ached to hold her until her tears subsided, Luke kept them fixed to his side.

He and God might be on speaking terms. But Luke was under no illusions. His relationship with Daisy was another matter altogether.

When she reached across the couch and pulled him into her arms, Luke had to remind himself to breathe. He'd not understood the idea of the patience of Job until that moment, trying with all his might not to crush her in his embrace. But this had to be on her terms, not his. He allowed the hug but didn't reciprocate.

"I'm so happy for you, Luke." She released him and sat back, fiddling with a throw pillow beside her. "I've prayed for this for so long."

Though her smile was brighter than he'd seen in quite a while, her gaze bounced from him to the pillow to nothing and back to him on repeat. She was uncomfortable with her show of affection. But how could he put her at ease?

He sat back against the cushions and loosely crossed his arms in front of him. "I know. And I appreciate that more than I can express. You've been a better friend to me than I deserved, and I thought you should know you made a difference."

The silence spoke volumes about their tenuous friendship. He'd said his piece. Done what he could to smooth things over. Time would be the judge of whether it mattered at all. No. That was wrong. Apologizing mattered. Informing Daisy that her prayers had not been in vain mattered. If that's all this was, it was enough.

Luke stood and looked down at Daisy. "I'll let you get back to your evening. I just wanted you to know. Thought it might sand off a little of the awkward between us when we run into each other." He frowned. "More than that. You deserved to hear it from me."

He turned to leave. Anything else would put conditions on his visit. For once, Daisy deserved his love, even in friendship, without any consideration of what he might get from it.

"Talk to you later?"

He looked back over his shoulder with a gentle smile. "Yeah. I'd like that."

Then, he closed the door behind him.

Chapter Twenty-Seven

"See you at seven." Katie grinned from atop her stool at the Communi-TEA Barn drink counter. "If you don't, I'll never hear the end of it. I think you're Sam's new hero."

Luke laughed as he slid the order ticket across the counter to Daisy. "That kid is something else. I'll be there."

"Thanks for bringing my order by." Daisy stuck the receipt in her cash drawer. "This stomach bug is awful. And with Bekah down for the count, I couldn't make it out to Mike's before closing. You're a lifesaver."

"Tell her I hope she's back on her feet quick."

"I will."

Luke nodded with a tip of his cap and glanced at Katie. "I'll see you guys tonight at seven."

He swung the door open, edging to the side to narrowly miss Jill as she rushed through.

"Call me if you need anything else. Okay?"

Daisy nodded while Jill surveyed the scene with a frown.

"I mean it." Luke pressed.

"I will." Daisy rolled her eyes. "Don't be a mother hen."

Luke adjusted his cap. "All right then. Just as long as we're on the same page."

As the door shut behind him, Jill headed to the drink counter. She glanced over her shoulder, still frowning, before plopping her purse onto the wooden top with a sigh and claiming the seat next to Katie.

"Who was that?"

"Long day?" Daisy ignored the question in favor of responding to the signs of weariness in her friend. "It's early in the day for it to have already gone sideways. You nearly plowed into Luke on your way in, but you didn't seem to see him until he spoke to me. Then, you stared at him like he was an alien with three heads or something."

Jill's head whipped around to the closed door. "Luke? That was Luke, and I missed my chance to meet him? I should have known." Just as quickly, she spun back around to face Daisy. "Wait a moment. What was Luke doing here?"

Katie laughed and patted Jill's hand. "I can see you've not been caught up on the latest in the Luke and Daisy saga. You're going to love it, but since I'm already up to date, I'll head out. I need to stop by Kroger on my way home and pick up a roast, or Luke's going to be sorely disappointed at supper tonight. Not to mention earning my own guys' disappointment."

After a round of goodbyes, Daisy turned to Jill. "What are you having today?"

"Details, hon." Jill wiggled her eyebrows with a grin. "It seems I've missed quite a bit. Last I knew, Luke was gone once and for all. At least, that's what you explained when you stopped coming to the group. I figured if I wanted to see you, I'd have to stop in. Looks like I picked the perfect time."

While Jill didn't seem to hold a grudge about Daisy dropping out of her life, Daisy knew she owed her friend an apology. Before the words could leave her lips, the bell on the door chimed a customer's entrance. Daisy waved at one of her regulars.

"Morning, Patty." Daisy smiled. "You'll want to check out booth fifteen today. They brought in some new goat milk soaps you're going to love."

"You don't have to tell me twice." The woman bee-lined to the booth in question. "Terri's meeting me. Can you send her back to me?"

"Sure thing." Daisy let her pass from earshot before returning to Jill. "We do need to talk. But I'm not sure—"

The bell jingled once more.

"Patty's back at booth fifteen." She greeted Terri with a smile and pointed in the correct direction. "Just over there. Checking out some new goat milk soaps."

"I love goat milk soap." The woman shut her eyes and breathed deeply as if she could smell the scents as she stood there. She glanced at Daisy. "Before I forget, I'm out of tea. While we're looking around, can you fix up a bag of your loose-leaf, orange mint tea for me?"

"Of course." Daisy nodded. "Take your time. It will be ready when you are."

Daisy grabbed a small plastic baggie from a narrow drawer under the shelves of glass containers housing her various loose-leaf tea blends. Finding the right one, she scooped in the requested tea and set it on the scale to confirm the weight. Finding it just right, she sealed the bag and added a label before setting it aside.

"I'm sorry, Jill." She turned back to her waiting friend. "I never did find out what you wanted to drink. Or were you just here to visit?"

Jill waved away the apology with one hand. "Don't worry about it, hon. I'm not in a hurry. I do want something and to catch up, but with Bekah out, the tea may be easier than the chat."

"What'll you have?"

"Anything with caffeine. Sleep eluded me last night." Jill yawned as if in confirmation of her restless night. "Oh, and sweet. And cold."

"How about an iced maple chai tea latte?"

Jill sighed. "That sounds heavenly."

Daisy quickly mixed up the drink and handed it over. Jill's eyes slid shut as she took her first sip. Daisy couldn't help smiling. God blessed her with being able to help others enjoy some of life's simple pleasures as much as she enjoyed them.

Daisy allowed Jill a moment of peace with her latte. Savoring those first sips could reset a mood as quickly as anything Daisy had found. The bells on the door chimed, alerting her to another customer. She greeted the newcomer before giving her attention back to Jill, who'd polished off half of her large drink.

"What are you doing this evening?" Daisy wiped down the counter.

Jill took another sip of her drink. "Nothing. Why?"

"I planned on a trip to Giant City to walk the flower path. See if anything is blooming yet. I'd love to take a few photos." Daisy scanned the room. "With the sudden rush on goat soap, now isn't a great time for a chat. But, a walk along a park trail might be the perfect place for one."

Jill's mouth twisted to one side. "Hmm. I'm not much of a hiker."

"It's an easy trail, promise." Daisy held up her fingers in the familiar scouting sign. "All flat. And short. It's a great introductory path for those who want to enjoy nature without the exertion of the actual hiking trails. People with mobility issues use it."

"In that case, I'm game." Jill threw her cup into the plastics recycling bin. "What time and where should we meet?"

"The Arrowwood trail is right by the visitor's center. The

shop closes at four today, because before Bekah got sick, there was supposed to be a class. Will four-thirty work for you?"

Jill grabbed her purse and slung the strap over her shoulder. "Perfect. I look forward to it."

∽

DAISY PULLED her camera from the passenger seat of her truck and shut the door. Jill's tiny Soul pulled into a parking spot right after Daisy claimed hers.

"Ready to go?" Daisy adjusted the camera strap on her neck.

"As ready as I'm going to be." Jill shot her a pointed look. "This trail better be as easy as you claim."

Daisy laughed. "Would I steer you wrong?"

The pair kept an easy stride through the open prairie that made up the trail's beginning. Daisy paused to snap a picture of a butterfly flitting from flower to flower. In her periphery, Daisy saw Jill scanning the area with a sigh.

"Relaxing. Isn't it?" Daisy straightened and moved forward, Jill falling into step with her.

"This part is. But when the bluffs and creek beds come into it, I'm out." Jill removed her lightweight jacket and tied it around her waist. "Too much exertion for me."

"I told you, there's nothing like that on this trail. It isn't a full mile, and temperatures are mild for late June. Easy-peasy."

"Good. Then you can start spilling it about what's changed with you and Luke."

"It started with running into him at Mike's Landscaping about a month ago." Daisy moved to the edge of the path and aimed her camera at a branch with vibrant green leaves and bright red berries. While she captured the perfect image, she filled Jill in on the happenings with Luke.

"His relationship with God is good? And it's not manipulation?" Jill's questions held no judgment, only curiosity.

Daisy stared through the green canopy overhead as she considered her answer. "I think it's real." She continued down the level pathway. "If it was manipulation, I think he'd have sought me out, not waited until a chance meeting pushed the issue."

"That sounds like a solid conclusion."

"And, then there's Katie." Daisy stooped to capture a perfect tiny mushroom on the edge of the path. "Her husband, Nathan, has been a mentor to Luke through all this. If he weren't on the up and up, she would have hinted at it. I mean, she's not part of Luke and Nathan's conversations. But they all hang out. If his attitudes or actions were ever questionable, she'd discourage me from being around Luke."

"So, now you're—what?—friends again? Something more?"

"Friends."

"Oh, look up there."

Jill grasped Daisy's arm and pointed into a nearby tree. Daisy quickly spotted the hawk and raised her camera. It wasn't the first time she'd seen a hawk in the park, but this one was close enough for a good, clear shot.

"Thanks." She lowered her camera after a few snaps. "I love bird pictures, but I mostly find blue birds and robins and the more common birds. I did see a bald eagle once, but it was too far for a decent photo."

"Just friends." Jill jumped tracks back to the original topic. "Nothing else?"

Daisy shook her head. "Nothing else."

It took Daisy a few steps to realize Jill had planted herself in the path, refusing to budge. Daisy turned back to find Jill, brows high, waiting for an answer to her unspoken doubts.

"Really." Daisy laughed. "We're friends again. Nothing more."

"And how is your heart handling all this?"

Daisy chewed her bottom lip. "It's doing what it has to do. There's no other choice, is there?"

"What led to that conclusion?"

"Because there's no sense in wishing for what isn't going to be." Daisy stared into the spaces between the trees lining the path. "I'll always love Luke. I've prayed for God to take that from me enough times that if He were going to, it would've happened already. But that's my cross to bear. A love that isn't meant to be."

Jill's eyes narrowed. "What if Luke still loved you?"

Daisy shook her head. "I'm not sure what you think you know, but that ship has sailed."

"I wouldn't be too sure if I were you." Jill shrugged. "Hon, maybe I'm out of line, but more than friendship showed in that man's eyes. Didn't take a drawn-out conversation to see it. I'm not saying anything should come of it. I'm just suggesting you answer the what-ifs now before they become questions waiting for answers."

"You mean, would I be open to a relationship with a recovering alcoholic?"

Jill nodded.

"I thought I knew that answer in the time before Luke's restored relationship with God." Daisy removed the camera from her neck as they exited the path back into the parking lot. "Then, he showed up hungover. For the first time, I was faced with the real question. Relationships take trust. Could I trust Luke not to mess up again?"

"Have you considered you're asking the wrong question?" Jill waited until Daisy deposited her camera onto the truck seat and turned to face her. "Luke's just a man. Like the rest of us, he struggles, and sometimes there's going to be a fall. His temptations are different, but we all fail. I don't know many relationships where the couple hasn't hurt each other at some point."

"But—"

Jill held up a hand to cut her off. "I'm not talking about forgetting an anniversary or loading the dishwasher wrong. I'm talking deep hurts and misunderstandings. Hurts where the D-word hovers close to the surface if the couple isn't careful."

"D-word?"

"Divorce." Jill shrugged. "Too many are quick to speak it into their relationship, and that's never a good thing. But my point is, we all fail. The only thing we can trust from another person is that failure isn't just an option, it's a reality. It may be something other than an addict's addiction resurfacing, but there will always be hurts."

Daisy leaned against the side of her truck. "There's no hope, then."

"There's always hope." Jill's mouth curved in a bright grin. "We don't put our trust in people, in relationships, or any other part of life. Our circumstances don't take our hope. We keep hope because it's rooted in trusting God to work for good, no matter what anyone or any situation throws at us. God's who we trust, and He's an unshakeable source of hope."

"So, because I trust God, it shouldn't matter that Luke is a recovering addict?"

"I'm not saying that at all."

"So, I shouldn't be in a relationship with him because he's a recovering addict?"

"That isn't what I'm saying that either."

"What exactly are you saying?" Daisy huffed and folded her arms across her chest. "I'm getting whiplash here?"

"I'm saying it's complicated but not impossible."

Jill's quiet tone calmed some of the storm swirling inside Daisy.

"Go on, please."

"What you've seen as the main issue between you and Luke is resolved. His faith is, by all accounts, legitimate."

She waited for a nod of agreement before continuing.

"With that hurdle out of the way, it would be smooth sailing to a relationship under normal circumstances. But these circumstances are far from normal. There's more than just the typical baggage of the past to contend with."

"Luke's addiction."

Jill nodded this time. "A recovering addict isn't any less deserving of love and mercy and grace than anyone else. But recovering doesn't equate to one hundred percent freed, so it will affect the relationship in some ways."

"But what about those who never struggle again?" Daisy tried and failed to keep the helpless tone out of her voice. "Now that Luke's relationship with God is where it should be, couldn't that be the case for him too?"

"It could." Jill lifted one shoulder. "But you can't bank on that possibility. Someone who's been free of the temptation for years can relapse under the perfect storm of circumstances."

"Then why would anyone commit to a relationship with someone in recovery?"

"Love is a powerful motivator."

Daisy couldn't deny that simple truth. As many times as she'd been disappointed and hurt by Luke, she still loved him. Beyond wanting God's best for him, way past friendship, Daisy was still ridiculously, head-over-heels in love with the man.

"How do people figure out if it's right or not? That they're going to be one of the strong ones?"

"That's just it. You don't. Not for certain." Jill sucked in a deep breath. "You can use judgment about their sincerity, but that doesn't mean infallibility. Anyone contemplating a relationship with a recovering addict must be honest with themselves above all else."

"Honest? About what?"

"That relationships are never rainbows, sunshine, and puppies. Even less so with someone in recovery." Jill pushed her hair back behind her ear. "There are going to be earnest conversations about uncomfortable subjects. Complete honesty is a must, and the ability to provide a safe place for their partner to share, including when it's not what the other wants to hear. That includes a willingness to admit your fears when they crop up and your doubts. Sometimes it means couples counseling, individual counseling, or both."

An invisible weight settled on Daisy's shoulders, increasing with each statement. "And if they're willing to do all that ... then it's all good?"

Jill shook her head. "As with any relationship, those in a relationship with a recovering addict need to keep their relationship with God strong. They need His model of forgiveness and every drop of wisdom and discernment available. In fact, that's where anyone not already in a committed relationship should start."

"Prayer?"

"Yes, ma'am." Jill nodded. "I suggest time seeking God's will. A relationship with a recovering addict is a harder path in many ways, and it isn't a path for everyone. But, as with any relationship, there's the potential for a wonderful love story. Ask God. He promises wisdom for those who seek it."

Daisy licked her lips and stared down at the trail they'd taken just minutes before. Easy peasy. Isn't that what she told Jill? Did she expect her path in life to be that smooth? Could she handle the more rugged path a relationship with Luke might bring? How was she to know without living it first? Everything was hypothetical at this point.

Jill unlocked her car door. "I can tell I've given you a lot to think about. And I can't help with this part. You know what you need to do."

"Pray?"

Jill plopped into her front seat and looked up at Daisy. "Pray."

Chapter Twenty-Eight

"Thanks for coming with me tonight." Luke leaned back on his elbows on the large quilt spread out under the fading shadow of the Gateway Arch.

Daisy spritzed herself with all-natural bug repellent and plopped down cross-legged beside him. "I've lived in southern Illinois all my life and never once considered driving two hours to watch the fireworks over the Mississippi River. Thanks for inviting me."

"Just another small way to say I'm sorry for all the trouble I've caused you through the years."

Regret pooled in his eyes, deepening their green. Seeing it there pinched Daisy's heart. Her hand looked small as she placed it over his. Hopefully, it wasn't too insignificant to offer a measure of comfort.

"You can't keep carrying guilt over what's been forgiven."

He adjusted his hand to weave his fingers together with hers. "I can be sorry about it, just the same. I may not have intended harm, but I hurt a lot of people. You more than all of them. That's something I'll always carry with me."

"I guess it makes sense." Daisy gave his hand a little

squeeze. "But, please, don't get caught in the trap that you have to make up for or earn the forgiveness you've been given."

Luke shook his head. "I could never do enough for that. I'm just trying to be worthy of it going forward."

A high-pitched whistle drew their attention to the dark sky over the glassy surface of the Mississippi. A burst set off a kaleidoscope of color mirrored in the water below and reflected in the stainless steel of the arch.

Conversation forgotten, Daisy lay back, resting her head on the small pillow Luke'd brought for her. The care he took to ensure her enjoyment of the evening stood in contrast to his concern that he wasn't worthy of her forgiveness. As much as their past cut deep, forgiveness was the salve allowing those wounds to close and heal. Eventually, though she'd carry deep scars, those wounds wouldn't be so tender to every touch.

Daisy pushed those thoughts aside. Though their outing to watch fireworks was nothing more than two close friends enjoying the Fourth together, there still wasn't a place in the night for the pains of their past. For the first time in years, their friendship had found solid footing. Nothing was going to steal that joy.

The clock ticked close to 2 a.m. by the time Luke pulled his truck into Daisy's driveway. She stifled a yawn. Luke smiled.

"Sorry for the late night." He brushed his hand through one side of his hair. "Didn't consider how crazy St. Louis traffic might affect our drive time home."

She yawned again, this time unable to tame it. "I figured it would be a late one. But now, I'm going to bed. And I'm not setting my alarm."

It didn't register that Luke had gotten out of the truck until he walked next to her. That she'd managed to get out before he could open the door for her was a feat in itself. Basic chivalry was a trait his Pops had ingrained in him that didn't fall by the wayside easily.

"You don't need to walk me to my door."

"It's two in the morning. I'm going to make sure everything's fine before I leave."

His concern warmed her heart, and she took his hand. "That's why I love you. Always making sure those you care about are okay."

Luke stopped dead, yanking her arm in the process. Daisy frowned. The gripe she prepared to give him stopped just as short as he had at his expression.

He swallowed hard. His eyes, illuminated by the front porch light, held an unvoiced question.

Daisy scrambled to figure out what caused the change in him. Love. She wanted to smack herself upside the head. She'd just admitted the not-so-secret secret of her heart. Despite everything, she still loved Luke. And now, he knew it beyond a doubt. Only one question remained. Was she okay with that?

A ROGUE SPARK from a firework could light Daisy's house on fire, and Luke doubted he'd be able to move to put it out. *That's why I love you.* Those were the words he'd never allowed himself to hope he'd hear again.

Did he know she loved him? Sure. But she carefully avoided all references to it. For all he knew, she didn't even admit it to herself. But now?

She'd spoken it out loud.

She obviously hadn't meant to. And she could have meant it like she loved her friend or her job. Luke told himself that's all she intended. It was the only way to restart his heart and kick those lungs back into action. But then, she turned to stare at him.

He could pinpoint the moment her words came back to her. The irritated starch in her posture and the frown marring her gorgeous face morphed into wide-eyed surprise. She rubbed her lips together, and Luke could swear he saw the wheels turning in her mind, trying to find something to say.

"Daisy." His voice was raspy. He cleared his throat. "Daisy, it's okay. You didn't mean it that way."

Was it wrong that he hoped she had? That Daisy *did* mean it that way? Then again, did he want her to love him like that? As much as his heart screamed yes, his mind reminded him that he was significantly less than Daisy deserved.

Why was she being so still? Had she not heard him?

"Everything's cool. You didn't mean it like that." He gave a little nod, though reassuring her that friendship was where they ended was the last thing he wanted to do. "We're just friends."

Daisy scrutinized him, laying him bare right there on her front lawn. He lifted his chin, hoping he was an Oscar-worthy actor. He couldn't let her see how much he really cared. How much he still loved her.

"What if I'm ready for more than friends?"

He might have missed the whispered words if he hadn't seen her lips move. Lips that slowly, cautiously lifted in invitation. They worked like a magnet on his heart, drawing him closer. A small step.

One hand still cradling hers. The other brushing her upturned cheek with his thumb.

He lowered his head.

She loved him. He paused before their lips met.

She loved a figment, a dream. He straightened, dropped his arms, and stepped back. He didn't need to see her fierce frown to realize he'd confused her. No, worse, he'd hurt her once again. But he wouldn't claim love, couldn't pretend that's what he felt for her without her knowing the truth. Without letting her see who he really was.

His eyes slid shut. "I'm so sorry."

"Did I do something wrong?" Pain laced each word.

"No." He met her gaze, kept it, and refused to let go. She had to hear him. She needed the unfiltered truth. "No. Please, don't think that."

A tear slid down her cheek. "You don't love me like that anymore." She swiped the offending moisture away. "It's fine. I understand."

He grasped her hand, like it offered life itself. "No. You don't understand at all. My feelings for you haven't changed. I've loved you since we were kids. That's not going to stop."

"Then, why?"

The pitiful sound tightened Luke's throat. "Because love demands the truth."

Her brows dipped low.

"I love you. But I'm starting to understand what that really means." Luke led her to the porch and dropped onto the swing, guiding her down beside him. "I can't claim to love you the way you deserve if I'm hiding the worst of who I am. To really love me, I have to let you know who I am."

A sad chuckle accompanied Daisy's slim smile. "I know who you are. I've known you since we were kids. I've seen you at your worst. And, Luke, I still love you."

Luke looked away from the hope and understanding in her gaze. He couldn't make it through this if he had to look her in the eyes, watch her reaction to the worst he had to offer. "No. You only think you've seen it. But that doesn't touch how bad it really is."

Chapter Twenty-Nine

Acid churned in Daisy's stomach as the urge to vomit clawed its way up her throat. She'd been witness to the fact that drunk Luke hadn't exercised self-control when it came to women. The image was seared into her brain, as much as she'd tried everything to bleach it out. But sleeping with a married woman?

After his father, he'd hated anything hinting of adultery. Oh, Luke always had charm with women, but if a ring was on the left hand, he refused to feed an infatuation, theirs or his. And he'd known plenty of drunken years to test the theory. But his fall wasn't the result of a weekend-long bender or even a time when being drunk was more common than sober. No. His plummet came on the heels of months of sobriety. The day before she'd sent him packing. Apparently, that afternoon in her garden was a sick walk of shame she was unaware of at the time.

He'd finished the sordid tale without looking at her once. Now, he sat beside her with his head in his hands. What was she supposed to do with this information? She had no clue.

"Say something, anything." Luke didn't lift his head, just angled to look her direction. "Please."

Completely barren. The look in his eyes would make Death Valley look like a rainforest teeming with life. But Daisy wasn't sure she possessed the words to bring life, or at least hope, back into the wasteland. Only one thing could come close.

"God's forgiven it."

He swallowed. "But?"

Daisy gnawed on her bottom lip while she racked her brain for something to say. The combination of his sordid tale and the early morning hours did nothing to aid the process. Still, he waited, watching her.

"I don't know." She looked over his head to the night sky, where stars gave their own performance to rival the fireworks from before. They brought neither comfort nor clarity. "I don't know what you need me to say here. I'm not sure what there is to say."

Daisy sat still as Luke unfolded himself from the swing. He took a step backward toward the stairs without turning from her. Daisy frowned.

"It's a lot." Luke quietly cleared his throat. "I'll go. You sort through it however you need to."

"What?"

"Take all the time you need." He broke eye contact, blinked. Then, shifted back to her. "And don't feel like you have to keep it to yourself. While I'm not for you broadcasting my failure to the world, I understand you might need to talk it through with a trusted friend."

"I wouldn't. It's your story to tell."

He looked her in the eyes. "But it affects you. Deeply. Just know I'll understand. I won't call or stop by or anything. When —if—you're ready to see me again, you've got my number."

Luke trudged to his truck. Daisy's heart dropped to her stomach quicker than the coasters fall at Six Flags. Why couldn't she put him at ease? It wasn't like he needed her forgiveness. He'd not sinned against her when he was ...

Nope. She couldn't finish the sentence without the urge to be ill. Better not to focus on that aspect of their conversation.

Regardless of what he'd done, she'd spoken the truth. God forgave Luke. The moment Luke asked, God erased his debt. This sin could haunt Luke's future in myriad physical ways, but he didn't need to cling to the shame.

"God, did I make it worse?" Daisy whispered the prayer. "Was there a way to avoid making Luke revisit the shame of it all?"

Silence. Daisy trudged into her house. No amount of stewing would force answers. It was late, and despite the shock Luke's admission jolted through her system, her body needed rest. Stopping only to kick off her shoes by the front door, Daisy padded down the hall to her room, lay on top of the quilt, hugged her extra pillow to her chest, and cried herself to sleep.

Chapter Thirty

Daisy's alarm broke through the haze earlier than she was ready to face the day. It didn't matter that the sun was peeking through the space where her blackout curtains came together. Daisy reached for her phone and swiped an empty spot where it should be on the bedside table. Where was that thing? And why was it softer than usual?

Daisy tried to clear the cobwebs and listen. She groaned and fished the phone out of her back pocket. She'd slept on her clean covers in worn clothes and skipped the essentials like brushing her teeth and putting her phone on the charger.

"I guess the shock of a lifetime will do that to you."

Not any more ready to face that thought than she was to face the day after a few hours of restless sleep, Daisy rolled onto her stomach long enough to scrounge the charging cord off the floor and plug in her depleted device. She flopped onto her back and used her toes to grab the edge of the fleece blanket at the end of her bed. She bent her leg at an odd angle until she could just snatch the blanket with her fingers.

It would've been easier to sit up and grab it. She simply did not have the will to do it. Anyway, she had it now. Snuggled under its fuzzy comfort, Daisy let her heavy eyelids close once more. Restful or not, she needed more sleep.

EVEN AFTER A CUP of warm milk, sleep eluded Luke. What was up with that? Every movie and television show ever created assured viewers that sleepless nights were best solved with warm milk. All it left Luke with was a sour milk taste in his mouth and more queasiness added to what was already swirling in his stomach.

So his foolproof falling-asleep-when-he-didn't-want-to plan hadn't worked. Scrolling social media on your phone while lying in bed didn't work so great when your mind didn't get the memo that it wasn't supposed to be thinking.

He glanced at the unhelpful device. Seven in the morning.

"What's the use? I'll have to wake up in an hour. Who decided the Fourth of July should be on a Saturday? People stay out late on the Fourth of July. Do they not want people to fill the pews on Sunday?" Not usually one to grumble, Luke kept up his cranky monologue throughout his shower and the brewing of a strong cup of coffee. Didn't matter that half of what he griped about wasn't logical. His mind kept churning out new things to be upset about.

"I guess it keeps me from thinking about my real problems." Luke reasoned as he took his first sip of coffee. As the hot liquid made its way down his throat, Luke leaned his head against the back of the seat and blew out a sigh.

Equal parts keyed up and exhausted, Luke knew his tired body would lose the fight to his overactive mind. He was up, and sleep wasn't anywhere on the horizon. He finished his coffee, rinsed the mug in the sink, and grabbed his Bible from the top of his dresser.

It was Sunday, and that meant church. Knowing fatigue could

hit at any moment, Luke took care driving to church and waited until the call to worship began before taking his seat. No sense in nodding off before things got going.

Luke stifled a yawn during the announcements. Maybe he should've stayed home. Glancing around the sanctuary, he noted many had made that choice. And with every second that passed, his chances of falling asleep mid-sermon grew. And if he was honest with himself, praising was the last thing Luke felt like doing.

"When you don't feel like praising, those are the times you need it most." Luke smiled as he mouthed the words Pops had frequently touted. The memory was bittersweet. But for the first time, thinking of Pops didn't cause the urge to drown his misery with his old friends in the bottle.

"Thank You, Father, for small blessings." Luke kept his head bowed as he whispered the praise. He'd be delusional to believe a day in his lifetime existed when he wouldn't miss Pops, but the hope of seeing him again made the ache manageable without the self-medication.

If only hope worked the same way with Daisy. Technically, it did. He would see her in heaven, but his heart wanted hope of their friendship in the here and now. Despite sharing the same faith and admitting their love for one another, hope of anything other than a polite greeting when they ran into each other seemed an impossible dream. After their post-fireworks discussion, all the progress they'd made vanished into the night like the smoke from the fireworks.

The choir began their first song, and Luke realized he'd zoned out all through the announcements. He rose and sang with the congregation, but his mind lagged behind. Lack of sleep was enough to cause the problem, but considering how heavy his heart was in his chest, his concern over Daisy was the most likely culprit.

"Did you come to church to hear from God today?" The

worship leader posed the question before the final song of the set. "Did you come expecting?"

Murmurs of agreement sounded around Luke.

The worship leader scanned the crowd. "You come wanting. Seeking what God has for you. But what are you giving Him? You've come into the King's house this morning. Are you really giving Him your praise, or is your mind on the roast cooking in the Crock-Pot at home?" He paused, allowing time to reflect. "We want God's best today. Let's start by giving Him our best just because of who He is."

Luke might not have lunch cooking at home, but at this point, he wasn't focused on God either. "I'm sorry, Father." Luke's prayer was for his and God's ears only. "No matter what's happening in my life right now, You deserve my attention in this moment. No matter how things work out with Daisy or how tired I am, You deserve my praise."

Taking control of his thoughts, Luke joined in the final worship song. This was God's time, and Luke refused to steal it from Him. After the song ended, Luke settled into his pew with renewed focus.

"Love that first song we sang today." The pastor took his place behind the pulpit. "I do look forward to the day we'll see Jesus face to face. The day our tears will be wiped away and the troubles of this earthly life will be no more."

An *amen* joined the message from a man in the second row.

The pastor set his Bible on the pulpit. "But what about now?" Silence. "Is your life with God, your life of faith, free of turmoil and strife?" He shook his head. "If it were, would the promise of heaven be so desirable to you?" He held up one hand. "I know. This world contains immense beauty. We all have wonderful memories of times spent with family and friends. But these don't begin to compare to heaven's joys. And, sometimes, the heights of our joys don't seem to balance out the lows of our pain."

Luke sat back in his pew.

"I'm sure no one in this place, no one as faithful as those who make up our congregation, has ever dealt with a loss so deep it feels a piece of ourselves has been stolen from us. Not one has faced dire circumstances and couldn't quite find their way in the darkness."

Only the occasional squeak of old wood under the weight of someone shifting on top of it broke the silence. The pastor seemed to take time looking at each congregant.

"I'm positive no one in this room has been trapped in the muck of their own sinful choices without an understanding of how to make things right again. Or experienced a pain so deep it pulled you under until you weren't sure how to reach the surface again." The pastor opened his Bible. "Then again, if we're honest, maybe we've all been there at one time or another. And maybe that's why the promise of heaven is so powerful."

The day's scripture flashed on the overhead screen while the pastor read Psalm 27:13-14. "'I would have despaired unless I had believed that I would see the goodness of the LORD in the land of the living. Wait for the LORD; Be strong and let your heart take courage; Yes, wait for the LORD.'"

Despair. Luke knew despair. He and the poisonous fellow were drinking buddies before Luke's newly recovered faith kicked despair to the curb. Or so he thought. But the pastor indicated that those who'd never walked away from their faith could still find despair on their doorstep.

It made perfect sense. People were people. Believers and nonbelievers alike lost loved ones and jobs, lived with the physical consequences of sins even when forgiven, and faced the unknown at times. Being human came with a great capacity to hurt and to hurt others. Why wouldn't the faithful still wrestle with the pain?

"But hope isn't only for the future."

The pastor's words drew Luke back to the message.

"And God has more for His children than despair. The

psalmist, David, had more reason than most to despair. Anointed king of Israel, he lived for years on the run, living in caves, hiding from King Saul, who alternated between wanting him in the palace and trying to run him through with a spear. His sin brought the death of his newborn son and the promise of unrest in his family line. He fled the kingdom he'd nurtured as one of his sons tried to usurp the throne, his daughter was raped by her half-brother, and son was pitted against son as one sought revenge."

King David had loads of trouble in his life. Luke couldn't argue.

"But." The pastor held up one finger. "But with all this turmoil and pain, David was able to rise above the pull of despair. Why? It wasn't the promise of heaven that pulled David through. Let's look at that again. 'Unless I had believed that I would see the goodness of the LORD in the land of the living.'" He paused, letting the words settle in the room. "David believed, despite everything he went through, that he would experience the goodness of God, not only in heaven, but in the middle of his messy life, in the land of the living."

Luke couldn't help smiling as the pastor's words reminded him of the encouragement Sam gave Frodo to fight for good in the world in *The Lord of the Rings*. Not that he'd ever share the comparison. Comparing God's word, even if only a summary given by a man, to a book would probably be discouraged.

Besides, fighting for the good in life was all well and good in books, but how did David fight for it? Did he believe that if he waited, as the next verse instructed, God would turn everything around? His kingdom would be secured? The breach in his family healed? If David found an answer, Luke wanted the secret too. Plenty in his life needed straightening up after the messes he'd made.

"David continued seeing his choices bring painful physical consequences."

Luke frowned. Not the news he wanted to hear.

"We don't know exactly when this psalm was written. But David's entire life was marked with difficult circumstances. So, where was the goodness of God in the land of the living for the king after God's own heart?"

Luke flashed through all the stories of David he'd learned as a child in Sunday school. None held the answer to the pastor's question.

"I believe our answer can be found in the New Testament, many years after David's reign." The pastor flipped the pages of his Bible. "Romans 8:28-29 encourages us. 'And we know that all things work together for good to those who love God, to those who are called according to His purpose.'" The pastor looked up from the pulpit.

"Don't misuse this passage to claim a life free from the earthly consequences of your choices. Don't quote it to reassure yourselves that the things you want in life will happen because you've been forgiven. David repented. His infant son still died. David repented. His family was still marked by lust and revenge. But David also experienced God's goodness in the land of the living."

Luke sat up straighter. He continued to face the consequences of his choices. The loss of Daisy looming largest of all. But could he still see God's goodness before heaven? God forgave him now. He didn't have to wait for it. God blessed him with a new job and renewed his friendship with Mike. That was God's goodness too. But was there more for him even without the promise of Daisy's return?

"God continued using David right up to the end of his life. God didn't declare him unfit for service. God's goodness at work." The pastor held up his Bible. "But more than that, God used David to encourage Solomon in how to lead the people. David pulled from the lessons he'd learned to help someone else.

God used the pain and heartache in David's life to make the life he lived more powerful for God's use and glory."

The pastor's gaze roamed the room. "And God will do the same for you. When you allow God to make you more like Jesus despite the hurts and disappointments, He can use you to comfort and encourage others as they face similar circumstances. That is the goodness of God. Using the ashes in your life to grow something beautiful, both in you and those around you."

The pastor's words stirred in Luke. He could fight with God over Daisy, but he'd warred with God before. He'd find nothing worthwhile on that desolate battlefield. Luke wanted more.

Luke stood with the rest of the congregation for the song of invitation, but the pianist hadn't yet played the first note when Luke moved to the aisle. With no thought to those looking on, Luke strode down the aisle and fell to his knees in front of the altar.

"Lord, I'm ready. Daisy or no, I'm still choosing You. Let me see Your goodness in the land of the living."

Chapter Thirty-One

A persistent knock interrupted Daisy's lunch. She placed her ham-and-Swiss sandwich back on the paper plate and headed to the door. Another series of knocks sounded before she reached it. "Give me a minute. I'm coming."

"Where were you this morning? And why weren't you answering your phone?" Bekah hurled the questions as soon as the door opened. She entered without waiting for Daisy's response or invitation. "You always answer your phone. And you never miss church without a good reason. Are you sick or something? Do you need some soup? Soda?"

Daisy rolled her eyes. "You breathe, and I'll try to answer your questions. No. I'm not sick." Daisy rummaged through her pockets and found them empty. "And I didn't answer my phone because I apparently left it on the charger in my bedroom."

She went down the hall to retrieve the forgotten device with Bekah traipsing close behind.

"You aren't sick. So, why weren't you at church?"

Bekah wouldn't let it go until she answered.

"I was out late last night." Daisy disconnected the phone

from the charger. "I slept in." She headed back to the kitchen. "Want a sandwich?"

"No. I don't want a sandwich."

With Bekah trailing after her, Daisy imagined one of those irritating little yappy dogs nipping at her heels. She smiled despite knowing it was an unfair comparison. Bekah would not be flattered.

Daisy resumed her lunch without answering the unasked question. It would be voiced soon enough and followed by a lengthy conversation. Having a little fortification for the conversation would serve Daisy well.

"You've stayed out late a million times." Bekah planted herself in the chair across from Daisy. "You've never missed church because of it. So, what gives?"

There it was. Not as to the point as Daisy expected, but asked just the same.

"Nothing. I was tired. I slept in. End of story."

Bekah snorted. "More like end of one chapter. A chapter that comes after a pivotal point where the heroine thinks there's no hope in going on."

"You're being ridiculous." Daisy took a bite from the sandwich Bekah's visit had managed to suck the simple pleasure from. "You, my friend, are the definition of dramatic."

"Maybe so." Bekah shrugged. "But I know there's something you're not telling me. So, you might as well spill it."

"Fine." If only to put an end to the inquisition, Daisy would share. But Bekah would be sorry. Luke was still far from her favorite subject. "You knew Luke and I went to see the fireworks in St. Louis last night?"

Bekah nodded while her eyes narrowed.

"We didn't get home until around two in the morning." Daisy smiled, thinking about their time in St. Louis. "It was beautiful, magical. I've never seen such an amazing display. But traffic getting back out of Missouri was a nightmare. So, we were already later than we should have been before …"

Daisy wasn't sure where to go with the next part. Much of what transpired between her and Luke was private. Luke's story, not hers, whether he gave his permission or not.

"Before what?" Bekah lifted her chin. "Before you kissed? Before Luke proposed? Before, oh—tell me he didn't pressure you into anything. Daisy, you know better."

Daisy's eyes widened with the implication. Her mouth dropped open. "I do know better, and you shouldn't have entertained that thought."

"If it were you and anyone else, I wouldn't have." Bekah crossed her arms over her chest. "But Luke's got a reputation."

"Hopefully," Daisy said eyeing her friend, "I'm not ever doomed to be a slave to my old sins even though I've been forgiven and am trying to grow in my faith."

Bekah held up her hands in surrender. "Point taken. Luke's not the same guy he was. And you're right. I was wrong to assume the worst."

Once she knew, the worst would seem like child's play. It didn't matter that Luke's downfall happened before his return to God. That Daisy refused to share the details wouldn't matter. Nothing between Bekah and Luke was ever easy and rarely positive.

"You're forgiven." Daisy finished off her sandwich and rinsed her plate. "I only paused because I was trying to figure out what I should and shouldn't say. We had a long talk, but part of it is no one's business but Luke's."

"Just start at the beginning and skip what you need to. I'll understand."

"Luke still loves me as much as I love him."

"Duh."

Daisy glared. "Do you want me to tell you or not?"

Bekah made a show of zipping her lips and locking them.

Daisy licked her lips. "I let it slip that I love him while we were in St. Louis. It was one of those throw-away sentences you say without thinking, only to realize it's far from disposable."

Bekah nodded, keeping her lips shut tight.

"I half-way hoped he'd forget about it by the time we got home, but we ended up on the porch talking about how our feelings have never faded. I admitted I might be ready for more than friendship."

Bekah's eyes widened. Daisy marveled at her restraint in staying quiet.

"It surprised me too." Daisy laughed. "But God and I have had several heart-to-hearts about what it would mean and whether my mindset is where it needs to be for the challenges a relationship with Luke would bring."

Daisy peered out the kitchen window. Sunshine and blue skies dotted with fluffy white clouds stood in contrast to the stormy seas swirling inside her since her time with Luke ended. She'd been at peace with moving forward in their relationship. But now? Daisy couldn't make sense of her feelings.

"And?" Bekah's question brought Daisy back to the current conversation.

"It was perfect." The memory brought a wistful smile. "A wonderful evening together. Finally admitting our love and finding hope for our relationship. I was so ready for it when he leaned in to kiss me." Daisy swiped a sudden tear from her cheek. "But then he stopped."

"He refused to kiss you?" Bekah threw her hands up in question. "Why?"

"He said first, I had to know his worst."

Bekah's huff ruffled her bangs as she shook her head. "Worst? Haven't you seen his worst for the last several years?"

"That's what I asked." Daisy brushed stray strands of hair behind her ear. "He assured me it wasn't." Daisy looked back out the window. "He was right." She looked back at Bekah, knowing there was no way to hide the pain from her friend. "Bek, I was so stunned. Despite what you think of Luke, he's never been a horrible guy. He's funny and caring. And he's always had lines he wouldn't cross."

Bekah covered Daisy's hand with her own. "I know I've been tough on him, but it's not because I think he's the scum of the earth. The opposite, really. I knew there was enough to like about Luke that it would be easy to fall for him, even with the bad. He'd caused you so much pain. I couldn't stand that you'd let it continue or get worse."

Daisy pulled one of her hands free and swiped it across her cheek. "Until last night, I didn't believe it was possible." She shook her head. "I was wrong. What he shared ... I don't know what to do with it."

"How did Luke react?"

"He left. He said I needed time to figure out how I felt about it." Daisy bit her lip. "He said he won't call me or stop by or anything. It's all up to me."

"Wow." Bekah sat back in her chair. "A Luke that doesn't push. I don't know what to do with that. He's always downplayed his drinking and everything that went with it. He really is changing for the better."

"Right?" Frustration surged until Daisy had to stand to relieve the pressure. She crossed to the sink and leaned against the counter, hands splayed at her sides. "Luke's becoming the man I always prayed he'd be. It's what I've hoped for all these years. And now, I'm unsure what to do with it, with this new information."

Bekah twisted in her chair to face Daisy. "Okay. Let's look at this objectively. You already knew a lot about Luke's bad habits. Drinking too much. Regularly hooking up with women."

"Right."

"And as much as you can see, you know he's got a relationship with God and is trying to grow in it."

"True." Daisy shoved off the counter and grabbed a glass from the cabinet next to the sink. "You want a cream soda?"

"Sure."

Daisy pulled a second glass from the shelf before retrieving the soda from the fridge. She set one in front of Bekah and sat back in her original seat.

"What else?" Daisy asked as she raised the glass for her first sweet sip.

Bekah ran her finger around the rim of the glass. "Plus, you've known he's going to meetings, and you've learned a ton about being in any type of relationship with someone in recovery from going to your own support group."

"True."

"Do you feel like you know the pros and the cons? Understand how all that works?"

"I guess." Daisy set her glass on the table. "I mean, in my head, I understand it. And I do have experience with the frustrations and struggles and setbacks, just not in a romantic relationship."

"And you said you'd come to terms with all that and still decided he was relationship material, right?" Bekah drained her glass and picked up both hers and Daisy's to put in the dishwasher.

"But that was before."

"Before the big reveal last night?"

Daisy nodded.

"With all this other stuff dealt with, can it be that bad?" Bekah walked from the kitchen, leaving Daisy to follow or be left behind. "Not that I'm pushing for a relationship or anything. I'd never tell someone they were prepared for those issues in addition to the normal relationship issues."

Bekah claimed the recliner. So, Daisy flopped on the couch and spread out across the cushions. The image of a psychiatrist and patient flitted through her mind, but she swatted it away. If peace in her situation eluded her, she could at least be comfortable while trying to sort it all out. Besides, she'd rather not be eye-to-eye with Bekah for what came next.

"You're not wrong. I had decided." She took a deep breath. Not good enough. She slipped her feet from the couch and righted herself. Apparently, weighty conversation demanded full attention. "But, and I say this only because I'm not sure we're going to get anywhere otherwise, that was before he told me the last time he got drunk, he ended up in a hotel with a married woman."

Bekah sat back, staring at her, but did Bekah actually see her there? She seemed to look straight through Daisy. The silence started chafing.

"He didn't know she was married." Daisy offered the olive branch. "Found out the next morning."

"Ugh." It came out on a breath as Bekah cringed. Her lips twisted to the side, a sure sign she was biting her cheek while she figured out what to say. "That's rough."

"I know. Now, you see why I was thrown for such a loop."

"No. I mean, yes, I do." Bekah's hands gestured in front of her, emphasizing her explanation but not clarifying it at all. "But no, that's not what I meant."

"Then, what's rough about it?"

Bekah lay her head back against the recliner and stared up at the ceiling. A moment later, she met Daisy's gaze again. Were those tears in her eyes? No. Not about Luke. He'd been public enemy number one in Bekah's mind since, well, forever. But she'd just confirmed her statement wasn't about Daisy's predicament. It had to be Luke, though it made no sense.

"I know it must have been a shock for you." Bekah licked her lips. "But it isn't so much of one for me. I always wondered how he avoided it. He was a reckless drunk. It was bound to happen at some point." She paused again, shifted in her chair.

"But as much of a shock as it is for you, think about what it must have been like for him."

Daisy was ashamed to admit, even to herself, that she'd really only given thought to how Luke's admission affected her and her decision.

Bekah wasn't finished. "Luke's dad's infidelity tore up their family. Destroyed Luke's relationship with him too. I can't imagine how he felt when he realized he had a part in inflicting the same pain on someone else's family. It had to be devastating."

"I think it was." Daisy reached for a tissue from the box on the table and handed it to Bekah, taking one for herself in the process. "It was what prompted his return to faith. I mean, it was a process, not like he came back to God immediately. But it opened his eyes to his need."

"Well, that's the blessing in the middle of a great big mess of heartache. I'm sure he'd rather been smart enough to come to it without what I assume was a truckload of shame and desperation, but even then, it was a gift. A blessing."

"But—" Daisy started and stopped in a breath. She didn't want to discount what Luke went through. Yet, a very real fear was hounding her, and had been since Luke confessed. "But what if it happens again. Not so much the drinking. I've handled that for ages, and I'm learning how to do it better every day."

"You mean, what if Luke cheats?"

Daisy nodded. "I'd dismissed the possibility, even knowing how willing he's been in the past. Told myself that he might drink, but he'd not cross that line with women anymore. But this? This has been his line in the sand since before he started drinking. I know a person in recovery might fall off the wagon or whatever they call it now, and we'd deal with that. But if he crossed the line with a married woman when drunk, how can I trust he wouldn't cross the line and cheat if he happens to drink again?"

"You can't." Bekah shook her head. "But Katie and Erin can't either."

Daisy hugged the couch's throw pillow against her middle. "But Nathan and Paul don't drink. So, that lowers the chance they'll get drunk and cheat on their wives."

"You, my friend," Bekah said with a point at Daisy, "are missing the point."

"What's that?"

"It doesn't take drinking to tempt someone to cheat."

"I know that."

Bekah smiled. "I know you do. But you're not thinking about it that way. You're stuck on it because Luke has the added temptation of drinking, and when he drinks, good choices are harder to commit to."

"But it does complicate things more than they have to consider."

"Maybe." Bekah's brow raised. "Maybe not. You don't know what goes on behind closed doors in their relationships. For all you know, one of them could thrive on trying to save everyone and find themselves in a fix with the damsel in distress. Or, since I'm sure that's not the same level of probability in your mind, one might struggle with a secret porn addiction. That addiction's got a sexual component all on its own."

Daisy picked at the pillow's edging. She doubted either of those situations plagued her friends' marriages, but Bekah's point was still valid. Still, what did any of it mean for her?

"I don't know, Bek." The weight of the choice forced a sigh. "I love Luke. I do. But where does it leave me if I can't trust him?"

"I think, overall, you can." Bekah rolled her eyes and chuckled. "And that's saying a lot coming from me. But that doesn't mean you're trusting him to be perfect. He can't do that any better than you can. Relationships are filled with one person letting the other down. If it weren't true, there'd be way fewer country songs on the radio."

Despite the seriousness of the topic, Daisy grinned. Leave it to Bekah to infuse some levity into the hard stuff.

"Jill said something like that." Daisy set the pillow aside. "Said I was putting my trust in Luke being perfect. Instead, I needed to trust God to strengthen me through whatever crisis came my way."

"Jill sounds like a very wise woman." Bekah puffed out her chest and brushed a hand over each shoulder. "Like someone else I know."

"You're too much."

"But you love me."

Daisy laughed. "I'm sick that way."

"Hey!" Bekah moved from the chair to grab the pillow and bop Daisy in the shoulder with it before she could protect herself. Tossing the pillow at the far end to avoid retribution, Bekah moved to retrieve her purse from the table in the nook serving as Daisy's entryway. "Seriously, though. Could Luke get drunk or cheat or both if you get together? Yes. Can you and God handle that, and is that a position you want to put yourself in? Only you and God can answer that. And the only way you're going to figure that out is if you spend some time with just you and Him."

Daisy nodded. "Thanks for everything."

"Any time." Bekah opened the door. "Call if you need me. I'll be praying for you."

Chapter Thirty-Two

Luke adjusted his cap. "I wouldn't know. I haven't talked to her in a while."

"How long?" Nathan hefted a bag of garden soil out of the back of Luke's truck.

Luke grabbed another bag from the bed. "Three weeks, two days."

Nathan snickered. He must find the specificity pathetic. Luke wasn't going to clue him in that he actually knew the time down to the hours.

"No word at all?"

Luke's bag thudded to the earth beside the edging stones running the length of Nathan's wrap-around porch. "Nope."

"And you're not going to try to reach out to her?" Nathan deposited his bag on top of Luke's and retrieved the final bag.

Luke shut the tailgate. "Nope."

"You doin' okay with that?"

"Nope."

Nathan ripped the top bag open and grabbed a shovel. "That's a lot of nope."

"Yep."

"Gotta get back to work?" Nathan tossed the shovelful of soil into the halfway-filled bed before sticking the tip of the blade into the grass at his feet and leaning on the handle.

"Nah. I clocked out before I headed this way with your load. Though I'm not sure why you're making a garden now. Shouldn't you have done this in the spring?"

"Usually. But seeing as these are brand new beds I'm puttin' in and that Katie's got a ton of bulbs to plant this fall, I figured now is as good a time as any." Nathan nodded toward the barn. "What d'ya say you grab a shovel and help me fill these gardens. Katie's got a roast in the Crock-Pot, and she'll be home with Sam before long."

Luke crossed the yard to the barn and grabbed a shovel from the tool and tack room and rejoined Nathan. The bag remained untouched. Luke gave a wry smile.

"You didn't have to wait for me to return."

"Sure I did." Nathan scooped another load of soil. "Gotta earn it if you want dinner tonight."

Luke filled his shovel as he eyed the two dozen bags of dirt. "Somehow, I don't think a lack of work is going to be a problem."

"It's good for you." Nathan laid his shovel aside and picked up a rake to spread the piles. "Builds character."

Luke raised a brow. "You don't think I have an abundance of character? You're the first."

"Guess you're right about that." Nathan laughed. "But enough about that nonsense. Why don't you tell me about all the nope going on in your life? It seemed like things were going good for you two."

"I told her about that last night."

"Oh."

Luke scooped out another shovelful. "Yep. She was all ready to get back together, and I got an attack of the conscience. She needed to know so she wouldn't be blindsided in the future."

"That's admirable." Nathan laid the rake aside and grabbed his shovel again. "It's never wise to start a relationship with secrets dangling between you. That's a good way for someone to end up hanging themselves in the future."

Luke snorted. "Instead, I found a way to do it now and avoid the wait."

"Said it was over, huh?"

"She didn't say anything." Luke wiped his forehead with his forearm. "I left. Gave her space to think. Told her I'd let her reach out whenever, if ever, she was ready."

Nathan threw the empty bag on top of the other empties and slit a new one open with this pocketknife. "How long you gonna wait?"

"Long as it takes for her to call."

"And if she doesn't?" Nathan folded the blade back into the handle and retrieved his shovel. "How long will you wait to call her?"

"I won't."

"Never?"

"Told her I wouldn't. I'm trying to respect whatever she decides." Luke dragged another bag toward the far end of the garden. Half the bed was at capacity. With Nathan working from the middle and Luke from the end, they'd finish the work in no time. "It's not easy, though."

"D'ya think you might change your mind on that later?"

"On what? Thinking it's difficult?"

"No." Nathan heaved a shovelful into the garden. "Change your mind about seeking her out. I mean, is there an expiration date on never?"

"Wouldn't be never then. Would it?" Luke took a few steps closer to midway. "Why? Do you think I was wrong telling her that?"

"I'm not the one to say. Just asking the questions."

"But?"

"But nothin'. I've never been in this situation before. I just can't see your feelings changing. And I imagine lovin' her from a distance ain't gonna be easy."

Luke tossed his last empty bag on the trash pile. "That's an understatement."

A honk sounded behind them, drawing their attention to the driveway. Katie's Jeep pulled up behind Nathan's truck. Sam waved wildly from the passenger seat. As soon as the vehicle reached a complete stop, the door flew open, and the pre-teen bounded across the yard toward them.

"Uncle Luke!" Sam stuck one closed hand up for a fist bump. "Guess what happened in practice today?"

Luke rubbed his chin and squinted at Sam. "Well, I suppose that depends. Were you practicing baseball or basketball today?"

"Ha ha." Sam rolled his eyes. "You think you're so funny. You know I'm on the swim team."

Luke ruffled his still-damp hair. "That's right. Let's see. Did you do a belly flop off the high dive?"

"No."

"Win a gold medal for synchronized swimming?"

"Be serious, Uncle Luke."

"Kiddo, the only swimming I do is a dog paddle. I don't have a clue. If you wait for me to guess, we'll be here all night."

"I got picked for the championship team!"

The excitement radiated off him. Luke drew him into a tight one-armed hug. "That's great, Sam. I'm proud of you."

Sam pushed away. "Eww. You stink, Uncle Luke."

"Sam." Katie's mom-voice caused all three males to stand at attention. She shifted the baby on her hip. "That was totally rude. I think you owe Uncle Luke an apology."

Luke sniffed his shirt and grimaced. "I'm not one to interfere with parenting. 'Cause"—Luke looked at Sam—"there's always a polite way to say things. But I have to admit the kid's right. Your husband roped me into slaving away in this hot sun with the promise of roast at the end. But I'm not sure I'm gonna be fit to sit at your table."

Katie hitched her thumb toward the barn. "There's a shower next to the tack room in the stable. Sam can fetch a shirt and some clean jogging pants from his dad's drawer, and you'll be presentable in no time."

Sam ran up the steps and into the house without waiting to be told.

"I guess that settles it then." Nathan laughed. "You can shower in there, and I'll go inside to grab one myself. Then, we can finish our talk after dinner."

"I thought we were done."

Nathan shook his head. "Not by a long shot."

"THAT'S ENOUGH FOR TONIGHT." Katie countered Sam's complaint about heading inside. "Uncle Luke and Dad need to have a talk."

"But I wanted to whip Uncle Luke in another game of horse."

"Not tonight, buddy." Luke bounced the basketball once before passing it off to Sam. "My ego can only take so many losses in a day."

Sam smirked. "Then you better work on toughening up. I've seen the way you play. You're going to need it."

"Sam." Katie's tone was sharp, even as she fought a grin.

Nathan held up a hand. "No need to get Sam in trouble for that one. You missed all the trash talk comin' outta Luke a few minutes ago. Just a little fun ribbing between buddies. Isn't that right, Sam?"

"Yessir."

"Now go on and do what your mom said. Uncle Luke and I've got to talk."

"Yessir." Though this agreement was less enthusiastic than his first, Sam fist-bumped Luke goodnight and headed inside with Katie.

"You've got a good kid there." Luke nodded in the direction of the house. "Never know he's not your biological son. It's amazing."

"I am blessed. Sam was young enough when Katie and I got together that I don't think he really remembers a time when I wasn't his dad, or at least in his life." Nathan turned his focus from his home to Luke. "The way you are with him, you're going to make a great dad someday."

Tightness pinched Luke's chest. "I didn't have such a great relationship with my dad. Don't know that I'd know how to be a good one, much less a great one."

"What do you say we go light up the fire pit in the backyard? Perfect night for it."

Though Luke knew the way, Nathan led them to the patio behind the house. He added some kindling to the pit and arranged a couple of small logs over it before lighting the easier-burning material at the base. Sparks flickered into a flame, which soon set the pile to blaze.

Away from the floodlight shining on the small basketball court out front, evening quickly settled around them as they settled into the cushioned patio chairs scattered around the fire pit. Luke breathed in the smoky air and listened to the sounds of frogs and crickets chirping from their hideouts in the trees and nearby pond. Peaceful. If only the feeling could be replicated in the rest of his life.

"You underestimate yourself." Nathan stretched out his legs and crossed his ankles. "Your dad wasn't a great example. But God didn't leave you without. You had your Pops. From what I know of him and what you've told me, he was more dad to you than anyone else. A great, godly example."

"He was."

"And I've seen you with Sam and Angeline." Nathan smiled. "You're going to be just fine."

"Not that it matters." Luke raked a hand through his hair. "I've given Daisy time and got nothing but silence. I don't blame her. But I gave her my heart a long time ago. Whether she wants it or not, it's still hers."

"So you've said."

A stream of light fell over Nathan's shoulder. Luke looked to the source where Katie exited the house with a glass in each hand. The light narrowed and disappeared as the door swung shut behind her. Nathan rose as his wife made her way to them.

"Don't worry." Katie smiled. "I'm not crashing your party. I just figured you might want something to drink."

She handed one glass to Luke before offering the other to Nathan. He thanked her with a kiss to the cheek that stirred a pang of jealousy in Luke. His mistakes cost him the opportunity for a love like theirs. The fault rested with him alone, making the sting sharper. He took a drink, the sweet, iced tea giving him a moment's distraction as Nathan settled back in his seat.

"Earlier, you admitted it's not as easy as just letting Daisy go." Nathan jumped back into the conversation. "Are you struggling?"

Luke didn't need Nathan to clarify the question. They both knew Luke's hang-ups, and losing Daisy had been a trigger to relapse.

Nathan eyed him. "I don't ask as a mentor or sponsor or for the program. Tonight, I'm just asking as your friend."

The answer would be the same either way. Still, Luke had experienced enough years without a godly man as a friend that hearing the affirmation strengthened his resolve to come through this time unscathed.

"I was scared, at first." Luke wiped a bead of sweat from his glass and flicked it into the night. "Those first few days, all I did was go to work, read my Bible, and pray."

"Not bad ways to spend the day."

"No. But that first group meeting I attended after it all went down reminded me I'd come through the worst of it without giving in to temptation. Daisy wasn't going to leave me any more than she already had. If I got through those days without drinking, I could keep making it through."

A look of regret marred Nathan's expression. "I'm sorry I wasn't there for you that night or in the following nights. This stomach bug going around hit our house hard."

Nathan had already told him how every free minute had been spent taking care of the kids while Katie dealt with the bug, then minding the baby while Katie took care of Sam when he ended up with it. Family first. The way it should be.

"No need to apologize." Luke looked out across the field where lightning bugs twinkled like low-hanging stars as they searched for the perfect mate. "I had support from the group. And Mike. He's become a real friend through all this. Though not even he knows about the night that shall not be named."

"You're doing okay, then?"

Luke sighed. "I'm taking it one day at a time."

Chapter Thirty-Three

One more day. Daisy reached for a banana. She would give it one more day before she started eating real food again. She didn't have enough energy to make something more substantial. She'd heard the stomach bug that had laid her out for the last four days was a doozy, but nothing adequately prepared her for the reality.

Though she'd been free of the virus's effects the full previous day, not eating properly left her run-down. But, ready or not, work couldn't wait another day. She couldn't expect Bekah to run things on her own any longer, even if Jill had jumped in to help some. While they could both ring out sales and bag up any teas a customer might want, neither knew how to tend the garden or make the drinks that brought in the majority of her income.

Friday and Saturday were Communi-TEA Barn's biggest days for those types of sales. Her bills wouldn't allow her to miss them.

"One for the road." Daisy snagged another banana from the bunch before retrieving a coconut water from the fridge. "And something to wash it down."

If she ate these on her way to work, it might perk her up enough to make it through at least part of the day.

DAISY EYED the banana on the truck's seat beside her. She'd made it to lunch, but how remained a mystery. Now, the meager meal meant to sustain her for the afternoon looked about as appetizing as one of the mud pies she'd fashioned in the front yard as a child.

"Why can't a cheeseburger be easy on the stomach?" Muttering as she drove, Daisy navigated toward Mike's Landscaping.

The nursery would be open during lunch hours. Daisy's shop would usually be, too, but Bekah convinced her to take a break, perhaps catch a nap, to make it through the day.

"But what she doesn't know won't hurt her." Daisy would've smiled if she had the energy. She'd agreed to closing for two hours, but not to rest. A quick look around her untended gardens demanded a trip to Mike's. Her herbs and flowers suffered in her absence. The best way to ensure her precious plants would still flourish was to add some extra food to their water. Food Daisy didn't have in her stash in the greenhouse.

A power nap waited for her as soon as she got back. Then, after the store closed, she would tend the plants the way they deserved. There was only one hitch in her plan.

"Please, Lord," she prayed out loud. "I can't deal with Luke right now."

Was it wrong to ask God to intervene when she was doing something behind her friend's back? True, she didn't tell Bekah she would nap, but that was the idea behind the extended lunch hour, and they both knew it.

Bekah wasn't the boss. She didn't own the business. It wasn't hers to decide how the day should go.

Daisy's groggy brain waffled between guilt and absolution. "It's not that big a deal. In and out and I'll still have time for a nap." She shoved off the pesky dilemma as the parking lot came into view.

∽

"Daisy." Luke kept his voice neutral despite the surge of anticipation flooding through him. If she was here, where she knew he would be, then she must have reached her conclusions about their relationship. However, business was likely too. Better to let her set the tone. "What can I do for you?"

"I need some of that plant food Mike keeps in stock for me. Enough for all the gardens. They're looking a little worse for wear right now."

Her plants weren't the only thing, though Luke would never admit it out loud. Daisy was pale, more than usual. Dark circles shaded the area under her eyes.

Luke nodded to a couple of chairs up against the wall. "You go ahead and have a seat. I've got to rummage around in the back and see what I can find. It may take a few minutes."

The way she accepted without argument and fell into the chair like it was a lifeline convinced Luke he wasn't imagining things. The cause was a mystery, but something wasn't right in Daisy's world.

Though he'd told Daisy it would take a few minutes to find her plant food, Luke didn't really expect it to take as long as it did. Usually, Mike's storage system was orderly and easy to understand. For some reason, the food wasn't where it should have been.

"Good. Gives her a couple extra minutes to rest, anyway." Luke would've taken his time, even if he'd found it right away. Now, he had to convince her to allow him to carry it out to her truck for her. He snorted. "That's going to be like wrestling a fresh cut of meat away from a hungry crocodile."

An idea struck as he was about to enter the shop. Instead, he made a U-turn and headed out the back door and around the building to the parking lot. All he needed was one package to scan the UPC. He deposited the rest in the bed of Daisy's truck before heading back where she waited for him inside.

Daisy didn't glance his direction when he came in the front door. Her head tilted back against the wall, eyes closed, though Luke doubted she was asleep.

"I've got everything loaded up." Luke gingerly touched her shoulder.

In one fluid motion, Daisy's head snapped forward and eyes popped open as she sprang up from the chair. Luke was biting back a laugh at her surprise when her already pale face turned two shades whiter than white.

"I'm sorr—"

Luke's minor concern flared into fear as Daisy's body swayed and her eyes slid shut. A quiet moan escaped her lips as she began to crumple in front of him. The plant food thudded to the wood floor as Luke dropped it in his haste to catch Daisy before she made it that far.

"What in the world?" Mike rushed toward them as he entered the room.

Luke gathered Daisy in his arms. "I'm not sure. She stood up and then went down."

"There's a sofa in my office." Mike took charge. "Lay her in there. Stay with her. I'll watch the front."

Luke rushed through the door Mike held open and headed to the office right inside the employee section of the store. Daisy began to stir before he reached the doorway. Instead of fighting, Daisy snuggled into his chest. Warmth and pain radiated through in equal measures, neither overriding his fear for the woman in his arms. Though her slight movement helped dissipate the riot of nervous energy that filled him as she fell.

He carefully laid her on the sofa. The disturbance pinched her expression into a frown, and she rustled without opening her eyes. With feather-light movements, he brushed her silky bangs away from her face. Her full lips curved in a soft smile. His responded in kind, though no one saw it.

Her eyelids fluttered and opened.

"What?" Her quiet question accompanied the return of her frown.

She glanced at what Luke knew was an unfamiliar space for her.

"It's okay." Luke stepped into her line of sight and placed a hand on her shoulder. "You passed out. I brought you into Mike's office until we figure out what's going on."

Daisy groaned. "Did anyone see?"

"Only Mike. And I assure you, he'll be the picture of discretion." Luke stepped away long enough to swivel Mike's chair around the desk next to Daisy. "How are you feeling?"

"Embarrassed."

"Other than that. Do you have any idea what happened?" *Please God,* Luke petitioned. *Don't let it be from the stress of seeing me again.* He could handle a lot, had been recently. But Daisy experiencing this level of anxiety due to his presence was more than he wanted to consider. He'd already hurt her enough.

Daisy rubbed her face with both hands and slowly propped herself up against the arm of the couch. "I should've eaten the banana."

Luke frowned. "What?"

Maybe she wasn't okay after all. She might not be coherent.

"The banana. My lunch." Daisy shook her head. "I knew I should've eaten it on the way over here, but it just didn't appeal to me."

"Missing lunch shouldn't cause you to pass out." Luke

wouldn't add that a banana was a pathetic excuse for a lunch. What was Daisy thinking, eating so little for her meal?

Daisy yawned. "No. But I've been sick. Stomach bug. Other than bananas and toast, I've not eaten much of anything for a few days."

"Why were you at work if you weren't eating yet?" Disbelief sharpened his words.

"Excuse me." Daisy's glare put Luke in his place. "It's not your job to release me to return to mine. I have bills like everyone else and need to pay them."

Luke sat back in his seat. Held up his hands. "You're right. I don't have any business telling you what you should or shouldn't do. Seeing you drop like that just scared me witless."

While he was glad to see a little color in her cheeks, Luke wished it wasn't brought on by embarrassment. Really, Daisy didn't need to apologize or be embarrassed. Even if she hadn't been ill recently, there were lots of reasons a person might faint.

"Didn't mean to scare you." Daisy bit her lip. "And you're right. I shouldn't skip lunch."

"How are you feeling now?"

Daisy lifted one shoulder. "Exhausted to be honest. And a little off."

"Stay right there." Luke jogged through the store and out to her truck. Lucky for him, she hadn't locked her door, and he was able to retrieve her banana. On the way back through, he paused in the break room and snagged a soda out of the fridge and a package of peanut butter crackers. He'd replace both for Mike later.

Daisy was sitting with her feet on the floor when he entered Mike's office. Her color looked better, but still not quite her normal.

"Here." Luke extended his offering. "It's not much, but it'll sit on your stomach all right and give you a little bit of strength."

Daisy accepted it without argument and popped the tab on the soda can.

"You eat. Let me talk to Mike just a sec."

He didn't wait for agreement before heading out to find his boss behind the cash register, the container of plant food he'd dropped sitting next to it. Luke reached for his wallet and pulled out some bills.

"Here." He handed them to Mike. "This should cover that one and three more I already put in Daisy's truck."

Mike scanned the package. "What happened?"

"Apparently, she's been sick for a few days. She's pushed too much without enough food to keep her going." Luke scanned the empty store and glanced at the clock. One-thirty. It would be a big favor to ask. "I don't feel easy about her driving right now."

Mike handed him the change from his purchase. "Don't even need to ask. Just get her back to her shop and make sure there's someone there who can keep an eye on her. Rick is due in about half an hour. I'll have him swing by on his way and pick you up."

"Thanks, Mike."

"Don't worry about it." Mike put the food in a bag and handed it to Luke. "Just tell Daisy to take care of herself and feel better."

With that settled, there was only one thing left to do. Tell Daisy the plan and hope that she'd be on board.

Chapter Thirty-Four

"She did what?" Bekah huffed and turned her focus on Daisy. "I can't believe you'd come back to work when you haven't eaten anything. And trying to work all day without a break or a meal? Are you nuts?"

Daisy straightened her shoulders as her chin lifted. "It happens. And I've eaten now. So, I'm good."

"No." Luke drew both women's attention. "You've eaten a bit now, but you still need to take it easy."

"Oh, I'll make sure of that." Bekah punctuated her edict with her hands on her hips.

Daisy looked between the two of them. There would be no winning this battle, even if she had the strength to fight it out.

Luke watched out the front window. "I think I see Rick. I'll leave your stuff in the greenhouse." He glanced at Bekah. "But don't let her deal with it today."

"You don't have to worry." Bekah glared at her again. "She's going to plant herself on a stool behind the counter until closing time and only get up if we need her to make a drink."

He nodded at Bekah before turning to her. "You take care of yourself. I'll talk to you later."

It wasn't a question. Yet it was. Daisy nodded. "Later. And thank you, Luke."

The pull between them snapped only when he broke eye contact and turned to leave.

"What are you going to do about that?"

Bekah's question waited until the door shut firmly behind Luke.

"What do you mean?"

"Don't misunderstand me." Bekah pulled a stool directly behind the cash register and pointed Daisy to it. "I'm glad Luke was there to play hero, but does this earn him a spot in your life again?"

Daisy plopped down on the stool. "I wish I knew."

"No decisions yet?"

"It's awkward, is all."

"Ah." Bekah nodded. "You're not sure how to tell him you don't want a relationship when you're going to have to see him again."

Daisy twisted so quickly she had to grab the shelf behind her to keep the stool from falling over. The last thing she needed after having Luke save her from a close call with a floor earlier was to end up there anyway.

"What?" Daisy's brows lowered in confusion. "No. I actually decided around week two that we needed to at least talk about the possibility of us."

Bekah sorted the teas on the shelf behind her. "I'm not seeing the awkward part."

"It's been over three weeks, Bekah. What if he's decided I'm not going to give him a chance? If he's moved on."

Bekah's immediate laugh drew a scowl from Daisy. Bekah wasn't there this afternoon. Didn't hear the discomfort in his voice when Luke greeted her. It cut her to the quick.

"Do you mind?" Her frustration bled through her words. "I'm serious. He was waiting, and I had my answer. But did I call? No. Stuff kept getting in the way, and then, I got sick and wasn't calling anyone."

"So what?"

Daisy steadied herself with a deep breath and counted to five. No, five wasn't enough. She added a couple of extra seconds for good measure. Bekah didn't get it, but that wasn't her fault. Bekah had never been in a position like this before. Then again, neither had Daisy.

"Luke went all that time thinking I was done with him." Daisy picked at a loose thread on her jacket. "Over three weeks, waiting. It'd be ridiculous for me to think he didn't take the unintended hint."

Bekah stopped sorting and looked at Daisy like she'd said one plus one equals applesauce. "Then you don't know that man as well as you think you do."

"But—"

"But nothing. Luke Masters has been in love with you since you were kids. You think a few weeks of going radio silent is going to change that? As much as it pains me to say it, he's made of sterner stuff than that."

"I don't know."

Bekah's shoulders dropped, her expression full of disbelief. "Yes, you do. And if you're not convinced, it's as easy as a conversation to clear it up. You're not going to sit here like a helpless heroine in a cheesy rom-com, missing out on love because you can't have a simple conversation. No misunderstandings or assumptions are going to destroy this chance. Not as long as I'm your best friend."

"What if he doesn't want to talk to me?"

"Seriously?" Bekah rolled her eyes. "He asked if he'd talk to you later, and you said yes. The man wants to hear from you."

Was Bekah right? Would a simple phone call be enough? Daisy dropped her gaze to the floor and shuffled her feet.

"There's just one question." Bekah waited until she had Daisy's full attention. "What are you going to do about it?"

Chapter Thirty-Five

Images from the last time Daisy showed up at Luke's house uninvited flooded her memory. Daisy swallowed.

"Take every thought captive." She repeated the instruction until she succeeded in pushing the unpleasant image from her mind. "Thank You, Father, for bringing Luke out of that time in his life. Help him be the man You want him to be."

Calm stole over her. Daisy knew it was God. Early on in her time with Jill, her mentor had shared that powerful secret with her.

"When the bad thoughts come," she had said, "take control. You're in charge of your mind, even when the enemy says you're not. It may take practice and a lot of prayer, but it will get easier with time."

Daisy had doubted that nugget of truth, but Jill wasn't finished.

"Then, pray. Whatever progress has taken place, praise God for that. Even if it's minuscule. Pray as a reminder of how far you've come. Then, pray for God to continue working in the future."

Jill's words had ushered in peace despite the storm more

often than Daisy could count. Whether the praise and petitions were for herself or Luke, focusing on what God had and could do instead of the circumstance always helped Daisy stay grounded.

Feeling more at peace, though no more prepared, Daisy left the sanctuary of her truck and made her way up the familiar stone walk to Luke's front door. Her knuckles rapped against the cool wood of the front door. After waiting what should have been an appropriate amount of time—though who was she to judge when time was standing still—she knocked again.

Footsteps echoed inside, growing closer. Daisy's stomach tightened. Attempting this so soon after being sick might not be the best option. No. Bekah was right. One conversation was all it would take to find the answers and allow her mind to rest, finally.

"Coming."

His voice sounded neither rushed nor anxious. Of course, he didn't know who waited for him to offer entry. Would that tone change when he saw her?

The door swung open. His mouth did the same. Daisy hoped her grin was more friendly than unhinged. With the nerves pinging through her, she couldn't be sure what won out in her expression.

"Daisy." Luke ran a hand through his brown hair, leaving messy little spikes.

It had to be a little damp for it to stay so obligingly in the way that made her fingers itch to comb back into place. Workout or shower? Considering the jeans and fitted T-shirt, Daisy would place her bets on a shower. Besides, that option created less ick-factor for running her hands through it.

"What are you doing here?"

Daisy's smile faltered. His tone wasn't dismissive, but it lacked the warmth he usually reserved for her. Were her worst fears coming true? Had Luke moved on? A rock settled in her already queasy stomach. What if he was getting ready for a date?

"I wanted to thank you." Daisy forced the words out as her mind swirled like a storm. Stop it. Remember what Bekah said. A simple conversation to clear up misunderstandings. That's all this is.

"You shouldn't have gone out of your way."

The rock grew into a boulder. Daisy bit her lip.

Luke stepped back from the doorway and motioned her inside. "You've not been feeling well. You need to rest, not traipse all over the county."

His reasoning eased some of her discomfort, allowing Daisy to accept his invitation without added guilt from having pushed her way in where she wasn't wanted. The scent of his cologne teased her into taking a deep breath of its unusual pairing of fresh citrus highlights and warm woody base notes. It wrapped around her like home, urging her to stay in its embrace.

Daisy followed Luke into his living room and took a seat on the brown leather sofa he'd purchased at her urging before their relationship went off course. The absence of wear on the fabric was a testament to the void of real friendships he'd had since then. The types Luke brought home during that period of life weren't the kind to spend time in the living room.

Pushing the thought from her mind was easier than Daisy imagined possible. Luke was a new man. Each day made it plainer than the last.

"I didn't have to." Daisy's fingers fidgeted. "I wanted to. You could've just made sure I had something to eat and sent me on my way. You didn't. That means something to me."

Luke settled into the opposite end of the couch. "You mean something to me."

He raised his eyes to hers and let the connection linger. He'd gone the extra mile because she was Daisy. In his mind, she was his Daisy. The message was clearly spoken in his gaze. Though

Daisy knew, if she walked out the door now, he wouldn't push the issue. Luke's love for her was constant and protective, but never possessive. He would let her go.

"But I don't want to." The words tumbled out without permission.

Luke frowned. "What? I didn't ask anything."

She'd not meant to speak the words. But now that they were out in the open, Daisy knew it was time to take the leap or dive into the deep end or whatever other tired cliché her mind could concoct.

"Thanking you isn't the only reason I stopped by."

Luke swallowed but remained silent.

"It's been weeks, but I didn't mean it to happen that way. I realized we needed to talk after just a few days. I didn't. Then, it just seemed like it was too long." Daisy blew out a frustrated breath. Rambling was not getting them anywhere. "I couldn't face you after taking so much time. And I was scared I'd waited too long."

"Never." Luke's response was so quiet Daisy almost missed it.

"But you don't know what I decided."

"Doesn't matter." Luke shrugged. "Whether you want to give us a go or," he cleared his throat, "Walk away forever. Even if you stay away for ten years, I'll always be here for you when you need me."

Daisy smiled as the warmth of his words spread through her. "I do. And I hope you do too."

Luke's crooked grin pushed his dimples to show through his constant five o'clock shadow in a way that raised Daisy's heart rate. She'd always loved his pirate smile. Nothing was as irresistible, especially when his green eyes twinkled with just a hint of mischief as they were now.

"Do what?" His grin grew. "Want to walk away forever or stay with me forever?"

Daisy laughed. "I don't recall committing to forever."

"If you were going to walk away forever, I just assumed the opposite would be on the table too."

Daisy wanted to agree. Give in to Luke's levity and simply enjoy being with him from now until forever. But there was so much they needed to figure out first.

"You don't know how appealing that is."

One brow rose. "We can head to Vegas and take care of that right now."

She knew he was kidding, sort of. "Luke, we can't jump into this."

His grin faded.

"We've got a rapid rushing beneath our feet, and the bridge we're crossing isn't as sound as it should be. We've got to deal with the issues, then cross."

Luke rubbed his hand over his stubble. Nodded. "You're right. To be honest, I question how you're even considering us. Especially since I can't promise I won't fail you in the future."

"You will."

"Um … thanks for that."

"It's true." Daisy wanted to beg him to understand. "You'll fail me, and I'll fail you. We're human that way."

"But your mistakes—"

"Will hurt you, just like yours will hurt me." Daisy brushed a strand of hair behind her ear. "Marriage, relationships in general, are hard. Even the best are marked with misunderstanding and hurts."

"Sure, but the issues that come with me aren't the run-of-the-mill problems."

"No. But they're not insurmountable either." Daisy paused to gather the right words. "Unlike others, we're aware of some of the issues we may face, and we can take measures to minimize the occurrence and damage."

Luke leaned back, arms crossed. "Rules and stuff?"

"Not rules exactly." Daisy shook her head. "More like safeguards. You value your house and your belongings, right?"

"Sure."

"You don't want your things destroyed or stolen."

"Who would?"

"Just stick with me here." Daisy stood and paced in front of the couch while she spoke. "To protect your home and belongings, you have locks on the windows and doors. You can choose to use them or not, given the situation."

"I see where you're going."

"And if there are measures a person can take, like motion-sensing lights, doorbell cameras, and alarms. Those kinds of things don't keep bad out, but they warn you that bad is trying to sneak in."

Luke's expression was less guarded than when she'd begun. A positive sign, right?

"Our relationship is more valuable than our possessions. Why wouldn't we take precautions and set alarms to warn us of known dangers in our neighborhood?"

"What are you thinking?"

Daisy shrugged and plopped down on the sofa cushion next to him. "I'm not entirely sure. I mean, we need to commit to honesty, particularly when it's uncomfortable. Not just you, me too."

"You?" Luke grinned. "I'm sure you're not going to go get drunk and need to confess."

"No. But some subjects are sensitive for you. I might be tempted to push down a fear or question until it grows into a bigger problem than it needs to be. Whether it's to spare you more hurt or to avoid frustration or whatever, I can't make excuses."

"Would that be a problem for you? You've always been able to tell me anything."

Daisy bit her lip. If they were going to do this, the safeguards had to start now. "This is so much bigger and harder than anything I've had to deal with. It's easy to say I understand we'll be dealing with these things indefinitely, and I only need to trust God to take me through. But right now? Right now, seems so big, and I feel so unprepared. It's scary."

"What scares you most?"

"That I'll wake up one day to find you've not come home. And I'll know where you've been and what you've done, even who you were doing it with is a mystery."

Daisy's eyes closed as Luke's thumb wiped away a tear from her cheek. It seemed impossible that a man as gentle, loving, and loyal as Luke could ever make a choice like that. But she had to be honest with herself. If he gave in to his addictions, it was a very real possibility.

"I'm so sorry." Luke's already deep voice was lower and rougher. "I want to promise you it will never happen. Not if we're together. But I can't. I don't want it to. You don't understand how much I don't want it to. But I'm not living one hundred percent free of the temptation to drink at this point. I may never experience life without the occasional temptation."

Daisy opened her eyes as the couch cushions shifted with Luke's movement. He'd angled himself to face her. She looked down at the floor, fighting the tears his truthfulness provoked. His touch was warm as his fingers lifted her chin and turned her face to his.

"I can't promise I won't fail, but I do trust God is with me, helping me take each day at a time. I want us more than anything. You know that. But I can't ask you to take this risk."

Daisy offered a bittersweet smile. "That's what I came here to tell you."

Luke's eyes dimmed before he looked away.

"No." Daisy took his strong hand in hers, gaining his attention. "I meant, you don't have to ask me. I want to take the risk with you, for you, and for everything God has for us in it."

"And if I fail?" Luke shook his head. "I can't doom you to a hopeless relationship."

"Who said it would be hopeless?"

"You think if I make what would be the worst mistake of my life—"

"Yes. There would be hope even after."

The wanting in his eyes was too much. Daisy had to look away and compose herself. Luke looked like he'd been promised the greatest gift in the world and was waiting for someone to snatch it out of reach to taunt him with it. The reality of his addiction, of what it cost him, inspired fear in him too—fear of hurting her.

Daisy framed his face with her hands, his stubble scratching her palms. "I have hope, no matter the circumstance, because I serve a God who can bring beauty from ashes." Still doubt shone in his eyes. "Can't you see it? God's already doing that in you. I prayed I'd see you come back to Him, but I never dreamed you'd do that and become better than the Luke I loved as a teenager. God used the ugliest thing in your life to open your heart to His forgiveness, to His love."

"But if I fail again—"

"Forgiveness will be waiting there to start again."

"It won't be easy."

"No. And it will hurt deeper than anything either of us has experienced before. But there will still be the promise of forgiveness and the hope of restoration to something more beautiful than we can imagine."

Luke pressed his cheek into her palm. "And you want to risk it?"

"For the man I've always loved?" Daisy leaned in close. "Always."

As Luke's arms slipped around her, Daisy's hands moved from his cheeks to the nape of his neck, where she meant to pull him toward her. Luke didn't give her the chance, closing the distance between them without any help from her. His lips were soft against hers. His touch mixed with his fragrance was heady. Their kiss deepened, freeing the love they'd fought against for so many years.

Daisy's heart beat furiously in her chest. As her hand slipped from Luke's shoulder to his chest, she felt the same rhythm pounding in his. They'd kissed once, in her garden, but that hesitant comfort-driven kiss was nothing in comparison to their current embrace. Every missed opportunity poured through her. The realization that she didn't have to fight her love for Luke any longer fed the flame between them until it blazed.

Cold soothed her lips as Luke moved away from her touch. Daisy opened her eyes and stared at him in confusion. Why pull away when they'd only just found each other again?

"We can't." Luke's voice was raw. He raked a hand through his hair.

"We won't." She leaned in again, sure of her words and eager to return to his embrace.

Luke stood abruptly. "No. You said honesty. Always. Honestly, if we don't go someplace else, I'm not sure I can keep my mind from going places it shouldn't. And while I'd never push you, neither of us is thinking clearly while wrapped in each other's arms."

The urge to argue fled in the face of Luke's honest appraisal of the situation. He was watching out for them, even in the face of her naïve confidence in their ability to avoid crossing the lines. Daisy added Luke's protection of their relationship to the list of things she loved about him.

Luke took her hand and pulled her up from the couch. "How about we grab a milkshake at Sonic and head to the park for a walk?"

Daisy gave a wry smile at his attempt to bribe her with one of her favorite summer-time treats. "Don't think I don't recognize your tactics."

"What?" One brow raised in challenge. "You don't want a milkshake?"

Daisy laughed and followed him out the door. "I always want a shake. Just don't think you've pulled one over on me. You're trying to distract me."

"Is it working?"

"Milkshakes and a man who's going to fight to protect our relationship?" Daisy lifted their joined hands and kissed the back of his. "Not at all. I'm falling in love more by the second."

Luke squeezed her hand. "One can only hope."

Epilogue

Eight Years Later

Daisy paced the kitchen floor, careful to avoid the squeaky board. Little Luke didn't need help waking up through the night. For that matter, neither did his older sisters.

"I should be in bed." Daisy tried to slow her breathing. "I've got work tomorrow."

How could she go to sleep when her husband was having such a hard time? In the last eight years, she and Luke had kept to their relationship protection plan. Added to always being honest was checking in if one was going to be late and continuing regular meetings even when they believed life was under control.

They'd faced hard situations. Living paycheck to paycheck sometimes created stress. They had disagreements and misunderstandings like every other couple. This was different. One month without work. When Mike's Landscaping closed a month prior, Luke held up like a champion.

God would provide. They both believed it. Prayed for His leading to the next opportunity. Now, going several weeks

EPILOGUE

without work was chipping away at Luke's optimism. The dwindling savings account and mounting bills taunted them. The Communi-TEA barn was doing well, but while it was enough for one to live on, it wasn't adequate to support a family of five.

Stress and frustration hounded Luke until he was cranky with her and the kids. His attitude prompted her to send him to town this evening when she realized they were out of toilet paper. But that was hours ago. One short text informed Daisy that Luke had met Nathan at the store and he'd be home in a bit.

A bit. A few minutes. Not three hours.

"God, what do I do?" Daisy didn't want to be the nagging wife who called to check up on her husband. But fear was grabbing hold and refusing to let go.

Daisy grabbed a glass and went to the fridge for some milk. Wasn't milk supposed to soothe? Or was that only warm milk? Since warm milk sounded disgusting, Daisy opted for cold. Before she opened the door, a plain black magnet with a quote in white calligraphy caught her attention.

"Of one thing I am perfectly sure: God's story never ends with ashes." Daisy smiled at Elisabeth Elliot's words. How long had it been since Daisy had to use the tried and true methods Jill taught her to handle her fears? Too long, perhaps.

"Take captive. God, I refuse to let fear consume me. No matter what comes, I trust You to bring beauty from ashes. I've seen it so many times before. Thank You for saving Luke. Thank You for using his darkest time to bring him back to faith." Daisy set the empty glass aside and traced a photo magnet with her finger. Her children last Easter. "Thank You for the wonderful father You've given my children. He's a man of faith who teaches them to follow You and loves them unconditionally every day."

"And thank you for providing me with such a wonderful husband. He's facing hard times right now, but You will bring

EPILOGUE

him through. He's fought hard to be the man You'd have him to be." Daisy sighed. "I love him more every day."

"Who do you love more every day?"

Daisy spun around and screamed before slapping her hand over her mouth. She glared at Luke for sneaking up on her, though she didn't dare speak yet. Instead, she listened closely to the silence around them. After it remained that way for several seconds, she deemed it safe enough to talk.

"Do not sneak up on me like that." Her furious whisper was reinforced with a smack across Luke's arm.

"Why aren't you in bed?" Luke set the toilet paper on the kitchen table and snagged the glass from the counter. He filled it with water, taking a long drink. "You work tomorrow, right?"

Daisy fought the urge to lash out and blame. Honesty was the foundation for their relationship's growth, and it would remain so. "I was afraid."

"Of what? I told you I was going to a meeting. Then, Nathan and I were going to talk."

What? Daisy frowned. "No, you said you met Nathan at the store."

Luke's brows rose like she'd just confirmed his statement. "Yes. And about thirty minutes later, I texted about the meeting and going out. I needed someone to vent to. You've heard it all so much already. I didn't want to bother you with it. Besides, fresh perspective."

"Luke, you didn't text."

"Yes, I did." Luke pulled his phone from his pocket and tapped it on. "Oh no. I'm so sorry, Daisy. I hit send and didn't think another thing about it. Just silenced my phone and put it back in my pocket. I didn't realize."

He turned the phone to face her. Sure enough, there was his explanation. Next to it, the bright red exclamation mark in its matching circle with the words "failed to deliver" under them.

Relief brought a rush of tears. Luke stowed the phone back in his pocket and pulled Daisy in close. He held her tight with one arm across her back and his other hand resting on her hair. Rather than shushing her, Luke let her cry it out.

"That's another reason I love you," Daisy mumbled against his shirt. "You put up with these crazy tears."

"They aren't crazy." Luke kissed the top of her head. "I'm guessing your imagination was running wild. Now, you're feeling the relief." He pulled back without relinquishing his hold on her and waited for Daisy to meet his gaze. "Next time, please, just call. I won't be offended by it. I'd rather you reach out than sit here in fear."

Daisy smiled and brushed the remnants of tears from her face with her fingertips. "God and I were working on that. It's been so long, I neglected what I knew to do to find peace in the unknown and strength if worse came to worst."

"That's why I went to a meeting tonight." Luke pulled her close once more and lowered his lips to hers.

Daisy accepted this kiss and all the love that went with it. Too soon, it ended. Luke brushed the back of his fingers down her cheek. "I pray we never see the worst happen. But—"

"But if we do." Daisy kissed him again before adding, "There is hope even after."

A Message from the Author

Dear Reader,

As a pastor's wife, youth group leader, and youth camp director for all of my adult life, I've been given the bittersweet blessing of an intimate look at the church and the families within the church. I've witnessed the deep hurts and difficult struggles of our families.

Addiction is wounding our families. Some addictions are more palatable and may be mentioned in prayer times, but others remain a secret shame. Addiction, whether to alcohol, drugs, sex (including pornography), or gambling, tears apart many families. And because the enemy thrives in fear, the issues don't come to light until the family has fallen apart.

We hurt silently because our secret shame subjects us to judgment. We are bad parents if our child's drug or alcohol addiction are known. We're failures as wives if our husband's pornography addiction comes to light. And what do people think when the woman singing praise songs beside them has failed once again in her battle against addiction? Hypocrite.

So, we fight and fail in silence.

Let's rewrite the playbook on dealing with addiction in our

churches. While these struggles are not something to wear like a badge of honor, we shouldn't force others to deal with them in silence for fear of judgment. As with any struggle, the families in our churches dealing with addiction need our understanding, loving support, and our prayers. They need hope.

My husband works in addiction counseling. The hardest part for him is knowing the teens committed to sobriety are headed back to the dysfunction that encouraged their addictions in the first place and now serve as triggers to relapse. Without a support system encouraging their recovery, their chances of success drop drastically.

As believers, called to love as Jesus loves, let's commit to being different. Let's stop judging families dealing with addiction or trying to pin the blame wherever we think it falls. Instead, let's come beside the wife (or husband) whose spouse is dealing with pornography addiction, offering love and support. Choose to support the alcoholic in their recovery through prayer or listening when they need to talk. For families dealing with drug addiction, offer prayers, resources on recovery options, and a safe space for them to hurt.

Let's be different to make a difference in the lives of those struggling with addiction. In doing so, we give them a gift that means more than anything else in their struggle—hope.

Blessings,
Heather Greer

Addiction Resources

Are you or someone you love dealing with addiction?

There are many places to find help. There are faith-based options as well as secular programs. The choice is yours. Though I will offer one word of caution.

Many times, addiction is the symptom of an underlying issue. As treatment progresses, past hurts can surface. If your treatment program doesn't have a mental health professional available, please find a qualified counselor you trust for godly advice in dealing with those issues.

While I can't share all possible resources, an internet search can provide other local options. Many mental health agencies also have addictions programs.

https://www.samhsa.gov—Substance Abuse and Mental Health Services Administration

https://celebraterecovery.com—Celebrate Recovery

https://www.aa.org—Alcoholics Anonymous

https://na.org—Narcotics Anonymous

https://saa-recovery.org—Sex Addicts Anonymous

https://fightthenewdrug.org—Fight the New Drug (pornography addiction resources)

Acknowledgments

As with all writing projects, Daisy and Luke's story couldn't have happened without the encouragement and expertise of others. I cannot name them all, but I want to thank a few that have journeyed with me in the writing of *Hope Even After*.

First and foremost, I thank God for the blessing of writing full-time and for the love of story He created in me. I pray everything I write is done through Him, for Him, and is used for His glory.

I also want to thank my husband, who is my biggest cheerleader. I couldn't have done it without you. Thank you for believing in me enough to let me chase this dream.

To my family and church family, I've appreciated every prayer and encouraging word. They make a difference in each page that I write.

To my local writing group and writing friends who have offered feedback, thank you. This book wouldn't be what it is today without your encouragement.

Finally, special thanks to Ben Wrase for reading *Hope Even After* in its early stages. Your feedback on the portrayal of addiction and recovery, along with that of my husband and my research, helped keep the story real. Thank you.

About the Author

As the wife of a drug and alcohol addiction counselor and pastor and having worked in a mental health agency herself, Heather Greer has witnessed the effects of addiction on individuals and families. Addiction has touched many families she loves both inside and outside the church, including her own. It is a subject Heather believes needs to be talked about with honesty, love, and understanding in our churches.

While Hope Even After tackles the hard topic of addiction, not all of Heather's stories dive quite so deep. Her novellas reflect her love of the lighthearted Christmas movies she enjoys, and her other novels always include some elements of the things she enjoys. Whether through setting, theme, or activities like baking, candy making, or enjoying a favorite drink, Heather has woven a bit of herself into each story.

Even more important is the faith element threaded through

each book. Heather's belief that faith should be who we are not something we do on Sunday morning or during bedtime prayers is evident in each story she writes. Heather's prayer is that each book she writes will provide hope, encouragement, and challenge to grow in faith for those who read them.

Also by Heather Greer

Faith, Hope, and Love Series:

Faith's Journey

Faith, Hope, and Love Series - Book One

https://scrivenings.link/faithsjourney

Grasping Hope

Faith, Hope, and Love Series - Book Two

https://scrivenings.link/graspinghope

Relentless Love

Faith, Hope, and Love Series - Book Three

https://scrivenings.link/relentlesslove

FROM THE STAINED-GLASS LEGACY COLLECTION:

Window of Opportunity

Faith and duty drive Evangeline Moore to protect her father's pristine image as a judge in Harrisburg, Illinois. Her resolve's biggest test? Dot, her childhood friend. With Evangeline beside her, Dot's desire for the Roaring Twenties' glitz and glamor leads the pair into questionable situations.

Born into a Chicago mob family, Brendan Dunne understands duty, but faith puts him at odds with his father's demands. Even when his brother James's propensity for trouble lands them in Harrisburg, the truth is undeniable. To their father, the lines he won't cross mean Brendan will never measure up.

When circumstances push Brendan and Evangeline together, unexpected events create an opportunity to break free of family expectations. Will they be brave enough to forge their own path before the window closes on their chance to change?

Get your copy here:
https://scrivenings.link/windowofopportunity

STAND-ALONE NOVELS
(CONTEMPORARY ROMANCE)

Love in the Squared Circle
by Heather Greer

Trinity Knight is not a professional wrestling fan. But with her husband gone, it falls to her to give their son the father-son trip they daydreamed about when he was alive. After Trinity causes them to miss a meet and greet with Jay's favorite wrestler, a random act of kindness saves the trip and starts Trinity on an unexpected path.

Universal Wrestling Organization Champion Blane Sterling hears whiny children at photo ops all the time. However, overhearing a young boy comfort his mother piques his interest. Touched by their story, Blane works to give Jay the experience of a lifetime.

Trinity and Blane are drawn to each other. But they live in different worlds. Trinity might learn to fit into his, but can those in her world look beyond Blane's profession to see his heart? Or will a lack of acceptance cause Trinity and Blane to lose their shot at love?

Get your copy here:
https://scrivenings.link/loveinthesquaredcircle

Cake That!

Competing on the *Cake That* baking show is a dream come true for Livvy Miller, but debt on her cupcake truck and an expensive repair make her question if she should chase it. Her best friend encourages Livvy to trust God to care for The Sugar Cube, win or lose.

Family is everything to Evan Jones. His parents always gave up their dreams so their children could achieve theirs. Winning *Cake That* would enable him to give them the trip they've always talked about but could never afford.

As the contestants live and bake together, more than the competition heats up. Livvy and Evan have a spark from the start, but they're in it to win. Neither needs the distraction of romance. Unwanted attention from another competitor complicates matters. Stir in strange occurrences on set, and everyone wonders if a saboteur is in the mix.

With the distractions inside and outside the *Cake That* kitchen, will Livvy or Evan rise above the rest and claim the prize? Or does God have more in store for them than they first imagined?

Get your copy here:

scrivenings.link/cakethat

NOVELLA COLLECTIONS:

Pets Amore

A novella collection—including "Pegboards, Parrots, and Pickup Lines" by Heather Greer

Pegboards, Parrots, and Pickup Lines—Charlotte Herring wants one thing—to prove she can succeed on her own. But to avoid failure, she needs the people of Brookview to accept her and her antique store. For years, Tyson Abbott's only goal was to realize his father's dreams for the family hardware store. After meeting the town's newest resident, he adds a new goal—helping Charlotte find her place in Brookview.

With a parrot named Cracker Jack paving the way for their partnership to become a romance, Charlotte and Tyson see more than the dreams for their stores coming true. But when their plans conflict and past hurts resurface, will they lose their dreams and each other?

Get your copy here:
https://scrivenings.link/petsamore

A Match Made at Christmas

A novella collection—including "The Santa Setup"

by Heather Greer

The Santa Setup—Turning friendship into love takes magic. Good thing Nicholas Eckert and Julie Clarke work at Christmas Wonderland. The attraction brims with holiday magic, not to mention four teenage elves determined that Mr. and Mrs. Claus stop playing a couple and become one. The teens will need more than mistletoe to pair up these two. Julie is seeing someone, and Nick won't risk their friendship for possible love. Only the elven employees' outrageous antics stand a chance of setting up Santa in time for Christmas.

Get your copy here:

https://scrivenings.link/amatchmadeatchristmas

Love Delivered

A novella collection—including "Sweet Delivery"

by Heather Greer

Sweet Delivery—After winning Cake That, Will Forrester thinks his Pastry Perfect Baking Dreams have come true. The sweetness fades when a chain bakery moves to town, and Will must adjust his plans to keep his customers. Hiring Erica Gerard is one of those changes. As they work together, Erica challenges Will and offers new ideas to improve the bakery. Soon, Erica and Will start bringing out the best in each other. But Erica harbors a secret, and if it's discovered, Will might never be the same.

Get your copy here:
https://scrivenings.link/lovedelivered

Love in Any Season

A novella collection—including "Sweet Delivery"

by Heather Greer

Sugar and Spice

Emeline Becker, owner of Sugar and Spice Bakery, loves New Kuchenbrünn, except for the gingerbread. As the only bakery, she supplies the annual Gingerbread Festival with the one treat she can't stand. It's gingerbread everywhere.

Things get worse when Ryker Lehmann is hired as the festival photographer. He was her secret teen crush, her sister's boyfriend, and witness to her worst humiliation. Plus, he broke her sister's heart and bruised hers when he left town after graduation. Now, he's back in town, determined to fix their friendship before the festival ends.

With gingerbread and Ryker together, can Emmie make it through the festival with her mind and heart intact?

Get your copy here:
https://scrivenings.link/loveinanyseason

∽

Stay up-to-date on your favorite books and authors with our free e-newsletters.

ScriveningsPress.com

www.ingramcontent.com/pod-product-compliance
Ingram Content Group UK Ltd.
Pitfield, Milton Keynes, MK11 3LW, UK
UKHW022237230426
12048UKWH00018BA/1303